Highland Fling on the Whisky Trail

Margaret Amatt

LEANNAN
PRESS
INDEPENDENT PUBLISHER

LEANNAN PRESS

First Published by Leannan Press 2023

Book Cover designed by Margaret Amatt

eBook ISBN: 978-1-914575-62-4

Paperback ISBN: 978-1-914575-59-4

CHAPTER ONE

Felicity

August

A high-pitched pinging resonated around the room and Felicity stopped speaking mid-sentence, clenching her fingers around her champagne glass. The chatter and laughter in the function room died. Well-coiffed heads turned to face the top table. Sequins from evening dresses glinted in the lights. Felicity glanced at her colleague, Ella. The limbo they'd worked in for the last two years was drawing to a close.

At the top table, Frank Sinclair stood framed by the French windows. He adjusted his bow tie and scanned the room with a warm smile, his grey head bobbing and his eyes bright. Rain battered the windows, mocking the fact it was still summer. Such fine Scottish weather. Felicity held her breath. Frank wasn't a wobbly old man and still looked fit and healthy despite him pushing seventy, but a frail edge lingered in his slightly stooped shoulders. A lump swelled in Felicity's throat. Frank's last few years at the helm of the Sinclair Brothers whisky chain hadn't exactly been smooth, what with a global pandemic and a recession to contend with. He'd put his retirement on hold, but now it was here.

His family and guests watched him closely, the beady eyes of his wife, Dorothy Sinclair, prominent among them. Where her husband was a good businessperson, a tough boss and a humane employer, Dorothy had a sharper edge.

'I wonder if she'll butt out now he's retired,' Ella whispered in Felicity's ear. Ella also had her eyes trained on Dorothy.

Felicity sipped her champagne. Most people knew Dorothy was the driving force behind many of the company's decisions. Would she disappear with Frank? 'I guess it depends if their son is any good at the job.'

As Frank began to speak, thanking people for the send-off and remembering times past, Dorothy put her hands on the arm of a younger man and patted him. His sombre expression looked better suited to a funeral. Felicity pulled a face and only just restrained an audible huff. He was the new boss, Frank and Dorothy's son, Gavin, and a man Felicity had barely got two words out of on the rare occasions they'd met. People in the office often described him as a plank in a suit and a stuffed shirt. All the rumours said he had no interest in running the business. He was a hotshot programmer and his interests were all computer based. Apparently, he had an apartment filled with screens and gadgets, and he didn't even like whisky. And yet he was here.

Further reminisces from Frank brought waves of laughter and Felicity held her hand to her lips. Ella looked at her quizzically and mouthed, 'Are you ok?'

Felicity nodded and flapped at her face. Her youngest sister, Caralyn, would have rolled her eyes and said she was soft in the head, but Felicity cried at everything – weddings, films, musicals, homeless people on the streets and apparently leaving speeches too. Blinking, she refocused and met the gaze of Julian Morrison, the executive manager, who was also at the top table. He looked away directly at the woman by his side, presumably his wife, and smiled. A hungry wolf probably observed his mate in much the same way, but Felicity doubted his wife was the object of his hunger pangs. Julian made no secret of his ambition and was in a good place to run the show if Gavin Sinclair was happy to have his strings pulled. Felicity took another mouthful of champagne. What had possessed her to leave her job as a tour guide at Glenbriar Distillery for this? It had always been fun; she'd made friends in the community and had left the claustrophobia of her childhood behind. Taking the position as the PA to the new CEO had seemed like a great opportunity but hadn't exactly gone smoothly – or quickly. So many delays had barred his takeover. And now she'd met him, she was even less certain she should have given up the job she loved. Sure, it was the promotion anyone would dream of, but the extra money didn't go that far when most of it went on extortionate Edinburgh rents and she was back to living in a cramped flat. The claustrophobia was edging back. Her heart ached for rolling hills and running rivers like the ones she'd left behind. She swiped away another crazy tear and laughed through it. *Listen to me,* the London girl who at sixteen didn't think she could survive anywhere more than a ten-minute ride away from a Primark. How quickly she'd adapted to life in the country, only to throw herself back into the city. The readjustment was so much harder than she'd anticipated.

Frank Sinclair welcomed his wife, son, and daughter to stand beside him. After thanking Dorothy for her behind-the-scenes support over the years, he turned to his children.

'My daughter, Emily, will continue her role as ad hoc PR if we need her, but she's currently devoting her days to bringing up her young family. Nothing more noble than that.' Frank patted her on the shoulder. 'And, now I'm retired, they'll get so much more Granny and Grandpa time too.'

Ella pulled a face. The Sinclairs were well known for their verging-on-obsessive family values. Felicity came from a big family she loved dearly but some of the Sinclair's ideas had always made her a little edgy – especially Dorothy's obsession with churchgoing. Felicity cringed, recalling a conversation where Dorothy had admonished her for wearing nail polish, something none of her churchgoing friends would ever do. *Eek.* Felicity curled her fingers to hide her latest style – silver glitter square tips with diamante studs.

'My son, Gavin,' Frank continued. A distant rumble set heads turning. Thunder? Felicity would have to remember to text her older brother, Joe, about this. He'd see it as a definite omen. Frank's eyes roamed around and he peered at the ceiling like he was warning it not to fall in. 'Wild weather out there, but where was I? Oh yes, Gavin. He's finally agreed to step into the role he was born to do. The Sinclair Brothers whisky chain has been run by a Sinclair for over a century now and we're pleased the tradition will continue.'

'Bit sexist all this, isn't it?' Ella whispered.

'A bit.' Felicity's gaze didn't leave Gavin. He looked like his dad, younger obviously, his hair light brown rather than Frank's white. Quite pleasant to look at. If only he wasn't so serious.

'Thank you.' Gavin's steely eyes flickered over the assembled crowd. 'I appreciate everything everyone here has done for my father over the years. He always speaks highly of all his employees.'

His voice was low and rumbling, but his tone was flat, verging on cold. Felicity and Ella exchanged another glance. 'Is he a robot?' Ella said.

Felicity pulled an uncertain face. 'Could he make it more obvious he doesn't want to be here?'

'I hope you'll extend the same sentiments to me. Walking in my father's footsteps won't be easy. I've given up a job I was deeply involved in and I'm quite sure this will be a challenging task for me.'

Felicity stared at him, tucking a long tendril of blonde hair behind her ear. If he was this disinterested, why not just refuse? Julian Morrison would love the opportunity to take over.

Gavin cleared his throat and straightened his tie. 'In the weeks to come, I'll rely heavily on all of you to keep me right.' Another thunderclap roared beyond. The tiniest of quirks played at the corner of his lips but was soon lost. He raised his eyes and scanned to the room. Briefly, his gaze touched on Felicity and she beamed. How could she not? It was like encouraging one of her younger siblings to keep going when they were afraid of tripping over their words in a school play. He blinked and lines flickered across his forehead. When his focus shifted, she snuck a peek around. No wonder he'd looked puzzled. She must be the only smiling face in a sea of dead pan expressions. Her throat grew thick and she rubbed at it. Change was coming. And while she didn't relish the prospect, perhaps the employees weren't the only ones stepping into unknown territory. She'd never had opportunities to prove herself and getting this job had felt like winning the lottery. Now it wouldn't matter that she hadn't had the chance to go to university and all she'd done with her life so far was guide tours at a whisky distillery. Claiming she was PA to the CEO sounded much better, but doubts wriggled inside her like eels. Something told her this wasn't going to be all shiny or plain sailing – Gavin Sinclair's grim face for a start.

The Sinclair family resumed their seats and servers appeared with food.

'I'm not looking forward to working for him.' Felicity pushed her dinner around her plate – *why were the portions so big?* – and eyeballed the back of Gavin Sinclair's head. 'He doesn't look like much fun.'

'I've heard a rumour,' Ella said quietly. 'That he's a bit of a playboy. Apparently, his family are desperate to have him settle down. I reckon this is part of it. My boyfriend works with someone who worked with him before and says he quite openly played the field.'

'Really?' Nothing about his buttoned-up façade screamed player but then you couldn't exactly tell. Her last boyfriend had seemed like the salt of the earth until the day he'd upended her dinner across the floor because she'd said she couldn't finish it. 'Stop being so dramatic,' he'd said. 'It's not like you need to lose weight. You're a skinny freak. Obsessed. Why don't you just eat like a normal person and stop all the, *ew, I-can't-eat-this shit*? Like it would kill you to try.'

She forced a mouthful of chicken. Now wasn't the time for her 'drama' either. A great tide of emotion rose up in her chest. How dare he talk to her like that when he knew nothing of her past? Why couldn't she find someone who liked her just as she was, someone who believed in her without the pressure of conforming to this or that? Uncertainty beat like a drummer rapping on her head. With this new job, the new boss and all the upheaval, so much would change. She'd already upended her world twice before, once when she'd moved from London to Glenbriar and now she'd left that lovely town and her BFF, Briony, behind. Calling Briony from her cold bedsit was a poor second to having her friend just a short distance away.

And she needed to talk to her. She snuck out her phone to message her. Briony always knew what to say, or she'd at least bring a smiley face and a warm hug to the party. Felicity rubbed a palm over her shoulder.

'Are you cold?' Ella asked. 'It's draughty in here.'

'A bit.'

At the top table, Gavin Sinclair put his arm around his mother's shoulder and squeezed it. His mother beamed at him. Felicity shivered, dropped her gaze to her phone and sighed. She was hundreds of miles from her family, detached from her best friend and about to embark on a new job – with a boss who looked like he had the potential to unravel the delicate balance of her life.

CHAPTER TWO

Gavin

October

Keeping a laptop open between him and Julian provided Gavin with the barrier he needed. His fingers tapped on the desk and he silently chewed his tongue as Julian spoke. There couldn't be much between them age-wise. Julian was maybe a few years older but he'd spent years working for big businesses in managerial roles. Gavin hadn't. Not that he'd been hiding all his life. He'd had his share of work for multinational companies and global organisations, but his strengths lay in the background, deep in algorithms and programs, silently weaving the magic for these businesses, not at the forefront, making the decisions. One mistake here wasn't something he could fix with another few lines of code.

The blinking cursor on the screen seemed to be beating a code of its own: *you don't have a clue what you're doing and you're completely out of your depth.*

'Did you tell my father this when he was still in charge?' Gavin adjusted the laptop screen and braced himself on his desk. His phone sat to his left, a pen holder and a desk pad to his right. Only a few brief notes sullied the otherwise clean white paper.

'Frequently,' Julian said with an air of superciliousness that made Gavin bristle.

'So, the core of what you're telling me is that some of the distilleries are doing better than others and the ones that aren't pulling weight should be cut loose?'

Julian held out his hands and rocked his head from side to side as if weighing Gavin's words against fact. 'Very loosely, yes. But it's not quite as simple as that. Cutting the deadwood won't necessarily work. Some of the bestselling lines come from the more obscure distilleries but the supply volume doesn't add up to the quantities sold from the larger distilleries. However, cutting off a bestselling line is never a good idea. We could gradually phase it out or look into ways of producing the same product at another distillery. The difficulty is that some of these lines sell on their uniqueness to a certain area.'

Gavin straightened his tie, considering the bouncing square screensaver travelling across his laptop. 'And do you have a solution for this problem?'

'I have some potential solutions, though we should have a proper meeting about it and gather opinions from every department.'

'Fine. Let's—'

The office door sprang open, bringing with it Monsoon Felicity. Gavin's jaw tightened and he glanced at the ceiling before fixing his eyes on her. He'd had a PA before who'd dressed in jeans, trainers and hoodies and been very efficient at taking calls, sending emails and liaising with clients. Felicity had given him no reason to doubt her skills in that department but she seemed to think it was necessary to dress like a model from Vogue magazine to do it. Today's grey sheath dress accentuated a willowy frame while sky-rise heels made her taller than most of the men. Blonde tresses looped over her shoulders with a just-stepped-out-of-the-salon bounce. When she smiled, her full lips sparkled rosy red.

Julian shook his head like he was only just holding back an eyeroll, then flicked through some notes on the desk.

'Sorry to interrupt.' Felicity stopped dead. 'I didn't realise you had a meeting.' Her brow furrowed and she blinked at the iPad in her arms like she must have missed something. Presumably rechecking his schedule. She was the one who organised his meetings, so she should know when they were.

'It isn't a meeting,' Gavin said, flexing his fingers.

'Just an informal discussion,' Julian added.

'Ah, ok.'

'Did you want something?' Gavin raised his eyebrows slightly.

'No. Well, yes, I have some, er, information for you, but it can wait.'

'I'm just leaving.' Julian rolled back his chair and stood.

'I'll schedule a meeting for next week,' Gavin said. 'In fact, you can do that now.' He signalled to Felicity with his pointer finger. As Julian passed her at the door, her lips quirked, and a sickening sensation twisted in Gavin's stomach. Was she laughing at him? Not out loud. No. She'd managed to hide it behind her perma-grin but seriously, why did she find him such an object of hilarity? Another time, he'd like to choose his own PA. And not one who dressed like a supermodel. He'd dated a woman like that before and she'd been completely obsessed with her appearance, though not greatly enamoured with his. Somehow he always messed up his chances with dates or had different expectations. He hadn't found the right person yet. But days, weeks, months, now years of swiping left and right with very little success had left him disheartened and he'd given up playing the game. He needed a break.

Felicity took the seat Julian had vacated and woke the iPad. 'Who do you want to attend the meeting? And what's its purpose?'

Good questions. Ones he supposed he should know the answers to. Maybe he would have known if he'd spent his life the way his parents had wanted, learning about this industry, ready to take over the reins when the time came. But he hadn't. Even now he was here, sitting in this office surrounded by beautifully framed pictures of all the distilleries he owned, plus slick advertising art and photographs of various Glenbriar and Sinclair Brothers' whiskies over the decades, he wasn't convinced he'd made the right decision. Family expectations always weighed heavily on his shoulders but so often he felt like he'd let them down. He wouldn't this time.

'The purpose is to discuss solutions and make an action plan for the future of the Highland Perthshire distilleries.'

Felicity tapped on her iPad screen. 'And who should I invite?'

He sat back in his leather seat, resting his elbow on the arm. 'The usual people.'

She glanced up, fingers poised over the screen, and a vague smile playing on her lips again. Lips that were oddly distracting, almost as much as the fragrance she'd brought in with her. The scent she wore was like a signature that marked the places she'd been. He could walk into a room and know she was there or had just left because of it.

'Who are the usual people?' she asked.

'Who have you invited before to meetings like this? Julian says he mentioned this several times to my father, so there must have been prior meetings.'

'I'll check back and see. I could invite the heads of departments, and would you like me to send Zoom invites to the managers of the Highland Perthshire distilleries?'

It seemed sensible. Courteous. But Julian hadn't mentioned them and he always seemed to know what he was doing. A little niggle in the back of Gavin's mind pushed him to wonder what Julian's motives were. For the moment, he would run with it, and give Julian the appearance of having got his way. But if this was a game, Gavin would soon figure out a way to win. He may not be well practised in this line of business but he knew a lot about games – he'd designed countless computer games, indulged in crippling dating games, and corporate games were just another level. He'd promised his parents he'd play, though he wasn't sure he was cut out for it.

'Check with Julian and see if he wants them there. Get him to make the agenda too.'

'Ok.' A slight frown imprinted on her brow as she tapped at the screen.

'What's the information you have for me?'

'Oh, that.' She slipped a long coiling tendril behind her ear and shifted in her seat. 'Some of the staff are organising a Secret Santa and were wondering if you wanted to take part. They, um, asked me to ask you.'

'Hardly information, is it?'

'No,' she agreed.

'And did my parents previously get involved?'

'As far as I know, but I haven't worked here for long – not in this office. I was a tour guide in the Glenbriar Distillery before.'

'Hmm.'

'But from what the people who are organising it were saying, I think everyone usually joins in.'

'Fine. I'll do it then.' He gave a little shrug. If that was what people expected. How hard could it be?

'Great, I'll let them know.' She tapped her nails on the iPad and smiled.

Did she enjoy this job? Or was that smile glued in place?

'You can go,' he said. 'Unless there's something else?'

She shook her head, got to her feet, and left. He kept his eyes down, but as soon as the door clicked shut, he loosened his collar. She needed to be replaced, preferably by someone twice her age who looked like his granny. Ah, screw it, he was the boss. He could have her shunted elsewhere if he wanted, couldn't he?

Who should he email about that? He woke his laptop. With a sigh, he clutched his face in his hands. If he got rid of her and hired someone new, he'd be in an even worse position. She might think him a joke, but without someone who at least appeared to know what they were doing in his camp, he'd be even further up shit creek. And right now, he needed all the help he could get.

CHAPTER THREE

Felicity

Felicity took several deep breaths outside Gavin's office. Those rumours about him being a stuffed shirt? All true. He had as much personality as an ironing board, in fact, not even as much as hers which collapsed every time she used it.

Could he not just liven up a bit? It would make life so much more enjoyable. Sometimes laughing at his irritating ways was the only way to get through the day – otherwise she'd cry. A lot.

She clicked across the floor. These heels gave her even more height and a bizarre sense of power. If she'd worn heels when she was a teenager to exert some control over her life, she might have saved herself years of hospitalisation and therapy. But what was done was done. Whenever the boss was about though, the old insecurities hit back. She was a pathetic shrimp in a sea of sharks. Still, that was all she needed to be. As long as she did her job, she had nothing to worry about. Only she wasn't sure she was doing it right. He always seemed to be annoyed with her. Could he fire her? What would she do then? She'd worked hard for this job and with her rubbish qualifications, she couldn't expect to get much better. Some people joked she'd only got this job because old Frank Sinclair always had a soft spot for her. The way Dorothy

Sinclair screwed up her face in her presence kind of confirmed it, but Felicity hoped she'd earned the job on some merit and not just because the old boss had liked her smile.

Back in the main office, she slumped into her seat.

Ella peered around the cubicle. 'Did you ask him?'

'What?'

'About the Secret Santa.'

'Yes.'

'And?'

'He said he'll do it.'

'Seriously? The plank wants to join in?'

'That's what he said.'

'Did you tell him about the rules and the budget?'

'No.'

Ella was obsessed with Christmas and October was still too early for Felicity.

'You can email him that information along with everyone else.'

'I don't like emailing him,' Ella said. 'He's not exactly approachable. You can do it for me. You get on ok with him, don't you?'

Felicity pulled a face. 'Hardly. He barely speaks to me and when he does, he never seems happy.'

'Worst thing that's ever happened to this business,' Winnie George said, appearing beside Ella and laying a stack of papers on her desk. 'I've worked here for twenty years. When Frank was boss, I wouldn't have minded asking him anything. He did a good job, and he was always around to help out if needed and he had such a pleasant nature, but Gavin... Well... I'd sooner approach a vampire bat in a lair of tarantulas.'

Felicity shook her head and held back a laugh. 'Ok, he's not quite that bad.' Just buttoned up with a way of making her feel small.

'Still, rather you than me,' Ella said. 'Did you hear that, Winnie? He wants to join in with the secret Santa. I bet he doesn't do it properly with my new rules.'

'They are a bit confusing.' Winnie pulled a side pout. 'My three facts will be so obvious everyone'll know it's me. You all know I have two kids, three guinea pigs and a fascination with cheese.'

Ella gave her arm a fake shove and Felicity opened her laptop with a smirk. Ella's new version of secret Santa was likely to backfire some way or other. The rules had got so ridiculously complicated that most people would forget or lie. Felicity scrolled through lists of emails, hoping to find one with a similar agenda and invitee list to the meeting Gavin wanted. Nothing presented itself. She'd have to ask Julian.

She knocked on his door and waited for him to call, 'Come in.'

'Hi.' Her heels clicked on the vinyl on the way to his desk. 'I need some information from you about the future of the Highland Perthshire distilleries meeting.' Her heart wavered as she opened her iPad. Saying it like that made it sound like their future wasn't guaranteed. She frowned at the iPad. She'd worked in those distilleries – had the time of her life taking tours around and meeting people from all over the world. The community around Glenbriar had been her home for three years and she missed it. It had been a gamble leaving her family in London when she was so young for a job in the back of beyond where she knew no one, but it had been the making of her, just as she'd hoped. What a way to repay that community by using her promotion to be part of this.

If it came to anything.

'What information do you need?' Julian steepled his fingers and peered at her. When Frank Sinclair was in charge, he would have known exactly who to invite. This situation would never have occurred. At the risk of sounding traitorous, she didn't think Gavin had a clue what he was doing.

'Who would you like to be present?' She poised, ready to add the details to the iPad. 'I have all the heads of department.'

'That'll do.'

'Do you want any management staff from the distilleries in question?'

'Does Gavin want them there?' A calculating look flashed across Julian's long pointed face.

'He didn't specify.'

'Then no. That won't be necessary.'

Why did that answer not fill her with confidence? 'He also wants you to make up the agenda.'

Julian shook his head and let out a sigh. 'Fine. I'll email one over.'

She left the office clutching her iPad. None of this felt right but she was just a PA to a puppet boss. What could she actually do about it?

At lunchtime, she fired off a message to Briony.

FELICITY: Hey. How's the festival?

She paused as an ache burned in her chest. Previously, she'd helped set up the Autumn Gold Festival in Glenbriar. The Glenbriar Distillery had sponsored the musical events in the village and surrounding area. She and Briony had put together displays at the Loch View Hotel that Briony owned. They'd had a friendship that clicked from the off. Felicity had arrived at Glenbriar, wide-eyed and excited, ready for her first solo adventure, only to discover the accommodation that came with her new job wasn't ready. In a stroke of serendipity, they'd got her a room at Briony's hotel for a week while they sorted out the living arrangements. The rest was history.

She glanced back at her phone and finished the text.

You know I told you I wasn't sure about my new boss? Now, it's worse. I don't think he knows what he's doing. I'm worried he's going to do something crazy... and I might get sacked. Eek! Let's talk soon.

A reply pinged back quickly.

BRIONY: I sure don't want you sacked but if it happens, come back up here and I'll give you a job. Miss you! The festival is going fine. Zach is putting up the banners, though I'm sure they won't be as perfect as they were when you helped him! X

Felicity smiled. Briony's partner, Zach, was a cutie and such a sweetheart. One day Felicity might be blessed with meeting someone like him.

On the morning of the meeting, Felicity stopped in the staffroom to start the coffee machine. Everyone worked better on caffeine. Several people were milling around, including Gavin and Julian. Why did it look like they were having their own private meeting? Had Julian grabbed him for a last-minute briefing before anyone else could?

'I need to get one of these for Christmas.' Winnie patted the coffee machine. 'The amount of drinks my family get through, it's quite ridiculous. I feel like a barista.'

'That's quite an ambitious Christmas gift. An industrial strength coffee maker? I'd be happy with a pair of new gloves.' Felicity pulled her worn through ones out of her pocket. 'I've had these since I was about sixteen and I love them. My granny gave them to me, and I can't find a good replacement in the same colour, unless I want to pay through the nose. But they're so cosy and waterproof. Maybe I'll splash out this year and invest in a new pair.'

'Are they the kind that have the touchscreen feature?' Ella asked, appearing behind her with a couple of other people.

'Sadly no. That would make them the ultra-glove.' Felicity grinned and shoved them back in her pocket.

'Beautiful colour though,' Lorah from payroll said. 'That sort of plum colour goes so well with grey.'

'Exactly.' Felicity handed around the mugs filled with steaming coffee.

'Are you in the meeting today?' Winnie asked. As head of advertising, she would be present.

'I'm taking the minutes, which reminds me, I should get everything hooked up in the meeting room. See you in a bit.' She slipped through the people mingling and enjoying their last few seconds of freedom before they started work. Funny how it was still a very traditional nine-till-five setup here. That was definitely because of Frank and Dorothy Sinclair. They'd instilled family values into the company. They closed over Christmas and took off bank holidays. They agreed to skeleton staff in the sales and distribution centres only to capitalise on the fact whisky sold well over the festive season and particularly in the lead up to new year – Hogmanay.

Was that all about to change? Felicity switched on the screen and rigged up the laptops. Of course, modernisation had to happen and if Gavin Sinclair wanted to increase working hours, change working patterns or open over Christmas, then he was well within his rights, but if he started shutting down distilleries to save money by crippling communities that couldn't be right. He'd already updated all the technology. That was his background after all. He'd ditched the old projectors for state-of-the-art Promethean boards and upgraded all the software, so some of it was 'space age'. Winnie's words.

The door clicked open and Gavin and Julian entered.

'Good morning,' Felicity said.

'Morning,' Julian replied.

Gavin made a noise somewhere between *hello* and a grunt, then carried on talking to Julian. Felicity returned to her setup.

Others started to arrive and Winnie tipped her a little wink as she took a seat at the boardroom table. Felicity moved to the door and welcomed people in. She caught Gavin's eye and he gave her a death look before sitting with his back to her. Such a charmer.

When everyone was in, she closed the door and turned to the table. Her gaze landed on the empty seat next to Gavin. Hmm, so no one wanted to sit next to him. Interesting. Maybe he smelled. Actually, he did. She'd noticed it in his office and she was still catching it now. That unmistakable heady fragrance of bergamot blended with woody spices. If she sat too close to him, that scent might drug her. She might fall asleep or... Well, nothing else.

The seat snagged on the carpet as she pulled it back. Gavin's gaze shifted her way for a second before he focused forward, sliding a pen through his fingers. Felicity slid her legs through the too-small gap between the table leg and Gavin's thigh. Her knee brushed briefly against the black suit fabric of his trousers and he instantly crossed his ankles and leaned over his open laptop.

'Good morning, everyone,' he said.

Felicity woke her laptop and opened her notes.

'The purpose of today's meeting is to discuss the viability of the Highland Perthshire distilleries.'

She typed into the minutes box. Viability? But nearly all the distilleries were in Highland Perthshire. They had one lowland one near the capital but the rural ones were where Glenbriar got its heart and soul. Even its name. Although their trade name was Sinclair Brothers, most people had heard of Glenbriar, and the smaller distilleries were part of the Glenbriar chain.

Mark from PR frowned and momentarily caught Felicity's eye before turning to Gavin. 'Can I ask exactly what you mean by that?'

'Some of the distilleries aren't bringing in enough profit. It seems to me their rural location makes everything cost more and it's no longer a viable model.' Gavin spoke to the Promethean board, not making eye contact with anyone.

Julian nodded, his expression barely changing, but the edge of something crept onto his face, like smugness; he'd done his job and got Gavin on side.

'But the rural distilleries are our bread and butter, no?' Mark said. 'They're our signature pieces. How can we get rid of them?'

'Financially, they're not the bread and butter,' Gavin said. 'And a signature piece is fine if it's bringing in the money. But if it's just there to look pretty in a picture, then it's not exactly pulling weight.'

Felicity frowned at him. Was that what he thought? Or was this Julian's spin on things? Gavin's focus travelled around the table; his firm jaw was set in a hard line with just a hint of stubble around it. Finally, he reached Felicity and mirrored her frown before looking away almost immediately.

'I don't get how you can consider shutting down the iconic places, that's all,' Mark said. 'The whisky may not sell in as big quantities but isn't that a fault of the marketing? Using the locations on packaging definitely sells.'

Gavin shucked off his suit jacket.

Completely unprepared for the waft of man scent, Felicity suppressed a gasp. The heat from his body was almost palpable.

He adjusted the cuffs of his pale grey shirt, revealing a glint of gold from his watch, and she sank her teeth into her lips, forcing her concentration onto her screen. But his proximity was interfering with her thoughts. So what if he was good looking and smelled nicer than the average man? Was she about to become a cliché PA and start fantasising about her boss? Ha, no danger. Even if it went with the territory, she wasn't about to fall down that hole. Nope. If her ironing board had more personality, she'd rather stick with that.

'This is what we need to talk about. Maybe there's a way to keep the buildings but centre all the production at the Glenbriar distillery.'

'But then you lose the uniqueness of each location,' Mark said.

'Not necessarily.' Julian leaned forward and made a decisive cutting movement with his hands. 'The Glenbriar distillery currently produces well but not all the lines are popular. If we cut the least popular lines, there would be room to produce some of the better selling labels. We could invest in transporting the raw materials from the original locations to Glenbriar as opposed to transporting the finished product.'

'But if you shut Inverbuie and Torrindhu, what about the local economies?' Felicity asked. The question was out before she remembered she was only here to take minutes, not contribute.

She was aware of Gavin side-eyeing her but she didn't dare look back.

'Not strictly speaking our concern,' Julian said. 'While we understand the impact of our distilleries to rural areas, we're not in any way duty-bound to ensure their survival.'

'In the event of any sell offs, we would try to limit the number of compulsory lay-offs,' Gavin added. 'But how many people are we talking about? Surely not enough to make that much of a difference.'

'I can find out.' Felicity clicked open a new tab, but he raised his finger.

'Email me the information. I don't need it this minute. I want to discuss other solutions before we get caught up in a scenario that may never happen.'

Yes, sir. She drew in a deep breath, catching Winnie's eye across the table. Winnie rolled her tongue into her cheek as if trying not to laugh and Felicity couldn't help smirking too.

The meeting dragged on as more people chipped in with suggestions and bandied thoughts about. Felicity tapped her foot, a thumping in her ears getting louder and louder. This was getting nowhere, but at the same time sounded more and more like it was almost a done deal. Instead of building on what they already had in the smaller distilleries, Gavin and Julian seemed intent on shutting them down. Why? For an easy life? Maybe they wanted to grow their lowland outlets; Edinburgh was an obvious hub when it came to international sales. But was he going to give up on the other distilleries so quickly?

'Right,' Gavin said. 'I'll take all these suggestions on board and maybe form a working party to flesh out the best way to move forward. Does anyone have any other business we should discuss?'

'Before making any decisions, it might be best to visit all the distilleries in question,' Felicity said. How could he decide anything based on places he admitted he hadn't visited since he was a child? 'It would give you the best insight into how they all work.'

He turned his head to her, rubbing his neck; his jaw tensed like he was trying to break his teeth. 'Good idea,' he said, though the words sounded more like he'd just told her to piss off, and it was about as good an idea as jumping off the Forth Road Bridge. 'Arrange that for next year sometime.'

'Certainly.' She beamed like he'd just handed her a month's paid leave and an all-expenses paid trip to Bermuda.

Adjusting his tie, he looked away and scanned around.

'Just make sure it doesn't clash with the international trip in February or the acquisitions in April,' Julian said.

'Ok.' Felicity jotted down the clashes. As if she wouldn't check the calendar before making plans.

'Nothing else?' Gavin scanned around the room.

People shook their heads and gathered their notes together. Felicity carried on typing as the room emptied. Gavin stood, lifting his jacket and moved off, but he was still nearby; his fragrance was unmistakable. She didn't dare look around but sensed there couldn't be many people left. Was it just the two of them? Her shoulders tingled. What was he up to? Was he waiting for everyone to leave so he could reprimand her for daring to speak out of turn?

The door closed and her heartrate tripled. Cold tingles ran down her neck and she peered around. The room was empty. She let out a sigh, though she wasn't sure if the squirm in her tummy was relief or disappointment.

Chapter Four

Gavin

December

Hot water gushed over Gavin's face and through his hair, washing away the chlorine and collecting in soapy pools at his feet. He lathered the gel over his arms and shoulders; they were no longer the weedy shape they used to be. Morning swims were great for building muscle and making him more toned than he'd ever been but the chlorine smell was cloying. Before he headed to the bus stop, he sprayed himself down with Tom Ford Venetian Bergamot, just in case.

Having already overheard someone calling him a plank in a suit, his image wouldn't improve by adding bleach-smelling to his list of nicknames. He buttoned up his blazer. His father had warned him not to expect universal popularity straight away. He hadn't. Just as well, because it felt like there was no one at the office who even vaguely liked him.

Some messages lingered on his phone from his past life, friends wanting to play golf. In December? He wasn't that die hard and his skills were low level. They wouldn't miss him. Plus, he wasn't sure he wanted to endure the dad talk. He didn't grudge them their lives but he didn't need reminding how he'd flunked the school of life so thoroughly. Not when most of them joked about him living as some edgy playboy – could they get much further from the truth? Still, it was an ego booster letting them believe what they wanted. He was tired of chasing just to discover most of the women he met were only in it for the hunt. Karma was what his ex would call it.

He hopped on the bus for the city centre, and it pulled into the nose-to-tail commuter traffic. Some days, he walked from his apartment in Leith to the office but it was too cold today. Taking an empty seat next to a man with earbuds in, he sighed. Had anyone at work noticed how completely out of his depth he was? Everyone probably. In years past, he'd either be working from home or travelling to an office where people talked to him and respected him. If they bitched behind his back, it was jealousy because he was a bloody good programmer. But now... The bitching was because he was incompetent. Did it show? Would anyone have the nerve to say it to his face before he had time to do something about it?

An older woman with sticks got on the bus at the next stop and the people closer to the front of the bus studiously ignored her. So rude. Gavin got to his feet and offered her his seat. She took it with a grateful smile.

'You're a lifesaver, young man. Thank you.'

'No problem.' He stood the rest of the way, leaning his shoulder on the pole, watching the city pass by in a haze of twinkling lights.

The air nipped at his neck when he got off and he marched along Princes Street towards the office. The sun was almost up now. No one could deny the beauty of Edinburgh, especially at Christmas, but the Glenbriar whisky label didn't originate here. An unhappy juxtaposition of ideas tumbled around his brain as it had done every day since the meeting with Julian. The continued identity of Glenbriar now rested on his shoulders. Shoulders that may have been strengthened by his swimming but were already weighed down with the responsibility of family history piled on them and the promise he'd made to his parents.

The glass-fronted Sinclair Brothers' office building up a side street from Princes Street always seemed incongruous with the older buildings in the block and didn't fit the image of Glenbriar whisky either. Not for him anyway. That name brought up visions of lochs, moors, hillsides covered in heather, stags clashing their antlers, grouse calling, Caledonian pines swaying in the breeze and romantic music drifting down the glens. He shook the idea from his head. The reality was likely very different.

He hadn't visited the rural distilleries since he was twelve. Now, he was thirty-six but it didn't seem like that long ago. How could it be twenty-four years?

'Good morning, Mr Sinclair,' a chirpy voice said; it could only belong to one person this early in the morning. Who else could muster that level of cheer before nine o'clock except Felicity, the smile machine?

'Morning, Miss Swan.' His father probably liked being 'Mr Sinclair' and would expect him to follow suit with the formalities but he found it all a bit old-fashioned. He lowered his briefcase and signed in at the desk.

'Did you get the email from Ella about the secret Santa?' she said. 'She's badgering me to ask you.'

He scanned upward, trying to find the patch of wall above her head more interesting than her face – not that he found her face interesting. Or if he did, he shouldn't really notice or care. 'It's your job to check my emails,' he said.

'Yes.'

That damn smile. Even when he wasn't directly looking at her, he couldn't miss it.

'And I did. I forwarded it to your personal address, so you wouldn't be left out.'

'I haven't checked. Why don't you just explain it to me?' Why did people care about pointless things like this anyway? The little Grinch inside him crawled into a corner and crossed its arms while a sweet little angel jumped out, shaking a finger and tutting. He didn't need to be so gruff. In days gone by, he'd have loved all this. When he'd been at work with friends and people he knew and liked, he'd have joined in as enthusiastically as anyone. Now he was in charge, it was a different dynamic. How could he effectively transition between friendly exchanges and keeping a beyond-reproach image? It was easier to keep out of it, though maybe he'd gone too far the other way. Striking a balance was so bloody hard.

Family Christmases had always been fun, mostly. Except one, but that was a long distant memory. And he always liked buying gifts, especially for his relatives. Well, who else was there?

He didn't have one special person. Not anymore. His niece and nephew would do. At least to them, he was a cool uncle.

'Of course.' Felicity signed her name in the registration book, dotting the *I*s with curly bubbles, then hoisting up the strap of her plum tweed shoulder bag. 'Ella thinks it's got far too easy to guess the identity of the secret Santas so she's come up with a cryptic version. The theory stays the same: you pull a name out of a hat, then you buy a gift for whoever you get, with a maximum budget of ten quid. We're doing that at five this afternoon, by the way, if you want to join us. Ella's rules have made the next bit more complicated. Once you have your gift, you wrap it up and instead of just writing *from Santa*, you have to write three random facts about yourself, and on the opening day we'll all try to guess who the giver is from the facts. For example, *to Mr Sinclair from someone who has two kids, three guinea pigs and a fascination with cheese.*'

Gavin closed his eyes and pinched the bridge of his nose. Not only was she an endlessly streaming cheer machine, but she could also spout a string of words longer than the human genome code without stopping for air. 'This game kind of defeats the purpose of it being secret. You should change the name to "Guess-who's Santa".'

Felicity smirked. 'I can put forward that idea, but it's just for fun really. I don't think it's meant to make sense.'

He sighed. 'Ok, fine I'll sign up.' He frowned as his gaze lined up with hers. Did she have two kids, three guinea pigs and a fascination with cheese? Who was he to judge? But he hadn't pegged her as having kids. Just went to show, you could never tell. 'And when is this for? A Christmas party?'

Please no. He didn't need that. As someone who'd worked in offices for twelve plus years, he was no stranger to the goings on at events like that. A quick hook-up by the photocopier wasn't his style, not these days.

'Well, I understand the tradition has always been that on the last day before the Christmas holiday, work finishes early and the last hour is a staff get-together, and the draw is done during that. But you might want to change that, of course.'

'No, I don't.' He slapped the button beside the lift, then clamped his jaw tight. His cheek twitched involuntarily. Why had he pressed the effing button when the stairs worked just as well? Now he was going to be stuck in a lift with... her.

'It's totally mad, that Secret Santa idea, isn't it?' Felicity slid a curl behind her ear and smiled. 'But it should be fun.'

Gavin's cheek twitched again, only this time it was his pitiful attempt at a smile. The lift doors opened and he flicked his head to indicate she should go in first.

'Thanks,' she said. As she passed him, he looked away, trying to avoid getting a lungful of that scent. Christ, it did things to him. Things it really shouldn't. Not when he was faced with an employee who was at least ten years younger than him and already had a perfectly normal life of her own. All of it set alarm bells going. This was classic stuff: getting trapped in the lift with the hot PA. *Hot?* Did his brain have to produce that word? And seriously, it might be the scenario most single guys dreamed of, but he'd bet his bottom dollar she didn't love this. No attractive young woman would want to get stuck in an enclosed space with the plank in the suit. She was probably freaking out.

She'd opened her bag and was pushing a pair of tattered gloves into it when he stepped in. He half expected her to launch into the glove story he'd heard her waffling about the week before, but when she looked up, she smiled, her expression almost teasing. No, no, no. *Of course it isn't.* That was his wayward brain interpreting her sweet-smelling perfume. The manufacturers would fist-pump with joy; their job was done. It probably had a dreadful name like Potion de Passion and an advertising campaign with a slay-all-day goddess seducing all the men she crossed paths with.

He punched three into the floor selection pad and the doors closed. His own fragrance hit his nostrils. Had he overdone the spraying earlier? The scent drifted around the space like he'd uncorked a vial containing his own essence; a wisp of vapour he couldn't get back in. And it met Felicity's scent somewhere between them. The two fragrances danced and blended, making such an evocative and erotic fusion he didn't know where to look. Heat burned up his neck and he loosened his tie, but not too much, nothing that might look suggestive or lechy. Christ, he didn't want that image circulating.

Felicity twirled a lock of hair around her finger. 'Will you see your parents over Christmas?' she asked.

'What?' He cleared his throat.

'I knew them quite well. When I worked as a tour guide at Glenbriar, your parents were often up there. Nice people.'

'Yes, I'll see them at some point.'

She smiled and carried on fiddling with her hair. Her eyes roamed about like she was searching for something else to talk about. Maybe he should ask about her kids but he couldn't summon the right words. The lift carried on up. He chewed his tongue. No more questions. Please, no more. He couldn't be sure if it was genuine interest or fishing for some titbit of gossip to spread. Or just small talk for the sake of it, which seemed completely pointless. He just needed out so he could breathe.

Finally, the doors dinged open and he held out his hand for her to go first. He must look like a traffic warden.

'I have a pile of Christmas cards you need to sign,' she said.

'Why?'

'So we can send them to all the companies we deal with. It's traditional for the boss to sign them.'

He let out a huff. 'Aren't you any good at forging signatures?'

Her lips quirked up and she gave a little laugh. 'Er, no.'

Probably just as well, he didn't fancy her attempt at his name... too many *I*s for her to put bubbles and hearts on instead of dots. 'Bring them in then. May as well get started.'

He'd barely taken his seat at the desk when his office door opened. Felicity had cast off her grey coat and had on a long-sleeved purple top, tucked into a belted grey tweed pencil skirt. The ensemble hugged her willowy frame. Ten years ago, he'd sported the male version of her physique – wiry and akin to a beanpole. Latterly, the swimming had given him a body he wished he'd had earlier, though he'd never be able to remove the cringy memory of one date laughing openly at his scrawny chest. Talk about a passion killer.

A vision of him ripping off his shirt like the Hulk to show off his perfectly toned pecs to the young woman leaning over his desk with that pretty smile and plump lips assaulted his brain. She laid down two boxes and a printed list, dragging him back to the present, just in time to kick the unwanted thought over a cliff.

'These are all the people who need a card,' she said.

'I have to write them individually?'

'Just their names and your signature. There's a company message printed inside.'

'This is going to take all morning.'

'Sorry I didn't remember sooner; you could have worn a Christmas jumper.'

'I have so many I wouldn't know which to choose from.' He opened the first box, flicking a quick glance at her and catching her uncertain smile.

'Really?' she said. 'I don't even have one.'

'Well, you better get one. I'm thinking of making it compulsory attire for the Secret Santa day.' He didn't look at her but sensed her smirk.

'Shall I put that out in a memo?'

'Go right ahead.'

She sashayed out of the office, swaying her hips, disturbing the air with her Potion de Passion. He didn't need to look up to catch the movement and feel its unwelcome effect on his body. With a determined cough, he flattened a card on his desk, quite convinced she'd actually send that memo. But he hadn't lied. He had several Christmas jumpers. For members of the Sinclair family, it was mandatory for the festive season. His parents liked a traditional Christmas. Even more so now they had grandchildren to share it with. He scrawled away at the cards, stopping now and then when his writing became illegible. He could type seventy plus words per minute and, in some of his more competitive jobs, he'd probably edged over a hundred, but handwriting? It was like walking a stubborn dinosaur up a very steep hill.

After the flash of banter with Felicity, he kept his head down. Passing pleasantries with colleagues was acceptable, but he still wasn't sure where the lines came for someone in charge. Would people misconstrue his words? Or did he just have to overthink everything?

Come the afternoon all the cards were done and he buzzed Felicity to collect them.

'That took a while,' she said.

'I haven't been doing it nonstop. I took breaks. It's mind-numbing, that kind of thing.'

'True. I'll get them all enveloped and posted.'

Rather you than me. He didn't fancy the job of addressing the envelopes and matching them with the names. Next year, he'd get a stamp with his signature and that was all they were getting.

Five o'clock had come and gone when he suddenly remembered he was supposed to be taking part in the Secret Santa draw. Felicity was so good at reminding him of all his engagements, he usually didn't have to think. Maybe she didn't think she should push this one. And maybe he'd have been annoyed if she'd barged in to remind him of something so trivial, but now he felt slightly irritated at being forgotten.

He whipped open the door to the staffroom. The chatter died and everyone eyed him like a wolf had just arrived at a rabbit-only party.

'Sorry, I'm late.' He straightened his tie and sat down, his eyes instantly landing on Felicity. She smiled at him like she was encouraging a child to take their first steps and he changed his focus to his shoes. They were quite nice, shiny shoes. Yes, very nice and distracting.

'You're not late,' a high-pitched voice said. Ella somebody... He really needed to make more of an effort to know who everyone was, especially after four months. There was a good chance he might pull a name out of the bag and he wouldn't know who they were, let alone what to get them.

'We've just started,' Ella continued. 'Remember, when you pull out a name, don't say who it is, or show it to anyone, or look at the person. We need it to be a complete secret.'

She moved around the seated staff and people put their hands into the bag, pulling out little bits of paper and smiling to themselves. Felicity pulled hers out and shielded it with her hand before reading it and placing it on her lap with a prim smile. When the bag got to Gavin, he put his hand in and fumbled about. Only a few slips remained. He caught one and drew it out. Unfolding it, he read the name impassively, then balled his fist over the top of it. The king of the poker face, he didn't react, but his heart walloped against his chest. Why, oh why, did it have to be her? As Ella reached the last person, he glanced briefly at his bit of paper just to make sure his mind wasn't playing tricks on him. Nope. There it was, plain as day. *FELICITY.*

CHAPTER FIVE

Felicity threw open the door to Gavin's office and held her arms wide, waggling her fingers like jazz hands. 'Tada.'

He glanced up from his desk and his eyebrows slowly raised as his focus roamed over her face and onto her bright red mohair jumper. The cute reindeer with its tartan scarf and sequined antlers seemed to shrink back. As his gaze roamed lower to where she'd tucked the jumper into a thick belt atop her grey pencil skirt, she wriggled her toes inside her court shoes. Bursting into his office probably wasn't her best idea. His most serious suit was on, matching his expression. What now? Shout Christmas fools' day and run off or grab the reindeer by the antlers and own it? The smallest quirk at the corner of his lips told her to roll with the latter.

She folded her arms. 'Um, what happened to the memo to wear Christmas jumpers on Secret Santa day? Where's yours?'

He got to his feet and adjusted his blazer cuffs. Something about the movement was arresting and slightly menacing. She edged her heel back as he moved round his desk.

'I said it was compulsory for the Secret Santa draw, not the whole day.'

Her chest eased and she exhaled long. *Phew.* 'Personally, I think that's cheating.'

He huffed a short laugh before his face fell again. 'No can do.' He strolled to the window, split the blinds with his fingertips and peered out. Sleety rain hit the glass. 'I had a phone call last night from some old friends of my parents. They live up near one of the distilleries in Perthshire but they're in the city this morning and want to meet for a coffee.'

Felicity bit her tongue before she told him how much more amusing it would have been if he'd had to meet them in a garish Christmas jumper. Perhaps one with a chimney where you could pull strings and make Santa's upturned boots jiggle. She suppressed a grin at the idea of a smartly dressed older woman leaning over to yank the string every few minutes. 'That'll be nice.'

'I doubt it,' he said. 'I suspect they have a hidden agenda and they're luring me out to talk business under the pretence of a gingerbread latte.'

'Oh dear.'

'That's why I need you to come with me.'

'What?' She gaped at him. 'Me? Dressed like this?'

His gaze raked over her top again, making her stomach swoop in a way she hadn't expected.

'Why not?' he said. 'As Christmas jumpers go, that one is erring on tasteful. If it had flashing lights or jingling bells, I might have had to reconsider.'

Great. So much for her private sniggering about him turning up dressed like Mr Christmas. *Joke's on me.* 'What kind of business do they do?'

'Geoff Harrington is in the renewables sector and I suspect he wants to drag us kicking and screaming into greener choices for the distilleries.'

'Doesn't sound like a completely terrible idea.'

'Maybe not, but there's enough going on just now without taking on anything else. If it's something we can easily integrate, I'll listen, but no new initiatives.'

'Fair enough. And what do you want me to do exactly?'

'Keep your ears open and take notes. Mental ones. Don't go whipping out a notebook or anything.'

'Ok. I can do that.' Not that she had a choice.

Ella almost spat out her morning coffee when Felicity told her where she was going.

'With the boss?'

'Yup, with the boss.'

Ella sniggered at her laptop screen. 'You poor thing. He's probably only taking you because he's crap at making small talk. I once got stuck in the staffroom with him. It was so awkward, he just didn't speak, or attempt to do anything. Eugh.' She shuddered.

'Hmm. He was like that with me at first. He talks a bit more now. Or maybe I just rabbit on for both of us. We're not going far. It's just—'

'Are you ready?'

Felicity spun around. Gavin was behind her in a mid-length navy wool coat, tugging on a pair of leather gloves.

'Yes, I am.' She buttoned up her cosy grey coat and pushed her hands into the pockets, turning back to Ella with a brief wince and sending her a telepathic message: *I hope he didn't overhear us.* Her favourite gloves had finally given up the ghost and she hadn't got round to replacing them. *Mental note to grab a pair later.* But as she was leaving for London as soon as the day ended, she might not have time. She could always save the glove buying for a Boxing Day trip to Oxford Street.

She shivered slightly as they stepped out of the building and onto the street.

'Bracing, isn't it?' Gavin strode forward.

Walking quickly in heels wasn't the easiest for her, even with her long legs. Residue of icy rain coated the pavement, making it slippery underfoot. She'd changed out of her court shoes into a pair of long boots, aware that once her coat came off, she was going to have a distinct Mrs Clausishness about her. What would these old friends of the boss make of her? Years of seeing a therapist as a young teen had helped her understand more about her obsession with the perfect figure and her desire to look immaculate even to the detriment of her health; understand maybe, but it didn't remove the butterflies that always woke whenever she was going to be 'on show'. Make-up, heels and smart clothes bolstered her confidence. Rudolf jumpers not so much. Why hadn't she thought to bring a change of clothes, just in case?

They strode down Princes Street, stopping at a busy side street and waiting to cross. Felicity looked right for traffic and was about to step out when Gavin's arm leapt across her. She stumbled back and he steadied her. What the? She gasped as a cyclist whizzed past. Where had he come from?

'Sorry.' Gavin let go quickly and held his hands up like he was surrendering. 'I thought you were going to walk out in front of him.'

'I was.' She rubbed her chest and puffed out a blast of air. 'I didn't see him coming. Thanks.'

'No problem. I once had to pull a woman back when she pushed a pram out in front of a bus. She thought it had stopped at the red light and she started walking. She got mad at me for putting my hands on her.'

'Seriously? She'd rather have had her kid hit by a bus?'

'That's what I said to her.'

'You're a regular Superman, aren't you?'

He grunted what might have been a laugh but more likely scorn. 'Hardly.'

But his presence was oddly reassuring, not just because of the cyclist. It was something else that she couldn't quite put her finger on, maybe just the fact he was taller than her. She was often eye-to-eye with guys and it was surprisingly nice to feel physically small next to him.

He stopped and tweaked his gloves at a glass-fronted coffee shop with a swirly sign over the door reading The Espresso Lounge.

'Do you think they're here yet?' Felicity rubbed her raw fingers together.

'Let's go and see.' He pulled open the door and held it for her.

Warmth hit her, along with the fragrance of freshly brewed coffee. The aromatic scent of cinnamon and other winter spices tingled in her nostrils, and she pressed the back of her hand against the cold tip of her nose. She probably looked like Rudolph now.

A server greeted them before she'd reached the *wait to be seated* sign.

'Table for two?' he asked.

'No.' Gavin fiddled with the edge of his glove. 'We're meeting a Mr and Mrs Harrington. They might be here already.'

Felicity scanned the dimly lit room with low glass tables and comfy chairs. Cityscape pictures hung from exposed brick walls and huge twisted copper lights were suspended from the ceiling.

'Yes, of course,' the server said. 'This way, please.'

'Oh no,' Gavin muttered, stalling, and Felicity turned to look at him.

'What?'

'Nothing.' He coughed and tugged on his tie. Even in the dim lights, his cheeks looked flushed. More so than when he'd come in out of the cold. Felicity frowned and carried on behind the server to a table in the corner where three people were seated. Her gaze instantly fell on the youngest person in the group. A woman about the same age as her or younger and, from what she could see, not dissimilar in build. A sheet of long caramel blonde hair fell around her shoulders, each strand perfectly straight. Her outfit was dark green and understated, unlike Felicity's reindeer jumper. Felicity fingered the hair she'd thrown into a messy updo that morning. Why hadn't she taken more time on it, like she usually did? Something prickled at her, making her squirm. Maybe the mohair?

The server put out his hand to indicate the table.

Three pairs of eyes landed on Gavin, then quickly shifted to Felicity.

'Gavin.' The only man at the table stood. 'You made it. Sorry for the short notice. We're not here for long. We're going back to Glenbriar this afternoon for Christmas.' He stretched out his hand and Gavin shook it. 'Who have we here?' The man smiled but it didn't extend to his sharp blue eyes. He must be at least in his fifties and had an easy-going debonair look about him. 'Is this your...' He looked back at Gavin.

'My PA, Felicity Swan.'

'Ahh.' The man nodded and his eyes twinkled. 'Of course. Well, Felicity, I'm Geoff Harrington, this is my wife, Hilary, and my daughter, Genevieve.'

'Pleased to meet you all.' Felicity smiled around the table, aware Genevieve was watching her with narrowed eyes.

'There was no need to bring your secretary,' Geoff muttered aside to Gavin. Felicity caught his words nonetheless as she unbuttoned her coat. Heat flared up her neck. Cups clinked at the neighbouring table, but Felicity tuned into Geoff. 'This is strictly personal, not business.'

'Indeed,' Gavin said.

Felicity slung her coat over the back of the chair, then sat beside Genevieve, pressing her hands together in front of her. Maybe she could hide the reindeer. Gavin took the seat opposite, beside Hilary, and Geoff resumed his place at the end.

'Very festive.' Hilary tucked a strand of blonde hair behind her ear, eyeing Felicity's top. She was almost the double of her daughter, only with a few more wrinkles and a little less make up.

'Thanks,' Felicity said. Clearly nothing could stop the sequins shining through.

'It's the last day of work.' Gavin flicked her a tiny smile. 'Felicity likes to spread Christmas joy.'

'Didn't work on you.' Geoff grinned at Gavin. 'As sombre as ever.'

'That's me,' Gavin said, his cheeks still abnormally red. His gaze roamed around, not settling on anything or anyone but most noticeably avoiding Genevieve. Felicity's teeth bore down on the inside of her lip, pulling back a smirk as she lifted the menu. This was a setup, and she was a mohair-covered, sequin-encrusted spanner in the works for the Harringtons. Gavin had got it all wrong. They didn't want him here for business. They were obviously trying to shove their very pretty daughter into the path of a very handsome, very eligible bachelor.

Gavin's evident discomfort at the situation set Felicity's mind wandering down speculation street. They ordered and small talk flowed. Geoff was quite in love with the sound of his own voice. Despite his insistence he wasn't there to talk business, he must have mentioned his company Harrington Energy Solutions about twenty times. And as for being friends with Gavin's parents, it sounded more like he wanted to make quite sure everyone at the table knew that his business was more successful – even if he didn't say so in quite so many words. Felicity smiled and laughed in all the right places, noting Gavin's hardened posture when Geoff Harrington said, 'Do you remember my son, Rafe? I tried to persuade him to take over the business like you did for Frank, but, oh my, he's having none of it. He runs his own company, you know, and has many projects and commitments of his own.'

'Good to hear.' Gavin took a sip of his drink with a clenched jaw.

Felicity glanced at Genevieve, whose expression was cool and impassive.

'I could always take over,' Genevieve said without looking up from her cup.

Geoff laughed. 'You could if you ever finish any of the degrees you start and get a proper job. She's a bright girl,' he added to Gavin, 'But this influencer thing isn't a real job.'

Genevieve stiffened and smoothed down her skirt.

'I have some ideas though.' Geoff tapped the side of his nose. 'We'll get her fixed up in a job soon.'

Poor Genevieve. Maybe she was desperate to meet a rich man who would sweep her off her feet and whisk her away from her parents and let her follow her own path. But was that just as bad as her parents choosing the man? Would it be Gavin? He was doing a great job of looking disinterested, his eyes wandering in every direction but Genevieve's. Not that Felicity should care, of course, but speculating about her boss's love life was as good a way as any to pass the time. And actually... Her gaze lingered on his well-honed jaw and pleasingly shaped nose; he was really good looking. Even more so than she'd noticed before and she had noticed once or twice.

As soon as Gavin swigged the last of his drink – a completely unfestive green tea – he lifted his gloves. 'So, sorry we can't stay longer,' he said. 'I'm due in another meeting, but it was great to see you all.'

Geoff slowly sipped his drink with such tight lips it was a wonder any liquid got in. His steely eyes fixed on Felicity and his nostrils flared. She understood his wordless accusation. *This is your fault.*

Maybe it was. Inadvertently. She hadn't invited herself along to pretend she was Gavin's date, and as far as she knew, he hadn't expected this either, so his inviting her had been a pure fluke. He could have brought anyone along and it would have scuppered the setup. But with Felicity's unfortunate similarities to Genevieve... Well, it had clearly annoyed Geoff. When he shook hands, it was with an ice-cold expression. Gavin settled the bill before hightailing it out of the coffee shop. He was at the side street where Felicity had almost been hit by the bike when she caught up with him, still tying her belt.

'Sorry about all that,' he said. 'I made a mistake. The business they wanted to talk about... Well, it was a different kind of business they had in mind.'

Felicity checked the road thoroughly for cyclists but also used it as an excuse to keep looking the other way while she smirked. 'Are they trying to marry you off to their daughter, by any chance?'

'Probably,' he muttered, striding off again. Subject closed and tightly tied up with sparkly Christmas ribbon.

Ella danced around the staffroom like a manic fairy come the afternoon, holding the Secret Santa sack and grinning as everyone took their seats. Felicity sat beside Winnie and tipped her head onto her shoulder with a sigh. 'Thank goodness it's holiday time.'

'I hear you were on a date with the boss this morning,' Winnie said, patting her leg.

Felicity lifted her head and gave Winnie a look. 'Oh, yeah. Only the top man's good enough for me. Why do you think his office door's been shut ever since?' Felicity winked. 'I've been keeping him busy.'

Winnie chuckled and shook her head. 'Very good. Where is he now? I thought he was joining in.'

'No idea. He told me he was on a call and not to be disturbed, so I didn't.'

Ella drew gifts from the bag and handed them to people. 'Don't read the notes,' she commanded. 'Everyone has to do it individually or it spoils the fun.'

She passed an oblong parcel to Felicity. It felt a bit like a book but was too narrow and light. The foil wrapping paper was high quality, with white snowflakes on silver; a neatly tied shiny bow fixed the tag to it.

Before the last gifts were handed out, the door opened and Gavin entered. Felicity covered her mouth as a giggle bubbled up. He tugged at the hem of a Christmas jumper in dark navy with snowflakes and a giant Christmas tree on the front decorated with 3d baubles and real jingling bells. Adjusting the neckline, he sat opposite and caught her eye. He gave her a resigned smirk and she beamed.

'That's unexpected,' Winnie muttered without moving her lips and pretending to look behind for something.

Ella flushed scarlet as she presented Gavin with his gift.

'Can I have everyone's attention for just a second?' he said. 'Not because I want you all to admire my, er, style choices.' He screwed up his nose at the jumper. 'But because I'd like to take this opportunity to thank you all for your work this year. And thank you, Ella, for organising this fun end to the year.'

Her cheeks were now so red, she looked like she had the mumps.

'I hope you all have a wonderful Christmas and a happy new year.' Gavin gave a brief smile and sat back in his chair.

'Thanks,' Ella said in a squeaky voice. 'Why don't you start us off?'

'Ok.' Gavin turned around the tag on his gift and read. '*To Mr Sinclair from someone who has two kids, three guinea pigs and a fascination with cheese.*' He raised his eyebrows slightly.

Winnie sniggered from beside Felicity and she nudged her. 'Shh.'

'Now open it,' Ella said. 'Then you have to guess who you think it is that sent it.'

Gavin's cheeks looked a little hot as he pulled off the paper to reveal a mug with the legend: Property of the Boss.

'So, who do you think it was?' Ella said. 'And remember, if he guesses right, the sender has to own up.'

He glanced around and his gaze settled on Felicity. 'I think it was Felicity.'

'What?' She burst out laughing and so did Ella. Winnie doubled over. A few other people joined in.

'Wasn't it?'

'No,' Felicity said.

'But you said…' Gavin mumbled.

'It definitely wasn't me. I don't have kids or guinea pigs. I quite like cheese but being fascinated with it is too much.'

'Ok. So, you got it wrong,' Ella said. 'Let's move to the next person.'

Gavin blinked at the mug with a slight frown.

Winnie typed something into her phone, then passed it covertly to Felicity.

Why the hell did he think that was you?

Felicity handed her the phone back with a shrug. She'd used Winnie's comment as an example. Had he actually thought it was her? Kids and guinea pigs – at twenty-five? Hardly. She hadn't reached that stage in life.

Slowly, they progressed around the room, barely anyone guessing right. Felicity fiddled with the tag impatiently.

Finally, it was her turn. She whipped it round and read the typed note aloud.

'To Felicity. From someone who:

1. Likes carrot juice

2. Enjoys wild swimming

3. Was once proposed to by the love of their life but turned them down and has regretted it ever since.'

She looked up and pulled a face, rippling her fingertips along her chin. 'Ooh, very cryptic.'

Ella's eyes popped as she scanned around the staff, clearly wondering who it was. Felicity slipped her finger under the perfectly aligned tape and unfolded the paper. Inside was a black box. She opened it and lifted a thin sheet of tissue paper to reveal a beautiful pair of plum-coloured gloves. 'Oh my god. Just what I wanted.' She pulled them out. Wow, the tips even had the touchscreen feature. 'No way. The ultra-glove.' She tried them on. Perfect fit and snuggly warm. 'Oh, this is someone very clever and kind. Or someone sneaky who was listening.' She searched around, trying to remember who had been in the room the morning she'd said she wanted new gloves. Winnie? But no. She'd obviously bought Gavin's gift and Felicity was pretty sure she didn't wild swim and was an unlikely candidate for a failed proposal. 'I'm completely stumped.' She squinted at the poker faces. 'Was it you, Lorah?'

'Not me,' Lorah said.

'Another wrong guess.' Ella shook her head. 'We're not doing very well with this.'

The focus shifted to the next person, but Felicity continued to stare at the gloves. Who on earth was it? Should she be worried? Maybe it was a stalker? Or should she be flattered? A secret admirer perhaps? But that proposal thing. It had to be a woman, right? Men didn't usually get proposals, but it was possible. Not to mention it seemed much more likely for a woman to have bought her such a considered gift. Her gaze raked the room.

Maybe she had a female admirer? That was possible too. Though she hoped not, for their sake. She was only into guys.

But one thing was certain: she was determined to find out who it was.

CHAPTER SIX

Gavin

Christmas Day

Gavin tossed a scrunched-up piece of wrapping paper into the fire. Flames crackled and fizzed as they chewed up the paper bomb. He lounged back, holding up a pair of black socks with the words *this meeting is bollocks* printed down the side. Emily, his sister, winked at him from across the room in between collecting armfuls of discarded paper as her children opened presents like mini whirlwinds.

'Accurate,' he said. 'If the last few months have been anything to go by.' He placed the socks aside and took a sip of Glenbriar's finest. He wasn't sure he'd ever acquire a taste for it but his father was intent on him trying.

'Oh dear, dear.' Dorothy, his well-dressed mother, tutted, stretching over the sofa and lifting the socks. 'That language is quite disgraceful. Who gave you them? Was it someone from work?'

'Um... Yes.' He didn't look at Emily, whose snigger went un-noticed as she pretended to laugh at her children's joy at opening so many presents.

'Put them under there.' Dorothy lifted his stack of presents and pushed them to the bottom. 'Don't let Artie and Cissy see them. They shouldn't be exposed to words like that.'

'Mum, they're four and two.' Emily held out her hands. 'They can't read yet.'

'Even so.' Dorothy got to her feet and bustled about, picking up more stray bits of wrapping paper.

The Sinclair family home may be old – *was* old; Frank and Dorothy Sinclair delighted in telling people the history of their arts and crafts home in Gullane – probably the poshest village in Scotland – but it was always immaculate. Having two cleaners no doubt helped. The deep wine carpet in the living room was a little dated décor-wise but matched his parents' austere and formal taste. At Christmas, it looked quite perfect. The entire house did. Dorothy hired an interior designer to ensure everything was just so. Real poinsettia plants bloomed in every alcove and green garlands interspersed with twinkling lights draped over the giant mantelpiece and coiled around the thick oak banisters.

Every year, the décor reached new heights but was always traditional, never tacky. Gavin swigged another mouthful of whisky. The heat from the fire was punishing now. He slipped his Christmas jumper off over his head, a different one from the one he'd worn for the Secret Santa. He smirked as he straightened out the t-shirt he had on underneath – red with a giant skating Santa on it. What would Felicity make of this? He downed another slug of whisky. Why was he thinking about her?

Problem was, he'd thought of her every day since the office had shut. At least once. Maybe twice. Ok, quite a bit more some days. He tried not to, but changing brain channels was challenging. Thoughts would creep up and spring on him when he wasn't expecting them or he'd suddenly realise he'd been thinking about her for an indeterminate amount of time. Certain facts kept leaping out more prominently than others. She didn't really have kids – or guinea pigs. She must have said that for a joke or to put him off the scent in case she drew him out of the bag. Made sense. She didn't really look like someone with kids. No judgement, she just didn't. And she'd liked her gloves. She thought they were from someone clever and kind. *She'll never suspect me then.* He took another sip. She wouldn't anyway. That cryptic note would make sure of it. Carrot juice was the most likely thing to give him away. He just had to remember not to drink it in front of her.

Who would think the stuffed shirt liked wild swimming? And he'd bet every penny he had they'd all think it was a woman who'd sent the note because of the proposal. But it was him. He'd been proposed to in this very house, at a Christmas dinner, on a day just like this one, when he was twenty-six, and marriage seemed like something for older people. Something he'd do in the distant future. He hadn't expected his girlfriend to propose. They hadn't seemed ready. And worse, his mother didn't like her. Dorothy had very fixed ideas on the 'type' of person she wanted him to marry but she hadn't settled on an individual yet. Thank god. It was enough having friends of his father trying to set him up with their daughters.

He pulled in a deep breath as scenes played through his mind. Holly, the proposer, had been his university sweetheart. They were the same age, did the same job, had similar interests and were good together in many ways. She'd gone to a big effort to make the proposal special by putting a note in a box atop a Christmas cake and ensuring he lifted the 'right' piece. He'd read the words aloud in shock, suspecting a joke. His mother's face had spoken volumes. Her dislike for Holly increased tenfold in that instance. With such an obsession with tradition and old-fashioned Christian ideals, it was unthinkable anyone should propose to her son. Men did the proposing and that was that. Flooded with fear and doubt, Gavin had taken Holly aside and declined. The relationship fell apart. Only now he saw what he'd missed. Holly had moved on and was with someone else. Gavin had stayed put, joined the dating game and failed.

'Hey.' Emily plonked herself down beside him. 'What you thinking?'

'Nothing, why?'

'I know that face,' she whispered. 'What's bothering you?' She glanced around, then lowered her voice further so Gavin had to lean forward to hear her. 'Is it work?'

'No, work's fine,' he lied.

'What then? Is it Holly?'

'No.' He rubbed his neck. 'She's in the past.'

Emily patted his thigh. 'I hope so, because it's time you moved on.'

'I have moved on. Years ago.'

'For real, Gav. Date whoever you like. You don't have to date the people they set you up with.'

'I haven't. I—'

'Dad told me about Genevieve Harrington.'

Gavin slouched back and massaged his forehead. 'Seriously? Let me get this straight. Dad set up that meeting with the Harringtons?'

'Didn't you know?'

Gavin shook his head. Great. Just great. 'No, I didn't.'

'Just as well it didn't work out. Mum thinks Genevieve is a harlot – her word, not mine – because she wears the devil's work on her nails. She only agreed because she thought she might have "grown out of that nonsense".' Emily air-quoted with a smirk.

Gavin snorted. 'Well, their plan backfired completely. I thought Geoff Harrington was hoping for some kind of business deal, so I went ready for a meeting. I even took my PA with me. I can't believe it was mum and dad's doing.' Unbelievable.

'What's this, what's this?' His dad nudged a footstool with his leg, then sat on it in front of Gavin. 'Did I hear you saying something about Geoff Harrington wanting a deal? What kind of deal?' Dad's grin made Gavin certain he was hoping to hear him gush about how wonderful Genevieve was and how he'd be seeing her as soon as he could come the new year.

'Turned out to be nothing,' Gavin said.

'Oh? But you met him, I understand.'

He understands! Because he set it up and they'd been merrily discussing it with Emily.

'Just a quick coffee. He wanted to say merry Christmas while he was in town.'

'Ah.' Frank nodded.

Gavin popped open a box of After Eights and offered one to his dad.

'Have you not had enough to eat?' his mother said.

'Always room for an After Eight.' Gavin slipped one from the packet. Usually, he stuck to an almost regimentally healthy diet, but on Christmas Day, well stuff it. 'Tell me. Did Julian suggest to you that we sell some of the Highland assets or downgrade them?'

Dad frowned and took another After Eight. 'He's not suggesting that, is he?'

'What's that?' His mother said.

'Julian suggested some of the Highland distilleries aren't viable anymore.' Gavin folded the After Eight wrapper.

'Why not?' Mum frowned and fixed him with a piercing stare.

'Good question,' Dad said. 'If there's a problem, then sort it. Selling up and downgrading should be an absolute last resort.'

'The problem is, I'm not an expert,' Gavin said. 'Solving this kind of problem is only possible if I know how. And I don't.'

'You know what you need to do?' Mum said.

'What?'

'Get out of your office and go and visit them. See what it's really like. Your father and I spent half our time here and half in the Highlands. It was by far the best way to see how things are going.'

'That's what my PA said I should do.'

'Ah, Felicity Swan.' Dad tilted his head to the side and smiled. His mum pulled a face.

'I hired her for you because I knew she'd be good,' Dad said.

'Though she was always a bit trashy.' Mum's mouth drew into a harsh line.

Gavin raised his eyebrows. Was she? She always appeared well turned out to him.

'That aside,' Dad said. 'She was one of our best guides at Glenbriar and I was loath to let her move from that, but I'm glad I did. I thought she would do well. So pleased she's working out for you.'

'I didn't say she was.' Gavin's insides winced. Where did that come from? Couldn't he just agree she was working out fine? On a professional level anyway.

'Isn't she?' Dad frowned.

'Yes, she is. She's good at her job.'

His mother tutted and let out a sigh. 'I know what you mean, son.'

'Do you?'

'Well, she's that certain type of woman, isn't she? Enthusiastic enough, I'm sure, but all the make-up is far too excessive. And her nails. That polish, ugh. Always looks a bit on the scarlet side, if you get my drift.'

Emily rolled her eyes.

'Right,' Gavin said. 'Have you seen Genevieve Harrington recently?' Her make-up was equal to Felicity's.

'No.' Mum swept a stray strand of hair from her face. 'But I hoped she'd have got over that stage by now. Still, I like Genevieve's family.'

Dad chuckled before Gavin could respond. 'Yes, these young ladies like to cake themselves in make-up, but as long as Felicity's good at her job, that's what matters. So, are you going to make a trip?'

'I guess I should.' Gavin slid out another After Eight. Of course he should visit. Having some knowledge of what he was in charge of seemed sensible but the practicalities made his stomach squirm. How long would it take? A week? A fortnight? A month? Learning more new ways, meeting more new people. He already had an international trip with Julian in February, plus several big acquisition meetings in April. When was he going to fit all this in?

'You can use the house, of course,' Mum said. 'We won't be going up until later in the year, so you may as well. I'll have June pop in and make sure it's clean.'

'Thanks, but hold off until I decide when I'm going.'

'Good.' Dad slapped his thighs. 'That's sorted. Just don't leave it too long. The sooner you go, the better. Now, who's up for a game of charades?'

January

'Happy new year.' Gavin laid his briefcase by his office door. Felicity was sitting at his desk, her back to him, ready for the first briefing of the new year. A sucker punch hit him in the gut. That fragrance was so intoxicating, and her glossy hair, straight at the top, working its way into coils at the end, was so beautiful. Just seeing her had a powerful impact on his heart rate.

'Happy new year,' she said, her voice soft and a bit too quiet.

Gavin straightened his blazer, marched across the room, and sat behind his desk opposite her. 'Are you ok?'

'Yeah, fine.' She dropped her gaze, then shrugged. 'Well, actually, not really, but…'

'What is it?' He steepled his fingers on the desk. This couldn't be good. Where was the ever-present smile? Her expression was flat and the skin around her eyes puffy. Had someone died over Christmas?

'It's not anything to do with work.' She didn't meet his gaze but glanced at her iPad on the desk.

'It doesn't matter. My employees' wellbeing is important too, so I'm listening.'

She blinked before looking up. He'd seen her with smoky eyes before but suspected this time the look wasn't on purpose. Vulnerability wasn't something he associated with her. She was usually so cheery and bright, so mature and assured, but now she looked her age – young and uncertain. Her demeanour cut like a blade to his heart. How could he take away her pain? He'd gladly suffer it for her if it would make her smile again. His fingertips twitched, begging him to reach out and offer her physical comfort, but he clenched them tightly together. He mustn't do anything silly.

'I went home over Christmas,' she said. 'To London.'

Gavin waited, not sure if he should prompt her to carry on. He never knew quite what to say when people were upset.

'Things have changed. My granny has dementia. She was always a bit forgetful but now it's got serious. It's so hard. My uncle has mental health issues and he lives with her. He doesn't want her to go into care, but he can't look after her. He can't even look after himself, so my mum's trying to do it all but my dad's not been well either. He's having all kinds of tests.' She glanced up at the ceiling, pressing her lips together. 'I'm the third of six kids, the oldest sister, and no one said anything, but I just have a feeling that everyone thinks I don't do enough. Or they think I don't care enough because I moved away. Like somehow, my living here means I've shut off and left them to do all the work. Does that make sense? I'm sorry if I'm talking shit. Pardon my language. I just didn't have a great Christmas.'

'It makes perfect sense,' Gavin said. 'Living up to family expectations is never easy and just when you think you've cracked it, the goalposts change, or they raise the bar another notch.'

The corners of her lips turned up briefly and she nodded. 'Yup.'

'So, what do you need? Time off? Or would you like to work remotely for a while so you can be down there, helping your family and maybe sorting some kind of care for your grandmother?'

'Would you allow that?'

His chest tightened. It wouldn't be half as nice around the office without her.

'Of course I would. In fact...' He opened his laptop and clicked on the calendar. 'The next few months have so many dates when I'm not here either, it hardly matters where you are. Right up until the end of April really. And that reminds me, I need you to organise the distillery tour. But I can't do that until at least May.'

'I'll sort that. How long do you want it to be?'

He tapped the desk. 'I'm not sure. What do you suggest?'

'If you really want to see how things work, you should spend at least a week getting to know the distilleries and the local area too. That would really help you understand the branding and the marketing. You could add your own blogs to the website and push up the social media ratings if you did posts from your visits, that kind of thing.'

Sometimes her non-stop chatter drove him round the twist but today his heart swelled. This was more like her. The energy and enthusiasm were back.

'Ok, well, you lay out an itinerary and see how long it'll take to do it properly. Once we get the international visits and the acquisitions out of the way, my head will be in a better place to think about it.'

'And you're sure it's ok for me to do this remotely?'

'Absolutely.'

'Thank you. I really appreciate it.' She got to her feet. Keeping her eyes on him, she ran her fingers along her collarbone, exposing her long neck as she disturbed the soft fabric of her top. Gavin held his breath. For a split second, his stomach swooped like a hawk with its eye on a pigeon. Was she going to come around and hug him?

He cleared his throat and jumped to his feet. 'No problem.'

She picked up the iPad, clutched it to her chest and left.

Now all he needed to do was survive the next four months without her. Easy, huh?

Chapter Seven

Felicity

May

Felicity's mum hugged her, then let her go, then hugged her again. Felicity laughed. 'I should get going, Mum.'

'I just can't thank you enough for coming back and helping out. That's the problem when my most helpful child lives so far away.'

'Sorry.' Her heart tugged, torn between wanting to stay and keep helping, and getting back to her other home and work. Not that work had stopped but she was keen to get back to the office.

'Don't you be sorry,' her mum said. 'I didn't expect you to do this at all. It's been great having you here and getting your nan sorted with care. You're very organised for such a young thing, but don't you be sorry about having to go back to your own life. I appreciate what you've done. Now get away and don't worry. It's time one of your siblings stepped up and helped out instead of expecting you to do it.'

Felicity grinned. Somehow she didn't see that happening but her mum was right. She couldn't let these guilt trips get the better of her or she'd end up leaving her job and moving back down. She hugged her younger sister, Caralyn, and her teenage brother, Elijah, before wrapping her arms around her dad.

He slapped her heartily on the back. 'Take care up in Scotland. A bit wild up there from what I've heard. And pack the car with everything you need. Stock up on all the things they don't have up there.'

'Such as?'

'I dunno... Do they have Cornish pasties?'

Felicity put her hands on her hips and frowned. 'Cornish pasties? Can you get them anywhere except Cornwall? I'm sure I can get a Scotch pie instead if I really want. But really, they've got everything up there that we have down here except the pollution levels.'

'Ah, righty-ho, that's good then.'

'You should come and visit when you're feeling a hundred per cent again. It'll do wonders for your chest.'

'What? All that fresh air? I'm sure it'd bring on an attack.'

'Dad, fresh air helps asthma. Didn't the doctor explain all that?' He may now have a diagnosis with asthma but he was still in denial and clearly ignorant about what to do to help himself.

Her mum rolled her eyes. 'Never mind him. I'd love to come. Maybe I'll leave everyone here and come up myself one day.'

'Please do. I'd love to have you.'

'I'll come too,' Caralyn said.

'Any time.' Felicity gave her another hug, hopped into her green Volkswagen Beetle, gave them one last wave, and drove off. She wasn't ashamed of where she came from but it made her smirk to think how backward some of her dad's ideas were about other places. Especially when he loved to think his ways were so superior. When she left the housing estate for the main road, she let out a sigh and relaxed her grip on the wheel. She'd spent all her formative years here with graffiti-covered walls and buildings crammed together. The only green space had a view of the motorway and high-rise flats overshadowed it. Much as it was familiar, she had no great desire to return. Not since living for three years with views of rolling hills, forests and rivers. And now she lived in Edinburgh – a much gentler city than this.

The nose-to-tail traffic curbed a restless urge to put her foot down and speed on the main road. Felicity's shoulders slumped and she groaned, but a little flame in her chest flickered stronger as she thought about going into the office on Monday. It wasn't something she generally looked forward to that much but this time it kept her smiling. Maybe just catching up with everyone. What else could it be?

With hours and hours of driving still to do, she tapped the wheel and weighed up the options. Music? Talk to herself – why not? She could rehearse her speech for when she let Gavin know the amazing itinerary she'd planned for the highland distillery trip. But once she'd done that, there would still be time to kill.

Or she could talk to Briony. Assuming she wasn't busy at the hotel with guests as was highly possible, if not likely, on a Friday morning, but why not try anyway?

She rang on the hands-free, putting up a silent prayer as she waited. *Please be there, please pick up.*

'Hello,' Briony's cheery voice said. 'Is everything ok?'

'Fine, yes. I'm driving back today and I'm bored.'

'Aw, bless. I remembered it was today. How are you feeling about it all?'

'I'm actually glad to be going back. It's not that I don't care about my family, it's just... Well, I miss Scotland.'

'You're an adopted Scot.'

'I think I must be.'

'Not long now until you'll be back,' Briony said. 'And you're coming to visit me.'

'I know. I'm so excited. It's the best excuse ever for a company-paid holiday. Hopefully I'll be able to get away quite a bit and we can catch up properly. My boss won't want me to hang about him in the evenings.'

'I've sorted him out with one of our new suites, so he'll have everything he needs in there.'

'Excellent,' Felicity said. 'I'll tell him on Monday.' She hadn't asked about his preferences on where to stay, only the budget, but how could he object to such a beautifully located hotel? And one with such an excellent location for visiting all the distilleries? She didn't have to let on her friend owned it. 'And how are you keeping?'

'Not bad, but I feel huge and everything aches when I'm on my feet too long.'

'Aw. Not long now. I can't wait until you have the little darling. I'll be first in the queue for a cuddle.'

Briony laughed. 'You definitely will be.'

Chatting to Briony passed a good forty minutes before Briony had to go and Felicity resorted to the radio.

Her mind wandered frequently, finding its way back to work more often than she meant. A job was a job. She'd never lived to work. Enjoying what she did was a bonus but she had a life. Moving to Edinburgh hadn't stopped her love of running, though it had scuppered her water sports. Maybe with a few weeks in Glenbriar, she could nip down to the loch and get out in a kayak again. Which reminded her of the cryptic Secret Santa. With everything that had happened at Christmas, then the mad dash south to help out her parents, she hadn't been able to snoop around and sniff out who might have been behind the gift.

As she hadn't worked in the office that long herself, she didn't know everyone and certainly not well. Whoever it was, she had them pegged as a lonely soul. Someone who was reasonably fit with their love of carrot juice and wild swimming, but also someone sad. They'd missed out on the love of their life. When she got back, she'd investigate more. Maybe the person would put themselves forward. That note could have been a cry for help. If it was someone who needed a friend, she could do that. She always had room for new friends and if they liked to stay fit and explore the wild outdoors, well, bonus! Maybe they could swim together. She'd never tried wild swimming despite her love of paddleboarding and kayaking, but she'd be willing to give it a go.

The distillery trip was the priority. Hopefully, it would be fun as well as do the job. She had to convince Gavin of the viability of the distilleries... Was she allowed to call him Gavin now? After Christmas, he'd thawed a little and been so kind about letting her work from home, and a faraway home at that, for one third of the year. They'd done calls remotely and he hadn't moaned or made any comments about having to set up meeting rooms on his own. He'd done his abroad trip with Julian and that had gone well. Or so it seemed, but Felicity suspected Julian had a hidden agenda. What if he'd persuaded Gavin to sell to some foreign investors? If she arrived back and discovered her proposed trip was up in smoke, she'd be gutted. The thought of that trip was part of the reason she was so chipper.

The flat was cold and had a horrible smell... Mould? Nothing would surprise her. With the heating being off for four months and a building not in the best of nick, it was only to be expected. She aired all her work clothes in the communal drying area. Hopefully the early May sunshine and the light breeze would do the trick. She couldn't turn up to the office smelling like she'd lived in a damp cupboard for several months.

Sunshine split through the window on Monday morning. Definitely a day for a summer dress. She liked bright colours but preferred to be muted at the office. Her sage green one with a ditsy white floral print was perfect. It gave her the illusion of curves when she was actually straight up and down, though not totally flat chested and with a good, padded bra, the dress scooped neatly at her neck, clung to her waist and flared in a pretty fashion over her non-existent hips. With a short-sleeved white linen jacket, she felt almost ready for summer, never mind late spring. But May in Scotland was always a beautiful month.

Princes Street looked bright and shiny as she made her way towards the office. The gardens were in full bloom and riotously colourful but her heart tugged. She so wanted to be back in the Highlands, surveying heather-clad hills and seeing foxgloves dancing on the moors. Not long now, assuming Gavin agreed. Should she call him Gavin? Or stick to Mr Sinclair? In the flesh, it seemed more of an issue than in an email or a phone call.

Nerves jangled in her tummy as she opened the main door. Why? It wasn't like she'd been off-radar. She'd spoken to people and kept in touch, but still, it was odd being here again, even though everything looked exactly the same.

When Ella pounced on her in the staffroom, Felicity laughed and breathed more easily.

'Thank goodness you're back,' she said. 'I've been so bored without you.'

'We can catch up properly later. I suppose I should go see the boss. Show face and all that.'

Ella screwed up her nose. 'Rather you than me.'

'Why?'

'Ah, you know?' She shrugged. 'I just don't get him. He's locked up in his office most of the time. It's so different from when Frank was boss. He was always in and out, helping if he had to and getting stuck in. He was friendly and chatty and people wanted to please him. But Gavin hardly ever shows face, so when I see him, I never know what to say to him. And he doesn't give anyone a word of thanks. Remember when Frank was boss, and Dorothy would always pop in with cakes on Fridays or arrange for catering for meetings? I can't see Gavin ever doing anything like that.'

Felicity fixed herself a coffee, an underlying layer of unease rippling over her shoulders. While she knew everyone would have a unique style of leadership, Gavin was acting more like a figurehead than someone leading from the top. And he was losing respect faster than whisky spouting from a broken barrel. Was it the same in the Highland Distilleries? When Felicity had worked at Glenbriar, Frank and Dorothy Sinclair had often shown up unannounced or appeared during busy times to help where needed. Everyone kept on top form and knew they were appreciated. Frank and Dorothy were generous and took time to get to know their employees. They paid for nights out and looked after their own. Who knew how the staff there were feeling now? Abandoned?

At the door to Gavin's office, Felicity took a long, deep breath, then knocked.

'Come.' That one monotonous word made goosebumps rise up her arms.

She pushed open the door and stepped in. 'Good morning.'

Gavin checked up from his laptop, blinked and looked like he was trying to rearrange his features. Into what she wasn't sure; maybe he wasn't either as he desisted and his lips twitched into a brief smile.

'Morning. Take a seat.' He indicated the seat opposite. He leaned back in his chair. 'So... Um, everything ok?'

'All good, thanks.'

'Good.' He nodded at his laptop. 'Yes. Good. So... It's good to have you back.'

'It's good to be back,' she said. Should they count how many times they could use the word good before one of them found something else to say?

'Well then, let's get straight to business. I need a conference room set up this morning. I'd like to start discussing the proposed new products this week.'

'Certainly.'

'And I'll email you some files I need made into a presentation. I've done some notes, but you can word it any way you like.'

'Ok.' Her heart tremored a little. He trusted her to do that. Or did he just not know what to put himself? 'Can I also tell you about the Highland Distillery trip? It's in the diary for next week and I have it all arranged.' She crossed her fingers under the desk. *Please don't say you want me to cancel it, please.*

'Yes, tell me.'

'So, over the fortnight, I've booked tours of all the distilleries and organised meetings with management and staff. You'll get to know how the distilleries work within the community.'

'Ok.'

'I've booked us a hotel that's close to all three distilleries and I'll be on hand to make sure you get everywhere you need to be. I know the area really well.'

Gavin raised his left eyebrow and ran his fingers along his cleanly shaven jaw. 'You're coming too?'

Felicity blinked and opened her mouth like a trippy fish. 'Well, yes... Am I not supposed to be?'

He looked back at his laptop. 'I, um... Just didn't realise. And a hotel?'

'You'll love it. It's the Loch View Hotel just outside Glenbriar. It has quite a history and it's linked to the distillery. You know about the theft?' Now she was babbling, but surely he wasn't going to go without her?

'Yes, I remember.'

It had been a big story for Briony and the local community not so long ago – a scandal linking the distillery and the hotel. 'I've got you the new executive suite there.' Felicity half-smiled at him... *Please say I can go.*

'Ok. And where are you staying?'

'At the hotel too, just in a normal room. Assuming you want me to come?'

'Yes, that's fine, but...' He let out a soft sigh. 'You realise my family has a house in Glenbriar?'

She frowned. *Shit.* Why hadn't she thought of that? Obviously Frank and Dorothy had needed somewhere to stay when they were visiting. 'I do,' she fibbed, 'but I thought maybe your parents lived in it.' Equally silly because, of course, they would allow him to stay with them for a couple of weeks.

'They're not there at present.' He tapped his finger on the desk. 'But if you're coming too, a hotel makes more sense.'

'I don't have to come.' Her heart sank with the words. She really didn't have to. He'd done trips abroad without her on hand, but she wanted to go back so much. 'Is there someone else you'd prefer to go with you? Julian?'

'No. It'll be easier with someone who knows what they're doing... I mean, where they're going.' He looked up and caught her eye. His pupils burned deep, forging a connection with hers that made her shiver. 'Right. That's settled.'

She caught her breath as soon as he shifted his focus. Her insides were dancing the conga. She was going on the trip. Only small problem was she'd be stuck with the boss for a fortnight... The conga dancing slowed. But she weighed it up against the thought of him not being there and the dance slowly started up again. Actually, it could be ok, maybe even fun, to see him out of his natural habitat.

CHAPTER EIGHT

Gavin

'That was an interesting presentation,' Julian said, taking the seat opposite Gavin in his office. 'I was pleasantly surprised by Felicity. I always thought she was a bit dim but she speaks well.'

'That's not really appropriate, is it?' She was many things but definitely not dim. Gavin had realised that early on. She'd just proved she knew as much as him, if not more. With a bit more experience, she'd be a rival for his job. She hadn't just given the presentation; she'd made it from his skeletal notes.

'You know what I mean,' Julian said, not giving him a chance to reply. 'And I'm a bit surprised by the direction you took the new product suggestions. Not entirely what I had envisioned from our discussions, but still, I like it.'

'Good,' Gavin said. Just as well really. Another instance of Felicity using her initiative. He'd been as in the dark as every-one else but being the poker-faced king he was, he'd kept his expression neutral. He just couldn't get excited about any of it. None of this was him. How bad would it be to tell his parents he couldn't do this, hand over the reins to Julian and go back to programming? He could walk into a job tomorrow. But that life had become stale in the last few years. This had seemed like a chance worth taking to inject something new into his life – as well as pleasing his parents. But so far it wasn't working. Seeing Felicity showcasing ideas for the future, beaming from ear to ear and clearly believing in the products and the business was enough to make him want to crawl into a box and hide. It should have been him. Why couldn't he muster the same enthusiasm?

'So, is that what we're running with?' Julian asked.

'Yes.' Felicity's ideas were as good as any. Better in fact.

'Ok. Should I get that up and running while you're away next week?'

'That would be perfect.'

Julian leaned forward, almost conspiratorially, which wasn't necessary as they were alone. 'Are you sure you want to bother with the rural distilleries trip? It almost seems unnecessary after the interest we got in Tennessee.'

'It's important that I go. Even if we end up selling one, it doesn't look good for the company's reputation if I haven't even visited.'

'Yeah, true. A formality then. Just watch Felicity.' He lowered his voice yet another notch. 'I'm worried she has her own agenda. She was a tour guide at Glenbriar before she got this job and I think it's made her soft about the place. I see now, she's intelligent and ambitious, so just make sure any decisions you make are your own. I wouldn't want her influencing you.'

'There's no danger of that. I'm perfectly capable of making up my own mind.' He folded his arms and frowned.

Julian nodded, slapped his palms on his thighs and got to his feet. 'Of course. Right. I'll set the ball rolling with the new products.'

Gavin watched him leave, letting out a long, slow breath as the door shut. Why did he feel like he was pig in the middle? Julian thought Felicity had a hidden agenda and he was sure Felicity suspected Julian of exactly the same. But whatever was going on with the two of them, Gavin was determined not to be persuaded by either. He was his own man and would make up his own mind.

Felicity had seen to everything for the trip. Not having to host her in his parents' house was a blessing. Mixing business with pleasure wasn't his thing. Not that he was going to be pleasuring Felicity in any way... Jesus. His brain was out on a bender. He just didn't want to have to see her off duty. No. He really did not want that. In a hotel, he could keep to his room. He could even sneak off to his parents' house alone if he needed to hide. And besides, Felicity knew people up there. She'd want to spend the nonworking hours with friends and that suited him fine. Just damn fine. To make sure there was no chance of being stuck with her, he was going to take his own car. He set her a quick email, telling her they'd be travelling individually.

The pictures of the hotel on its website looked stunning. When Felicity was off frequenting posh bars with her friends, he could nip off to the loch for a wild swim. He was used to dipping in the sea off the Berwick coast but hadn't tried freshwater. The loch would be a new challenge. Maybe it would inject some oomph back into his life. He'd taken up swimming to do that after his dating disasters, and it had worked... to a point. But what was the point of keeping himself in great shape when there was no one to look at it? Was it time to think about dating again? The idea made his stomach squirm. All those horrible first meetings, the stilted conversation, the sickening thoughts of how to end the evening. And if they ended up going home together, the partings got even more awkward. How many dates before he found someone he really connected with?

On the morning of the trip, he had his car packed and ready to go. He pulled out his phone and messaged Felicity to tell her he was leaving. Maybe he should have offered her a lift but she'd replied to his email, saying she was fine taking her own car.

He tapped out a brief message.

Leaving now. See you at the hotel later.

Sun split the sky as he drove north on roads he hadn't been on for years. His parents had often invited him to join them but he'd always declined. Going to the distilleries was like a mental block for him. He didn't fully understand it. It wasn't like he'd had any unpleasant experiences there or disliked the area particularly. It was a more indistinct link between it and the expectations that had always surrounded him. Like if he avoided going, then he could avoid taking on the family business. But he'd done that bit, so visiting the rural distilleries was just the next logical step. He tapped the wheel as he waited in a queue at a large roundabout near the town of Perth. Spiritual feelings, sixth senses and that kind of thing were not his style, but he couldn't shake an odd niggle of disquiet. It was almost like a warning light had popped on but he didn't know what it meant. Just a sense that something big was going to happen on this trip, though maybe not something good.

When he reached the small town of Glenbriar, familiar places triggered memories in the caverns of his brain. Just Desserts, the ice-cream shop, was still there. He remembered getting treats there as a child. The shop front was a lot more modern and trendier these days. In fact, the whole town appeared bright and clean, much more vibrant than he recalled.

He turned out of the village towards the loch side and carried on through a heavily wooded area. Hills climbed up behind the loch and reflected on its still surface, looking every inch the romantic picture he'd imagined. The hotel came into view, shining like a beacon with bright pink paintwork. It commanded a gorgeous spot at the top of the loch. If his room was at the front, what a view he'd wake to every morning.

The car park was at the back and he pulled in, spotting a bright lime green Volkswagen Beetle near the door. He didn't know what kind of car Felicity had but something told him that was hers. So, she was here already. He lifted his case, suit hanger and laptop backpack from the boot of his car and headed up the short steps to the door. He hesitated, swallowing and taking a deep breath. Feelings of being out of his depth weren't new. Over the past year, he'd had them almost every day, but a different sort of tension gripped him this time. He shoved his suit carrier into the same hand as his case and pulled open the door to the foyer, a panelled strip of a room off the main dining area, with a heavy wooden staircase bending off to the right. The unmistakable scent of Felicity sent his stomach into a flurry. She stood, leaning on the high part of the reception desk, her long thin legs encased in skinny jeans. Her top was lightweight purple chiffon, cut low at the back, and a pair of high-heeled grey ankle boots finished the look of casual perfection. Someone else was behind the desk but Gavin couldn't focus on her properly. Not yet. Felicity's long, immaculate barrel curls were pulled into a perfect ponytail, trailing down her back. She caught it and twisted it over her shoulder as she slowly turned around. Gavin's heart stopped. *Keep mouth closed and breathe.*

'Oh, hi,' Felicity said, standing straighter and linking her fingers in front of her. 'I wasn't sure when you'd get here.'

'Hi,' Gavin said, pushing the word out like it was a stubborn hippopotamus he was trying to squeeze through a narrow opening.

'Good afternoon,' the woman at the reception desk said, and Gavin shifted his attention to her.

'Good afternoon.'

'Are you Mr Sinclair?' she continued.

'Yes.'

'Excellent. I'm Briony. I own the hotel and I'm delighted to have a Sinclair staying here. You know the history of our families goes way back. Even if some of it is a bit dodgy,' she added with a grin at Felicity.

Felicity hadn't hidden the fact she had friends up here. Something told him Briony was one of them. A match made in heaven. Both had big smiles, dressed immaculately and apparently could talk about anything with anyone.

'So,' Briony continued. 'Let me get your room key, Mr Sinclair. You are in the Whisky Kisses suite, named after that very famous whisky from your very own distillery. The room has a beautiful view and I understand the weather this week is to be fabulous, so you'll actually be able to see it. Honestly, it's so misty here sometimes, it feels a bit cheeky saying any of the rooms have a loch view.'

'I'm sure it'll be' – his eyes darted to Felicity – 'fine.'

'Good,' Briony said. 'Now, if you wouldn't mind checking your info here, please.' She pushed an iPad in front of him.

'That's all fine.'

'I hope it is,' Felicity said. 'If it's not, it's my fault.'

Gavin winced at his date of birth. There could be no kidding on he was any younger. How the hell was he thirty-six? Had someone paused his life for ten years? Jeez, when he was twenty-six, thirty-six had sounded old. But he felt exactly the same, better in fact. He was a lot healthier, fitter, stronger. Just missing direction.

'Here's your key. Do you want a hand up with your luggage?' Briony passed him an actual metal key with a long white fob. He hadn't had one like that for a while.

'I can manage, thanks.'

'You shouldn't be doing anything like that anyway.' Felicity patted her own tummy and added aside to Gavin. 'She has a baby onboard.'

'Oh, right.'

'I'm hiding the bump behind the desk.' Briony smiled. 'Your room is at the top of the stairs, across the corridor and—'

'I'll show you,' Felicity said. 'I need to grab my phone anyway. It's upstairs.'

'Ok.' Gavin loosened the collar of his shirt and lifted his bags. Why was he wearing his suit? They'd agreed the first day would be settling in and not business but it just didn't seem right. The Christmas jumper had been fun but wearing casual stuff in front of Felicity was like... Well, letting her in to a secret place. His private life. And his private life was none of her business.

She was already on the stairs, her long, slender legs scaling them like a model.

'How do you like the hotel?' she asked as she skirted the first landing and started on the next section.

'It's nice,' he said.

She kept her eyes forward.

At the top of the stairs, she pushed open a door into a wide, carpeted corridor. Ahead was a thick panelled door with an elegant brass sign reading Whisky Kisses.

'That's your room.' She tapped on the wood with her sparkly nail.

'Tell me,' Gavin said, dropping his bags on the floor and pushing the key into the lock. 'Is Briony a friend of yours?'

Felicity pulled an innocent pout, her pupils sneaking sideways, and she flicked her index finger back and forward softly over the base of her neck.

Gavin's stomach swooped and he wanted to rip off his shirt and ravish her. The thought of her lips on his sent a frenzied spark zipping through him. An untamed animal was inside him, fighting to get out and it wanted Felicity.

'Um, yes,' she said.

Fuck's sake. He caught his breath, forcing it steady like he did when he was swimming in icy water. He must not think about her like that. Really, really must not. 'Thought so,' he muttered, turning the key.

'I hope you don't mind. The hotel is so lovely, I thought, it seemed...'

'I don't mind,' he said.

'Phew.' She relaxed her arms at her side. 'Do you want to have a drink after? When you're settled in... Or would you rather have peace? I'll buzz off if you want. I, er, will do whatever.'

A drink? With her? Just them? Not business. That couldn't work. 'I don't think so,' he said. 'I've got stuff to do.'

'Right. I'll see you tomorrow then. For the first trip.'

'Indeed.' He pushed open the door and almost flung his bags in so he could close it again quickly. He didn't want to see her face. This was work. And exactly the reason it should never be mixed with pleasure. It had to be one or the other. No blurry lines. He'd steered clear of making friends in the office for fear of breaking codes or rules but what Felicity made him feel was a whole new level of danger.

He crossed to the window and looked over the gorgeous glassy surface of the loch, unbuttoning his shirt. A dip in that clear water would be glorious. That would unclog his head and work off some tension. But if he did, he'd have to make sure Felicity was well out of sight.

A group of older people strolled along the loch side path towards the wood. Gavin pulled off his shirt. Walking would do if he couldn't swim, but he couldn't do either in his business clothes. He cast his shirt onto the chair beside the handsome four-poster bed. This was like a honeymoon suite, not a single-man zone. He sat on the end of the bed and cradled his forehead. What a dick he'd been to Felicity. She was just being polite and repressed-idiot Gavin had barked at her. How must she be feeling now? Christ. One drink and friendly chat wouldn't kill him. His father would have done it. In fact, his father would have asked first. He'd have made sure his staff were looked after.

He could still make it right. It wasn't her fault he found her insanely hot. But now wasn't the time for games. He had to master himself and find her.

Just as soon as he put some clothes on.

CHAPTER NINE

Felicity

Felicity sat on a picnic bench on the deck outside the hotel dining room in the sunshine, hugging her knees to her chest and staring at the gorgeous reflections of green hills in the glassy loch. She tossed back her head and tried to shake free her crazy moment from earlier. Ugh. The moment she'd asked the boss to go for a drink was going down as a high-ranking gaff. Just what had possessed her? He'd brushed her off like the lowly PA she was.

Idiot. Idiot. Idiot. She couldn't even bring herself to tell Briony. It would mean confessing things she didn't want to confess, like the fact her boss set her insides on fire and she couldn't stop thinking about him – in ways she definitely should not be.

The patio door behind her opened and she jumped, spinning around, forgetting this was a public place.

Briony came out chattering, followed by a tall man with broad shoulders and a somewhat roguish grin. He flipped his mid-length hair from his eyes and nodded. Felicity sat up. She recognised him as a local tradesperson, affectionately known as Brann the builder. His rugged good looks came alongside rumours that bored housewives in the town invented building work just to hire him and enjoy the view as Brann fixed up their houses. When he'd been hired to fix the viewing platform at Glenbriar Distillery, some of her colleagues had wet their pants about him and spent the week sneaking into the roped-off area to catch a sly glimpse of him at work. A tight t-shirt over taut muscles and a hefty tool belt worked wonders, and admittedly, he was quite a hunk.

'Oh, Felicity.' Briony rested her hand on her beach-ball-like bump. 'I didn't know you were out here.'

'Hey,' Brann said.

'Hi.' Felicity got to her feet. 'How are you?'

'Living the dream.' He quirked her a grin, friendly though possibly appraising as well. Her head was so full of Gavin Sinclair, this rugged specimen was nothing but a poor second. 'You? I haven't seen you about for a while.'

'I moved to Edinburgh for a new job. I'm back on business for a week.'

'Ah, I gotcha.'

'Brann's here to fix the railing,' Briony said. 'A couple of guys leaned on it last week and it broke. Thankfully, neither of them got hurt. It was just a bit embarrassing for them.'

'And they lost their beer,' Brann said.

'They were fully compensated for that.' Briony perched on a seat, cradling her bump.

Brann swaggered across the deck and surveyed a taped-off area. 'Ah, that'll not take long. Maybe I should take compensation in beer too.'

Briony chuckled. 'If you'd rather have that, I'm sure we could come to some arrangement.' She glanced over at Felicity. 'Would you like anything? A drink?'

'Nothing too strong this early.'

'Very disciplined,' Brann said.

'How about a lime and soda?' Briony suggested. 'You used to like them.'

'Ok. But I'll get it myself. You sit. You look like you need a rest.'

'No, really. It's better if I move about. Otherwise, it's hard to get up again.'

'If you're really sure.'

'Perfectly. Brann, do you want anything?'

'No thanks. I'm good.'

She got to her feet and made her way back into the main hotel. Felicity watched her with a slight frown.

'What do you do in Edinburgh?' Brann asked.

'I still work for Glenbriar distilleries but in the Edinburgh office. I'm just visiting this week. My boss is doing a tour and I'm organising it.'

'Is that the Sinclair bloke?' Brann levered off the old railing and it snapped with a sharp crack. He didn't look up but gave off a heavy aura of strength as he cast aside the broken wood.

'Yes. Gavin Sinclair.' The sound of his name gave her another whoosh in her tummy.

'He any good?'

'Yes.' It seemed traitorous to say no, but she wasn't sure she could honestly vouch for his greatness in leadership. Still, she wouldn't throw him under the bus.

'My mate works there. He says the new man's never showed face, morale's crap and lots of folk are looking to move on.'

'Really?' Felicity rubbed the tips of her nails over her throat. His words weren't news but hearing them straight like that was a blow.

'Yup. 'fraid so.'

'Well, he's here now and hopefully we can rectify the situation. It's not been the easiest of times to take over a business.'

Brann snapped off another bit of broken wood. His muscly arms had celtic-style tattoos decorating them and there was something of a warrior about him – a slightly dark warrior.

The door bumped open and Briony appeared with a small tray and laid it in front of Felicity. 'There you go, one lime and soda.'

'Thank you. Are you sure you're ok?'

'Fine.' Briony took the seat again. 'I've been getting pelvic pains on and off. Sometimes sitting helps, other times it makes it worse. The midwife says nothing will stop it except having the baby but I'm not due for another two months.'

'Do you know what you're having?' Brann asked. 'Boy or girl?'

'I do, but it's a secret.'

Brann smirked. 'Well, I've got one of each. Both have their moments, I can tell you.'

'I bet. And... oh my.' She raised her eyebrows at his demolition job.

'It has to get worse before it gets better.' He winked.

'I'm sure you know what you're doing.' She lifted a drink for herself. 'Like old times, isn't it?'

'Yeah.' Felicity sipped her drink to knock back a rising lump in her throat. 'I do miss it here.'

'I miss having you.' Briony patted Felicity's shoulder. 'Pity your boss doesn't want his office up here, then you could come too.'

'I don't see that happening.' It had taken long enough to get him to come for a short visit. But even just driving through Glenbriar earlier had woken memories. She was so much more attuned to living here than Edinburgh. When she'd had her little flat in Glenbriar, she could walk to the distillery on nice days. If she was needed at one of the smaller ones, it was a pleasant drive through the countryside, and the friendly staff welcomed her with open arms.

'Is it true they're selling out to some foreign company?' Brann cracked another bit of wood over his knee.

Felicity glanced up. Drat, he was listening.

'No. We always have business dealings with other companies and groups from all over the world.' Which was true but she felt like she was putting up a shield, a flimsy one made from what she hoped was true and not fact. 'Rumours like that always start up when the execs take a trip. Gavin and Julian were abroad earlier in the year, but it's as much PR as anything.'

'I see.' Brann nodded, but his eyebrow quirked up in a way that suggested he didn't believe a word of it. Felicity couldn't blame him. Gavin's indifference to what should be his top priority – in her opinion anyway – might prove very costly.

'Oh dear.' Briony pulled a face but clearly didn't want to say too much in front of Brann. 'I really hope things improve after this visit.'

'Yeah.' Felicity took another gulp of her drink, not convinced.

Briony stayed and chatted for a while. Back when Felicity had lived here, Briony had always been rushed off her feet and short staffed, but she'd pulled through and now had enough staff to allow herself shorter hours. Brann chipped into the conversation now and then but Felicity made sure she gave nothing away. She suspected he would be straight back to his friend with sensationalised reports that the Glenbriar distillery boss was in town trying to salvage his career, which might be closer to the truth than Felicity cared to admit.

When Briony had to go back to work, Felicity went down to the lochside and walked along the path. She'd changed into her trainers and kind of wished she'd put on her running gear. This was the perfect place for it. Many times, she'd run here from the village. Should she nip back and change? Maybe not. She still had two weeks. There would be other times.

The path wound into the trees and she tread the familiar route, smiling and swinging her arms as she breathed in the fresh air and listened to the twittering birds. But now she was alone again, the creeping disquiet in her tummy returned. Bad enough this mission could be a too-late attempt to save the distilleries, but she still had the Gavin situation to deal with. Somehow, she had to forget her moment of stupidity. *Eek.* And hopefully, he would too. If she just acted like nothing was different, surely, he wouldn't notice. After all, she was just being friendly. Nothing wrong with that. Nothing except the swoop in her tummy every time she thought about him.

At several places along the path, the undergrowth and bushes fell back, leaving a clear view to the loch and access points to get to the shore. With the weather being so fair, the water level was low, and the shore was wide. Most of it was pebbly, but in some places, there were sandy inlets like mini beaches. She'd seen it in summer packed with people picnicking and kids playing. At the other end of the loch, three miles away, was a water sports centre. Maybe at the weekend, she could nip along and have some fun there. She loved kayaking and paddleboarding and it would be something to look forward to because she doubted the majority of the week would be fun.

Voices from further along the shore caught her attention and she craned her neck to get a better view. It sounded like a child crying. Another voice spoke and she relaxed. At least it wasn't a lost child. She carried on, still trying to see where the voices were coming from.

The trees and bushes thinned, framing a view of one of the larger sandy areas. A woman held a crying toddler on her hip, soothing him and wiping tears from his red face as a man with rolled up grey cargo trousers waded into the water. Felicity stopped dead. It was Gavin. Her jaw fell slack. She'd never seen him in casual clothes before, unless she counted his Christmas jumper. But here he was, in a tight-fitting white t-shirt, looking every inch as muscular as Brann the builder. Bloody hell. If the clench in her tummy was bad before, now it was like a giant boxing glove had slammed her against the tree, knocking all the air from her body. What the hell was he doing? Then she spotted a yellow football floating on the surface of the loch not far from him. He leaned forward and teased it to him with his fingertips. As he lifted it, the toddler's sobs morphed into a breathy giggle and the woman laughed too.

'There you go,' she said. 'The man got it for you. It's ok now.'

Gavin paddled back to shore carrying the ball, a smile splitting his face. A smile like Felicity had never seen on him before. Genuine and warm. Enough to turn her to mush. He handed over the ball and the toddler cuddled it close.

'Thanks so much,' the woman said. 'I didn't know how I was going to get it back. Sorry you got wet.'

'It's fine.' Gavin glanced at the damp edges of his trousers. 'At least this little guy got his ball back.'

'Aw, thank you.' The woman beamed at him.

Felicity tried to quench the burning in her chest and the sudden desire to jump in front of the woman and take her place. What crazy nonsense was this?

'I think we'll play somewhere further from the water,' she added.

'Good idea.'

The woman thanked him again, then set off towards the path. Gavin dropped onto a large, flat boulder and rolled down his trousers. His trainers and socks were placed neatly beside it.

'Oh, hello.'

Felicity jumped. The woman with the toddler had reached her on the path and here she was hanging around gawping like an idiot.

'Hi.' Felicity smiled and started to walk. The voices must have alerted Gavin and he looked around. His gaze locked with hers.

Shit. What now? Should she walk on and pretend she hadn't seen him? Or wave and walk on? Talk to him? Or what? Since when had she been so indecisive and crazy?

She raised her hand in a quick wave, then looked away. Yes. She had to leave him alone. Putting her head down, she strode forward.

'Felicity,' his voice called and she couldn't pretend she hadn't heard. It was perfectly clear.

She turned and peered towards him. He was standing, trousers rolled down but feet still bare.

'Hi,' she said.

'Have you got a minute?'

'Of course.' Like she could say no to the boss.

'Two seconds.' He dropped onto the stone again and picked up his socks.

But Felicity couldn't wait to find out what he wanted. She nipped down the short embankment and her feet hit the sand, sinking slightly, and muffling her footsteps.

'Is everything ok?' she asked.

He spun his head abruptly, clearly not expecting her to be there. 'What? Oh, yes.' He blinked and pulled on his other sock. His broad forearms were very distracting. If he chose to rip up wood with his bare hands like Brann the builder, it would be some contest.

'Did you want me for something?'

He glanced up at her. 'Yes. Here.' He grabbed his trainers and shunted along the boulder, leaving a space for her. She sat, making sure her arm didn't touch his. If it did, she might have convulsions. Her skin tingled like it was trying to pull away from her and adhere itself to him.

'I should apologise.' He didn't look at her as he shoved his foot into his trainer and hauled the laces tight.

'What for?' Had she missed something?

'Being rude earlier.'

'Were you?'

'I was standoffish when you suggested a drink. I'm sorry.' He grabbed his other shoe and thrust his foot into it. 'It's just... You know?'

She didn't and her heartbeat leapt off the charts. Where the hell was this leading? 'Know what?'

'It's awkward for me... and you. We're used to working together.' He knotted his lace, then sat up, resting his wrists on his knees, his watch glinting in the sunlight, his focus fixed on the loch. 'I just wanted to keep things professional.'

'So did I.' Well, kind of. At least she knew she should. 'I don't think it's unprofessional having a drink with a colleague.'

'Exactly.' He glanced at her and his Adam's apple bobbed as he swallowed. 'That's what I'm saying. I apologise and if you'd like to have that drink now, or later, or anytime, then that's fine. In fact, it's good.'

She relaxed into a smile. He was hot as hell and also cute when he was tongue-tied and unsure. 'Of course I would,' she said. 'Shall we go now?'

'Yes. Ok. I should probably put on dry trousers. These got a bit wet round the edges.'

'They might dry,' she said. 'It's hot out here.'

'It really is.' His eyes met hers and lava erupted inside her. Energy buzzed between them. Did he mean...? No, he couldn't.

He jumped to his feet and rubbed the outer edge of his thighs. 'Nice place, this.'

'Yes, it is. How did you get wet?' Not that she hadn't watched the whole thing, but he didn't need to know that.

'A kid kicked his ball in just as I walked by. The mum tried to get a branch to pull it back but it had floated too far. I don't think she fancied getting her feet wet, or maybe she was worried the kid would follow her and get into trouble.'

'And you just happened to be passing at the right time, like the regular Superman you are.'

Gavin pinched the bridge of his nose and smirked as he started to walk along the shore. 'Clearly.'

Maybe she should tell him about what Brann had said. Or should she save that for official work time? Gavin might be good at rescuing people from speeding cyclists and balls from the depths of the loch but could he save the business from Julian's backward ideas?

Felicity got to her feet and stood beside him. 'Mr Sinclair. Do you—'

'Before you say anything else, can you not call me that here? It sounds odd being called that when we're not in the office. Gavin is fine.'

'Sure, of course, Gavin.' Her lip quirked up and she glanced sideways. Eek. Did that make things worse? It sounded much more personal. 'I just wondered if you'd like me to set up a meeting with all the highland distillery managers, maybe even some of the other staff, while we're here. I think it might be a good idea to give them a forum where they can air their views and share ideas, instead of just seeing them individually.'

'Do you think that's necessary?'

She let out a long sigh and blinked up at him, steeling herself. She had to tell him but he was going to hate it. 'I don't really know how to say this.'

'Say what?' He frowned. 'Whatever it is, spit it out.'

'I think there's going to be a lot of bad feeling from staff.'

'Nothing new there then.' The edge in his voice was clear. 'What do you mean?'

'Well, I haven't exactly been welcomed with open arms. Not that I expected it but, to be perfectly honest, some of the behaviour in the office is borderline bullying. In my first week there, I heard someone calling me a plank in a suit and that was just the start.'

Felicity's cheeks reddened. Shit. She'd heard people say that several times too – maybe even said it herself. She'd definitely thought it. But now she'd been exposed to exactly what he stuffed his shirts with and wow...

'And it's not just that.' He rubbed his arms. 'The general feeling is one of hostility. If the tables were turned and I behaved to employees like that or called them names, I'd be dragged through the courts. I know I'm not my father. I know I can't replace him or expect respect just because of my name, but it's worse than that. It's not like people just expect me to fail, it's like they want me to.'

Felicity nodded and fiddled with a strand of her hair. His hurt was real, and she got it. How could she not? She hated people getting upset but she had to go on. He needed to hear this and she couldn't leave it. If he arrived at the distilleries, looked around and said, 'that's nice', then they went home, it would be a complete waste of time. She had to make him see that wasn't enough.

'That might be true,' she conceded, scuffing her feet in the sand. 'I think it's quite common with a change of management, though I've never really worked anywhere else. People are afraid of what might happen. It's like venturing into the unknown.'

'Tell me about it,' he muttered.

'I am. And I need to tell you something else.'

'Oh?'

How could she tell him he needed to do his job better than he was doing it? Who was she, after all?

'Felicity.' He stepped in front of her and blocked the way forward. 'Tell me. I know I'm not going to like it. Christ, I could probably say it myself if I had the nerve to face it.' He wheeled away and let out a growl.

'You might not want to hear it but—'

'I don't have a clue what I'm doing. That's what you want to say, isn't it?' He glared back at her, one eyebrow poised high, pressing for an answer.

'I don't want to.' She pressed her lips together, holding in an ache. It shouldn't be up to her to do this. She hated it; every word was like beating him, each blow cutting closer to his heart. Most people in the office would laugh their heads off at the thought of her telling the boss how to do his job. 'I can see how difficult it is for you. I've seen it from the start. This isn't your usual line of business.'

He let out a dry laugh and strutted away. 'Yeah. You can say that again. Is that the word on the ground? That I'm incompetent.'

'Stop.' She sped up and grabbed hold of his arm before thinking about what she was doing. The charge that had been building in her all day almost blasted her off the ground and she let go. 'Maybe that has been said. Not by me.' She held her hands up. 'But I know you better than most of the others. I may be inexperienced in business but I'm good at reading people and situations. I can tell you're an intelligent man but you need to apply your intelligence differently here. You're working with people now, not computers.'

'You're an expert now, are you?' he grouched.

'No. But people have feelings and you can't ignore them. If you do, the dissent will get worse. Already there's bickering in the office. People are giving up or looking for an easy way out. Julian's idea to sell up might sound simple, but is that what you want for the company? Back in the hotel, I was talking to someone who knows people who work in the distilleries here. People who think you've abandoned them. People who think you don't care. And if you don't care, then why should they?'

Gavin stared at her, his sculpted chest rising and falling slowly beneath his tight t-shirt, and his fists balled. Felicity wanted to shrink into the sand and disappear, maybe cry.

'Right,' he said quietly, his jaw tense. 'That's a hell of a lot to unpick and I'm not sure I can do it in company. Let's put the drinks on ice. I need some space to think.'

He stalked away, but Felicity didn't move. He'd asked for space. She had to give it to him. Her heart pounded and ached. She rubbed at her face. Would it have been better if she just kept her big mouth shut? He was right; she wasn't an expert. She was a twenty-five-year-old with no experience and she'd just given the boss a talking to. It didn't get much worse and this was only day one.

Chapter Ten

Gavin

Gavin slammed the door to his room shut. He winced. He hadn't meant to close it that hard, but after his conversation with Felicity, his blood was boiling.

Who the hell did she think she was? How could she have the first idea of how to run a business? She was a twenty-something PA with next to nothing on her CV. Did she have any idea of the credentials he came with? Even if objectively, they didn't qualify him to do this job either.

He sat on the end of the bed and cradled his forehead. Ah, screw it. She wasn't the actual cause of his fury. It was himself and his own stupidity. Getting to his feet, he paced to the window, then back to the door. What he needed was proper advice, good solid stuff from someone who knew what they were doing. Who though? If he asked his father, he'd go straight into panic mode and think Gavin was incompetent – which he now knew he was, but Dad didn't need to know too.

I got myself into this. Against everything he'd ever wanted, he'd given in and gone for it, taken up his birthright and done what everyone wanted. Everyone except him. He should have stuck to his guns and carried on in programming. So what if it disappointed his parents? Why did that even matter? But it did. He always gave into what they wanted. Even if it took years, they got their own way and made up his mind for him. He couldn't live with the guilt of letting them down.

A knock on the door made him stop dead. He hadn't ordered anything but he hadn't put on the Do Not Disturb sign either.

'Who is it?'

'Felicity.'

Jesus Christ. What did she want now? His blood reached boiling point. He breathed deeply until it cooled, then opened the door.

'Hi,' she said. 'I'm sorry... I didn't mean—'

He held up his hand. 'I know what you meant and why you said it.' He motioned for her to come in. Having her in his bedroom for this discussion was only a small step up from the corridor. Less likely to be overheard but more likely to send his imagination on a bender.

She stepped inside and stood close to the desk, fiddling with a twinkling ring on her middle finger.

'You were right,' he said. 'On almost all counts. I didn't expect anyone to have the guts to say it to my face, especially, well...'

'Someone as unqualified as me.'

'Someone I underestimated.' He searched her face. She was stock still, like she was holding her breath. 'I thought I could do this,' he said. 'But I can't.'

'Of course you can, but not by doing what you're doing.'

'Maybe.' He nodded. 'But you got one thing wrong. I do care. I care about the success of this business as much as anyone, maybe more than most. I admit I didn't realise how much I'd bitten off, but if I seem indifferent about it, it's because I don't know where to start or exactly what to do.'

'Didn't your parents explain... anything?'

He marched to the window and leant on the sill. 'They probably spent years telling me. But I didn't listen at the time. I didn't want this job.'

'Then why did you take it?'

'Because there was no one else. And I didn't want my parents' life work being sold to the highest bidder. I wanted it to continue. My own career was successful and lucrative but I'd reached a stalemate. The contracts I was getting weren't as interesting to me as they were when I started out. I thought maybe a change would work in my favour. Guess I was wrong.'

'I think you have the potential to be a great leader, but you shouldn't have to do it alone. Your father was the head of the company, but he had your mother helping him. She might have been ok with him taking all the credit but she did a lot of the groundwork.'

'I know she did, but that's my mother for you. She's very good at getting things done.'

'Then let someone help you.'

'Who?' He turned to her and frowned. 'I can't very well ask my mother to help me.'

'Not her. Me.'

'You?'

'Why not? Your father didn't have a PA, but he had your mother. It was him who employed me to work for you. Maybe he wanted me to help you.'

'But you've never done anything like this before. Do you have any idea how to run a business on this scale?'

She raised an eyebrow. 'Do you?'

He glared at her, then a dry laugh escaped his lips. She smiled back, before looking away, covering her mouth.

'Sorry, I shouldn't have said that.'

'Don't worry,' he said. 'You're probably right.'

'Why don't we try doing this together?'

He looked at her for a moment, then bowed his head. 'Ok. Can't be any worse than it is already. So, what do you suggest?'

'Well...' She took a deep breath. 'When we go to the distilleries this week, you have to let them see they're your number one priority. Nothing in the world is more important. I'll make some excuse why you haven't been sooner. You also need to act like you're carrying out spot checks. Ask lots of questions, praise them, show them you're interested. If they complain about things that aren't working or are out of date, take those things on board and do something.'

He raised his eyebrows. 'You've really thought about this, haven't you?'

'I've just been listening and learning.'

'Sensible.' He folded his arms. 'So, how about dinner with me? We can work through everything I need to know. And I'll pay you a huge bonus for working overtime.'

'Sure, I'd like dinner, and I could use a bonus.'

'Great. How about six?'

Her lashes flickered.

'Six o'clock, for dinner,' he added, just in case she'd misheard him.

'See you there.' She smiled before crossing the room and letting herself out.

Of all the things he'd considered might happen on this trip, he hadn't expected to be getting lessons in management from his PA. He might have indulged in other fantasies – subconsciously and completely inappropriately – but this was like having the tables turned in his face. Still, he was going to swallow his remaining pride and see what she suggested.

The release of tension in his neck was like he'd been cut down from the gallows and could breathe again. Finally, someone was willing to help without the judgy looks and snide backhanders. Or so he hoped. Because, despite his repressed libido having its own opinion of her, she was someone who'd always been loyal and supportive. He needed her on his side.

Gavin double and treble checked his tie was straight in the mirror before heading downstairs the following morning. After dinner the evening before, he considered calling his father and telling him he should have given Felicity the role of company director. She had more ideas than he'd ever had or was likely to have. Her finger was on the pulse and she'd spent the whole evening explaining what she thought he should do. Now, he just had to do it. Insecurities hovered around like vultures, waiting to peck at him. This could still go horribly wrong and if it did, it would be entirely his fault.

Felicity was already at breakfast when he got down. She waved to him and he took it as an invitation to sit at her table. Had Julian, or his father, or a director from another company taken upon themself to give him the benefit of their wisdom the way she had, he could only imagine how smug they'd look and how awkward he'd feel. But her ideas weren't tried or tested. She had no prior experience to draw from either but she was in tune enough for her suggestions to have more merit than most he'd heard recently.

'Did you sleep ok?' she asked.

'Not really.' He let out a sigh and sat down.

She cocked her head. 'Don't stress, it'll be fine.'

'You think? I must look like a twelve-year-old on work experience.' He huffed out a sigh. 'Think about someone about ten years younger than you explaining your business to you and you'll understand what I mean.'

'Don't be ridiculous. You're a hundred times more intelligent than me.'

'It's not the same. You have a different kind of intelligence.'

'That's why we should do this together.'

'Indeed,' he said. 'But my brain's all over the place. Imagine I'd sat up last evening telling you how to program a game, including algorithms and logic, then asked you to remember it all this morning. How do you think you'd do?'

Felicity grinned at her yoghurt. 'I wouldn't have a clue, but this isn't the same. You have experience that I don't have. I'm just making suggestions based on what I've heard and read.'

'I'm not sure why you don't have a degree and your eye on a management role.'

She gave a little shrug. 'I didn't have that many opportunities growing up.'

'Well, I'm glad you're making use of your talents to help me.' Their eyes met across the table and he breathed in her scent. It settled some of the niggles in his chest but opened up a new vein, one that rocketed straight to his gut. He ignored it. 'And thank you.'

'For what? Being bossy?'

'Yes. I needed to hear it.' He scanned the breakfast menu, reminding himself his daily dose of carrot juice was off the menu until Felicity was elsewhere. 'You had the guts to say something to me that none of the SMT would have dared to. And it's possibly saved my skin. Even if it doesn't, I feel a lot more confident about this trip now I've got a better insight.'

After breakfast, they headed for the car park. His resolve to stay in separate vehicles seemed silly now and he'd offered to drive them both.

'You don't need the satnav,' Felicity said. 'It's just outside the village, not far and easy to find.'

'Would it shock you to hear I last came here when I was sixteen? That was twenty years ago.' Saying it like that sounded horrendous. He couldn't be *that* old. Old enough to have done something twenty years ago.

'It doesn't shock me. But I don't get why you haven't been back.'

He crunched out of the car park onto the road. 'Denial, I think. Hoping this day would never come. I didn't want the responsibility. I suppose I thought by distancing myself from it, my parents might not trust me to take over. And maybe they shouldn't have.'

'Don't say things like that. Be positive.'

'You really are bossy once you get started.'

'I expect my brothers and sisters would agree with you.'

'Ah yes, you have quite a few, if I recall.'

'Yup. Five. Three brothers and two sisters.'

The small talk that usually bothered him had the opposite effect today and his muscles relaxed. He could do this if he approached it in the same way as he'd approached countless other seemingly impossible assignments in the past. *Just stay calm, focused, and in control.*

He straightened his jacket as he got out of his car. The distillery was so familiar from the countless photographs he'd seen all over the office, an imposing long and low white building with a grey roof and the trademark twin cupolas on the drying towers that resembled bronze pagodas. Despite being within walking distance of the village, the mountainous landscape behind it and the small lochan in front gave it a remote feel. Beautifully kept hanging baskets flanked the front door and Gavin swallowed. His chest was full and a woozy moment of everything being too big to comprehend assailed him. Seeing it like this hammered home the tremendous responsibility he had to bear.

Felicity pushed open the glass doors and people engulfed her, hugging her and laughing. Gavin straightened his tie, hanging back and observing the fine finish on the polished floor of the reception area. A glass box on a table encased a model of the building. He squinted to read the bronze plaque but before he could finish, Felicity said, 'This is Gavin Sinclair, the new CEO.'

He attempted a perfunctory smile, hyper aware that 'new' wasn't exactly true anymore. The faces that had been so bright when talking to Felicity dropped and turned stony. He put out his hand and an older man with white hair and a beard shook it.

'I'm Jerry, the operations manager,' he said.

Gavin gave him a nod; the crawling sensation that he should know these people already made him squirm. Why had he left it so late?

'I'm Scott, one of the distillery operators,' the next man said.

'And I'm Victoria, I work on reception, front of house and admin.'

'Pleased to meet you all,' Gavin said. 'I'd like to have a chat with everyone individually at some point today.'

'Of course,' Jerry said. 'I think that would be sensible.'

Something in his expression told Gavin several people wanted to use this opportunity to air gripes. Probably about him.

'We're going to start with the tour,' Felicity said.

'Are you going to lead it?' Jerry asked. 'Like old times?'

'I could do. I really miss it. Remember when it was freezing outside and I'd go and cuddle up by the tanks?'

'Yes.' Jerry smiled. 'I think if we'd given you a sleeping bag, you'd have gone and lived in there.'

'I so would.'

Gavin cleared his throat. 'I'm happy for Felicity to do the tour but perhaps you could accompany us.'

'Certainly,' Jerry said. 'Follow me, we'll start in the Mash House.'

Chapter Eleven

Felicity pulled up the hood of the purple waxed jacket she'd borrowed from the staff room at the Glenbriar Distillery. The fleece lining was so cosy and familiar, and the little white Glenbriar logo shone like a badge of pride. She'd loved having one of these and wearing it out on days like this when she'd been running tours and the weather had taken a turn for the worse – usually well timed with the outdoor part of the tour.

She leaned on the railings above the stream that rushed down from the hills, crashing past the main building and into the lochan. Raindrops pattered on her hood. Beside her, Jerry did the same, tapping his fingertips together.

'What do you make of the new boss?' he asked.

She teetered on the edge of the truth and the tactful answer. She'd known Jerry a while and he was a kind man with a sympathetic nature who'd always looked out for her. Lying to him didn't feel right but after spending the previous evening brainstorming with Gavin, she'd realised just how little he'd bothered to learn about his new business until he'd almost left it too late. She'd overheard so much chat in her current job and her previous one that she knew what people wanted. Things needed to change and improvements were required. But not the easy get-out clause Julian was proposing.

'I'm not sure,' she said.

'Not like Frank, is he?' Jerry said.

'Definitely not.'

'Is this a bit of lip service?' he continued.

The phrase did nothing to help Felicity stave off wayward thoughts about Gavin that kept jumping out and grabbing her at the untimeliest moments. Lip service from him conjured a completely different meaning.

'I suspect it is, but I'm trying to convince him to focus his attention here.' She could think of other places she'd like him to focus his attention. *But just stop thinking about him like that!*

'But you're not hopeful?'

'It's been difficult to find time for a proper discussion so far, but we had a good planning session yesterday and he seemed more enthusiastic than usual. He's very intelligent and if he puts his mind to doing things properly, I'm sure he can.' The fact that he was usually aloof and detached, made her even more certain he wanted to do things right this time, otherwise he wouldn't have spent hours listening and talking to her. He could have walked away and said he was doing it his own way and that was final.

Jerry patted the back of her hand. 'Well, I remember you getting even the most sceptical, teetotal tourists to taste the whisky and say they liked it; you have a way with people. If anyone can turn him around, it's you.'

She chuckled. 'I'm trying my best. What did he ask you?' Gavin had decided to do the individual meetings without her.

It made sense. People might act differently if she was there too. Perhaps he wanted them to be brutally honest and thought they might hold back if an old friend was present.

'We had a good chat actually,' Jerry said. 'Frank was spot on when it came to making the distilleries perfectly pleasing to the eye. No complaints about that. Tourists get a tiptop tour here; the equipment is well maintained and the building is in perfect nick. But I can't help feeling it's got a bit superficial. We've lost a few staff recently and the turnover has got higher. Morale is low. Some of the systems we have are outdated and with Gavin not taking an active role in leading from the ground, there's a feeling of being adrift. I'm sixty-two, I won't be working here forever, but honestly, I don't see how someone new here would manage. I get on with it because I know how things work but without competent leadership, if you pardon my French, we're screwed.'

'Did you tell him all that?'

'I alluded to it, but I don't know I have the nerve to tell him outright that I don't rate him at all.'

'What would he have to do to redeem himself in your eyes?'

'Good question,' he said. 'Be present. I can't see any other way. He needs to be here, learning about how the distillery works and he needs to go up the glen to Torrindhu and out to Inverbuie and learn about them too.'

'We're going to them both,' she said. 'I want him to see all three for what they have.'

'Good, because they all have individuality and importance but the network has fallen apart. When Frank was at the helm, he had us all working together as well as individually. How often did you have to nip up and cover tours?'

'Ha, yes. Quite a few times.'

'And we didn't mind. None of us did. We were like a big family. Now, it's like three distilleries on different planets run by rival companies. We rarely see anyone from there and when we do, for bottling or supplies, there's hostility. Like somehow, we're causing problems for the other places. And I'm not blind to the possibility that we need to work on some of these problems even without Gavin but it's a time issue too. Frank helped out with this kind of thing or he and Dorothy freed us up to allow us networking time.'

'Oh no.' She rubbed her face and sighed. 'That's not good. In fact, it's worse than I thought.' In the back of her mind, she couldn't shake off thoughts of Julian and his wish to close or sell the other two distilleries. Was it possible people had got wind of these suggestions and now blamed Jerry and the Glenbriar staff?

'We should head in,' he said. 'Or I should. I need to see if Gavin is ready for the next person.'

'I'll come too. It's getting too wet out here.'

They went in through the back door and the heat hit her, along with the sweet malty scent she'd grown so used to. Sometimes she wondered if she'd got tipsy just from the fumes; it could be overpowering, especially in summer when it was already hot. But even the negatives hadn't stopped her enjoying it. The gushing sound of liquid cascading into the tanks peaked as they passed the giant copper stills and entered the reception area.

Gavin stood behind the high reception desk with Victoria, leaning his elbow on it and smiling. Yes, actually smiling. What the…? Felicity's stomach burned and she clenched her teeth. Victoria was beaming back, chatting and pointing at something on the screen. Gavin leaned over and his finger moved as he spoke, like he was describing a picture or a diagram. A hot twisting sensation burned inside Felicity. Since when was he ever that cosy with people? Why Victoria? *Why not me?* She pushed her hair behind her ears and smiled at Jerry. He put a fatherly palm on her back and nodded like he genuinely understood the pain she was feeling, though of course he didn't. Sheesh, she shouldn't even care. What did it matter? Gavin was her boss, not her boyfriend.

'Have you finished with Victoria?' Jerry approached the desk, making their presence known.

Gavin looked around and his eyes landed on Felicity first. She didn't smile; she couldn't. Lockjaw had taken over and her face had lost its ability to move. His focus shifted almost instantly to Jerry.

'We're nearly done,' he said. 'Who should I see next?'

'Matt, the barman, should be in now. You could see him.'

'Ok, let's do that then.' Gavin moved out from behind the reception area and Jerry led him through to the bar. He didn't look at Felicity. A happy balloon popped in her chest, leaving her feeling like he'd left her waiting outside in the cold. Maybe she should be pleased he was finally taking an interest in her old territory but it felt more like a brush off. Before she could face Victoria, a large tour party swung through the main doors and Felicity slipped out of the way. Memories swam before her of the days when she'd be the one to step out and lead them. Not someone called Brayden, who she'd never met before.

She hovered, pretending to examine the distillery model, listening as the smooth-talking Brayden charmed them with his low Scottish drawl. Felicity had always joked about her London accent and what made her qualified to lead the tour but Brayden didn't need to explain himself; he sounded made for the job. The tour moved through the door, following him like he was the Pied Piper.

Victoria clicked away on the computer for a moment, then looked up. 'What a day,' she said. 'I feel like we're being inspected.'

'How do you mean?' Felicity said.

'Gavin Sinclair.' Victoria let out a sigh. 'What a lot of questions he asked me.'

'Did he?' Felicity took off the jacket, shook it dry and draped it over her arm as she approached the desk. 'What about?'

'Well, apparently, Jerry had mentioned some of the systems being out of date, so Gavin wanted to know what we used for everything. Then he came and had a look. It sounded like he wanted to hire a software developer to invent something for the whole company. You should have heard his ideas. He's going to make us space age. I didn't understand half the stuff he was saying. My brain's fried. We might even be getting an app, but won't that cost a bloody fortune?'

Felicity sucked in a deep breath and let it fill her lungs slowly. It made more sense that Gavin's cheerful mood was nothing to do with Victoria and everything to do with the fact he was back on home territory.

'I don't think he'll have to hire anyone to do that. I suspect he wants to do it himself. That's what he used to do before he took on this job. Computer programming.'

'Ahh, that explains it,' Victoria said. 'The stuff he was asking me was so complicated, I thought it was a test. Oh, well, if he does all that, it might make our lives easier. I see where he's coming from. He wants one overall system that links to supply, finances, wages, bookings and everything really. Instead of using different things.'

'Quite ambitious.' Felicity tapped the desk. And maybe sensible. She remembered the faff they had trying to login sometimes and then when she went to one of the other distilleries, they had different systems.

Gavin interviewed staff most of the day and Felicity filled the time chatting with old work colleagues and getting more word on the ground. The same thing came up over and over – morale was low. Bickering had started between the three distilleries and the staff felt disenfranchised. When she and Gavin got back in the car to return to the hotel, she couldn't help wondering if he'd heard the same thing. Or had everyone pretended things were hunky-dory and walked around him on eggshells?

She took her seat, feeling a rush of heat in her neck and cheeks as Gavin got in. His raw man scent hit her, pushing her off course. That surge she'd felt earlier when she'd watched him laughing with Victoria swooped again in her chest along with words... *If I can't have you, no one will.* She almost let out a laugh, biting her lip hard, trying to stop hysteria from bursting out but also forcing herself back to sense. What was going on? This had to stop. What did she want to happen? If she answered that, it opened doors. But she couldn't walk through them. They led to places that might give pleasure and relief for a little while but beyond that was misery. Morning-after misery – made much worse by the fact there was no getting away from him unless she resigned. All of which took her back to where she'd been moments ago – she had to stop. Only she hadn't really started. Not consciously anyway. She hadn't woken up one day and thought, *hey, my boss is hot and I really want to climb into bed with him.*

'Jesus Christ,' she muttered, letting her head drop into her hand. This had reached ludicrous levels.

'Are you ok?'

'What?' *Shit.* She'd said that out loud. 'Me? I'm ok. Are you?'

'I am,' he said, his tone more relaxed than usual. 'That was a good day. You were right in suggesting this. I should have done it months ago. Already, I'm seeing where the gaps are and what needs to be done.'

'Do you mean the new software system?'

'Ah, someone blabbed about that, did they?'

'Was it a secret?'

'No, not really.'

'It sounds like a good idea.' She tried to look at him, though even his hands on the wheel and the edge of his gold watch at his cuff were oddly distracting. 'But I don't think that in itself will solve the problems.'

'I agree. In fact, that's a superficial solution and one I'm confident I can get up and running because of my background. Other things won't be as easy to put right, not without a lot of effort on my part.'

She swallowed. 'And are you willing to put in that effort?'

'I think so,' he said with a slight shrug, as though it was nothing. 'I took on the responsibility, so I have to make it work. You gave me some great ideas last night and I had some of my own today. Tomorrow, I'd like us to get together and make up some action plans for this distillery before we visit the next one.'

'That's fine. I scheduled it like that, so we had a day clear in between.'

'A wise move. Next week, once I've visited all three, I'd like to pull together all the managers and flesh out a bigger-picture plan for moving forward. Can you sort that for next Wednesday?'

'Of course I can.' She whipped out her phone and put in the details. How quickly he'd found his feet. He was a new man already.

Her eyes were on her phone but she had the feeling he'd glanced at her.

'So, um, are we done for the day?' she asked as he pulled into the hotel car park.

'Sure. Let's call it a day.'

She got out of the car, hyper aware of herself, in a way she hadn't been since the first few weeks of Gavin's takeover.

'Would you like…' He caught up with her, zapping shut his slick black saloon.

She blinked and made eye contact.

'I just wondered if you wanted to dine together again. Only no work talk this time.'

She raised her eyebrows. 'No work talk?' Why did her throat feel dry? 'What else do we have to talk about?'

His lip quirked up. 'Good point. That'll be a challenge, probably more so for me. You're good at keeping a conversation going.' He stopped and frowned, rubbing the back of his neck. 'Assuming you want to, that is. You're at perfect liberty to do as you please. I won't be offended if you don't want to speak to me at all outside of working hours. I'm not sure anyone would choose to eat with their boss.'

She smiled. His expression was so endearing and, really, if she said no, she'd spend all night wondering where he was and what he was doing. 'Of course I will. I can't wait to hear all about your life out of work.'

'Touché,' he said with a smirk. 'I better think up a damn good story.'

Felicity peered into the mirror, moving her head from side to side and teasing the hair tumbling over her shoulder for the umpteenth time. She puckered her lips and checked her teeth for any wayward lip gloss, then adjusted the straps of her black top. On its own it was way too racy for a dinner but she had a see-through chiffon top slipped over it to make it respectable. Casual but smart at the same time. Paired with dressy jeans and high-heeled ankle boots, she thought she'd done the job.

Or was it too brassy? She'd slicked on an almost-natural lip colour but maybe the eyeliner was too heavy. Grabbing a cotton bud, she dabbed some of it off, then blinked. Better. This wasn't a date after all. Dating the boss was out of the question. That would be crazy, as she'd told herself that afternoon in her pep talk. She had to stop all these silly thoughts but there was no getting around the fact she was having dinner with Gavin Sinclair – and he was her boss.

When she reached the foyer, she was the only person there other than Briony, who glanced up from the reception desk and wolf-whistled.

'Stop it,' Felicity said with a smirk.

'You look hotter than hot,' she said. 'Are you meeting someone tasty here tonight?'

'Just Gavin, my boss.'

'You have a date with the hot boss.' Briony grinned. 'Well, the two of you will set the dining room on fire.' She fake-fanned herself.

'Stop,' Felicity said, but she couldn't help grinning. 'It isn't a date. We work together. That's all.'

'Wait until he sees you tonight. He might have other ideas.'

'Seriously, stop it. Why are you working anyway and where's Zach? I thought you'd stopped doing evening shifts now you have more staff.'

'Zach's gone to get the shopping. He'll be back soon. I'm just covering while Janey's at a wedding.'

'Hmm.' Felicity eyed her. 'So you can spy on me?'

'Maybe.'

They both laughed before Felicity went into the dining room and took her seat. She'd only waited a few moments when Gavin came through the door. Oh god. He was in a crisp white shirt and tight black jeans. Totally, utterly, devastatingly handsome. Her insides melted into gooey liquid. His top button was open just enough to give her an agonisingly tantalising glimpse of his chest, sending a bolt of lust to her tummy and below. He adjusted his cufflinks and walked towards her. She couldn't take her eyes off him, though she felt like she ought to look away. Her mouth was dry.

He took the seat opposite and sat, his gaze flickering like he was trying to look her over and maintain eye-contact at the same time but not managing either. His mouth moved but obviously he couldn't settle on what to say. Eventually, he said, 'Good evening.'

'Good evening,' Felicity said, pleased at how cheery and playful her voice sounded. She'd half expected a croak. She crossed her legs under the table, forgetting how small it was and how both she and Gavin had long narrow pins. They collided and he visibly pulled back.

'Sorry,' they both said at the same time. Their eyes met for a few seconds before they laughed.

'I need a drink,' he said. 'A real one. For someone who owns a chain of whisky distilleries, it might surprise you to learn I don't really drink. Not much anyway.'

'Is that your first non-work fact?'

'Indeed.'

'It doesn't surprise me.' Though it intrigued her but, right now, everything about him was intriguing her.

'Recommend something for me then,' he said. 'Just not whisky.'

'This could get dangerous. What if I recommend tequila slammers?'

He looked up and raised an eyebrow. 'I think I last drank tequila at university and it's not an experience I want to repeat.'

'How about Prosecco? It's very drinkable and most people like it... I think.'

'Yes, that'll do.'

A server appeared at their table, lit a candle and took their drinks order. When the Prosecco arrived, the table became suddenly romantic. Gavin raised his glass, his face flickering in the candlelight.

'To us. I mean Glenbriar us... A working partnership... You know what I mean.'

She giggled and clinked her glass on his. 'I do.' She gulped a large mouthful. Why did that have to sound like she'd just married him?

He watched her closely as he sipped and she grew warm under his gaze. Now was the time to talk about anything, let her verbal diarrhoea flow, but she couldn't. Taking another glug, she forced her focus to the door where the server was talking to some guests who'd just arrived.

'So,' Gavin said. 'Your turn for a non-work-related fact.'

'Well, I... Hang on,' she frowned at the new arrivals. The server was leading them towards their table. 'Isn't that your mum and dad?'

'Pardon? What?' Gavin spun around in his chair and gaped. What were they doing here?

This may be an innocent working meal but Dorothy Sinclair's face was crimson and her eyes flashed like she'd caught her son in flagrante over the desk with his secretary. Felicity's blood ran cold.

Chapter Twelve

Gavin

Gavin shoved back his seat and jumped to his feet. The desire to hide Felicity burned him almost as much as the shock of seeing his parents.

'What are you doing here?'

'Surprise,' his mum said.

'It certainly is. But why? It's not my birthday or anything.'

'We know, we know.' His dad clapped his shoulder. 'We also knew you were up here this week and decided to drop by.'

'Drop by?'

'We're taking a holiday.' Mum took hold of Gavin's upper arms and beamed at him.

'Here?' Icy fingers gripped his lungs and squashed the air out. Having his parents here for the week would ruin everything. They'd interfere with business and... Well, dinners like this with Felicity wouldn't be happening. Like they probably shouldn't be anyway.

'No, not here,' Dad said. 'We're staying at the house tonight but we're on our way north. We're going over to Orkney for the week.'

A trickle of heat melted the icy fingers and Gavin breathed again.

'Oh, it is you, Felicity.' His mum peered around him and raised her eyebrow. She didn't need words to make her distaste known. Make-up was a pet hate of hers – unless it was on women she approved of and clearly Felicity wasn't one of them.

'Hi.' Felicity beamed. 'Nice to see you again.'

'This looks very...' She waved a long finger at the candle and the prosecco. 'Romantic.'

'Hardly.' Gavin coughed. The heat in the room was stifling.

'It does,' his mum said. 'I wasn't meaning you. I meant the setup. Why on earth have they put candles on the table and served champagne for a business dinner?'

'No idea.' Gavin tugged at his collar.

'It's prosecco.' Felicity held up her glass. 'I don't think it's a particularly romantic drink. Lots of people drink it.'

His mum glanced at her and the end of her nose twitched. She looked like she wanted to tell Felicity to be quiet but she cast her a withering smile. 'Indeed.'

'I've asked the waitress to make a bigger table for us over here.' Dad gestured to the corner. 'She said you hadn't ordered food yet, so perfect timing. We can all eat together.'

Gavin adjusted his cufflinks. 'Really, Dad?' Eating with his parents didn't appeal half as much as spending the evening alone with Felicity. No matter how wrong that may be. He licked his lips and glanced back at her. 'Is that ok with you?' He couldn't say no but he could give her an escape route. 'This isn't work, so if you'd rather not join us, it's up to you.'

'I, er, don't mind.' She glanced between him and his dad.

'Ah, join us,' Dad said. 'I'd love to hear how you're getting on.'

She got to her feet, lifting both her glass and Gavin's. He raised an eyebrow at his father. Dad had always had a soft spot for Felicity, though clearly his mum did not. Her eyes narrowed, and she looked away with a faint huff.

Something warm touched his arm, pressing the cotton of his shirt into his skin. He checked around to see Felicity, her upper arm causing the pressure on his as she moved between tables. With a weak smile, she handed him his drink.

'I think that's your one,' she said. 'You hadn't drunk as much as me.'

'Not yet,' he murmured close to her ear. 'I might need quite a lot to get me through this.'

She'd cocked her head up to hear him, exposing her long, slender neck. He almost crushed his glass, restraining the primal urge to kiss her. A throbbing ache pulsed through him and he ground his teeth. This was not wise. But as they shifted to a nearby table set for four, he couldn't stop thinking how coupley this must look – and felt. Nobody nearby batted an eyelid or had an expression of surprise or wonder. Felicity could be his girlfriend, his wife, his lover, whatever, and nobody thought it odd. But they didn't know the circumstances, the power imbalance, the age gap.

Gavin pulled out a chair and offered it to Felicity.

'Thank you.' She flashed him a smile before she sat.

His mother sat opposite, her lips set in a stiff line. She couldn't complain; she'd raised him to have good manners. He took his own seat beside Felicity, painfully aware of how close her thighs were to his. *Must keep my shit together.* Focus.

'So, how did the tour go today?' his dad asked.

Bang went the non-work-related chat. Gavin took a sip of his drink. Should he tell his parents they'd agreed not to talk shop tonight? Or did that make things look worse? They'd question what the hell he was doing dining with Felicity if they weren't talking about work. And maybe it was a good question. Right now, his brain, body and heart weren't on the same page and work was at the bottom of the agenda for all three.

'It was good.' Felicity blinked at Gavin with a slight frown on her otherwise perfectly smooth skin. Her long eyelashes fluttered and she gave him a half smile with her rosy lips. Everything about her face was gorgeous. 'Wasn't it?'

'What? Oh, er, yes. It was interesting. How did you know we were on a tour today?'

'Julian,' Dad said. 'I phoned him to find out your schedule for the week. And, Felicity, you have made a fantastic one. I knew you'd be good.' He winked at her and Gavin swigged back a mouthful of Prosecco. He was going to need a lot more of this tonight.

'I'm not sure why it's taken you so long to get up here, though Julian seems to think it inconvenient,' Dad went on.

'Does he? Why?'

His father leaned across the table. 'Because Julian is excellent at running the Edinburgh office but he's deluded about the work that goes on up here. He wants to modernise something that can't be modernised. Not in the way he wants.'

'Maybe I should arrange a tour for him too.' Felicity sipped her prosecco.

'Not a bad idea,' Dad said. 'Though he's had tours before and nothing changes. In many ways, he's the one who needs modernisation. He thinks he's moving things forward but he's ruthless at times. I've known him to propose strategies that are like cutting down a forest to preserve one special tree without a second thought for the devastation he's left behind.'

Gavin shuffled in his seat. That seemed exactly what Julian was proposing here. Why hadn't he listened to his father on this before?

'I like Julian,' his mother said. 'He's decisive but he needs to be tempered.'

'You were always good at that.' Dad's eyes twinkled as he looked at her.

'Felicity's good at that too,' Gavin said.

'Am I?' She gaped at him while his mother narrowed her eyes.

'You always give alternative solutions.'

'That's excellent,' Dad said.

'I'm not sure it's Felicity's place to be giving you alternative solutions, dear,' Mum said. 'Don't let my son have unrealistic expectations and push you into doing jobs that are way above your paygrade.' She smiled at Felicity as though commiserating but Gavin felt her sting and was sure Felicity would too.

'He doesn't,' she said. 'I just like to help if I can.'

'And I appreciate it.' Gavin took another mouthful of prosecco and didn't look at her. He wasn't lying but the heat in his body was going to make him spontaneously combust at any second.

'Well, I'm delighted.' Dad grinned at Felicity.

'Very supportive,' his mother said. 'But in future I suggest not worrying yourself about what the management team is doing. I'd stick to keeping Gavin's diary up to date. It'll be much less stressful.'

Gavin drew in a deep breath. 'Felicity isn't doing anything above her paygrade, Mum.'

'And I'll keep the diary up to date too,' Felicity said. 'I like the look of the salmon. What about you?' She passed the menu to Gavin and gave him a little smile that told him not to worry. He took it from her with such a release of tension he almost threw everything out the window and kissed her. Almost. He wasn't that far gone. After they'd decided what to order, he signalled the server and she bustled over.

'And more prosecco,' Gavin said before she left. 'A bottle, please.'

'I see you're drinking.' Dad smirked and lifted an eyebrow. 'What happened to the carrot juice regime?'

Bloody hell. That blew part one of his alias out of the water.

'That was a fad, you know,' he lied, aware of Felicity's gaze on him. She'd possibly already done the maths. But surely not? She'd never believe he enjoyed wild swimming. And as for the proposal. Nope. She wouldn't think that was him. But what if she did and realised he was the one who bought those gloves? The ones he shouldn't really have known about. The ones he only knew about because he was listening into her conversation. He couldn't help it. He never could. Wherever she was, he was drawn to her, even when he'd tried hard not to be affected by her. Being aloof and standoffish with her might have frightened her off but it hadn't stopped the raw attraction eating at him from inside.

Dad laughed and pointed to a picture on the wall, drawing Mum into a conversation about it. Gavin had a sudden inkling Felicity might ask for clarification about the carrot juice and he had to stop her. He leaned slightly closer, all his nerve ends springing to life as he took a long drag on her perfume before murmuring, 'Sorry.'

'What about?' she whispered, her breath tickling his cheek.

'This.' He motioned towards his parents with his eyes. 'And the constant work talk. After we agreed—'

'Gavin,' Mum said with a sharp bite. 'Do you see this painting? It has the distillery at Torrindhu in it.'

'So it does.' He straightened up.

The conversation didn't improve – or deviate. Work. Work. Work. Part of him was happy about that. Who wanted their parents discussing their child's private life? Those stories never ended well. But it was irritating. He tapped the table as the server cleared the plates. How much more pleasant would this have been if it were just him and Felicity?

Felicity declined a dessert. Maybe an indication she didn't want to prolong the evening further. Could he blame her? But her warm demeanour didn't slip and she chatted like this was the only thing in the world she wanted to be doing.

'I'm not big on dessert either.' Gavin closed the menu.

'He's a bit of a health freak,' Dad said. A ripple of unease made Gavin slap the menu on the table a little harder than he meant to. His mother frowned but Gavin had to intercept his dad before he blabbed to Felicity that his son's preferred workout was swimming.

'Not a freak, Dad. Just an average guy who doesn't fancy dying of a heart attack. Now, when are you heading off to Orkney?'

'Tomorrow morning,' Mum said.

Gavin checked his watch. 'You better not stay too late then. It's already after nine.'

'Is it?' Mum checked her own watch. 'Goodness, time really flies. Maybe we should pass on dessert too and make a move, Frank.'

'Yes, yes, that's fine,' he said. 'I'll settle for a coffee.'

'Oh, it's too late for me to have a coffee,' Mum said. 'It'll keep me awake all night.'

It had to be the longest coffee ever. Gavin needed them gone. He didn't think they'd ever timed a visit so badly before, though no one needed to know that.

'I'll foot the bill,' Dad said.

'That's very generous,' Felicity said. 'But shouldn't I contribute?'

'Definitely not,' Gavin said. 'This trip is all on expenses anyway.'

'No objections.' Dad pulled out his wallet. 'I'm paying for everyone.'

Dorothy nipped to the bathroom and suddenly, after all that, Gavin and Felicity were alone at the table. He glanced at her and she looked back with a half-smile.

'I honestly can't apologise enough. You're due another bonus for putting up with that.'

'Don't be ridiculous.' She shook her head. 'It wasn't that bad.'

'No?' He sighed and looked skyward. 'You've obviously got a higher tolerance rate than me.'

'I expect so. I've worked with people all my life and you... Well, you've spent a lot of time with machines.'

He laughed and dropped his face into his hand.

'Oh god, did that sound really nasty? I didn't mean it to. I think I've had too much prosecco and it's made me a blabbering idiot.'

He flicked his gaze towards her. 'I know what you meant. And you're right. As usual.'

'Hardly.'

'In my world, you're always right. No one makes the right decisions in life all the time but you make plenty of good calls around here.'

'Thanks.' She lifted her almost empty glass and clinked it on the edge of his.

He picked up his and downed the last mouthful. 'I bet I have a killer headache tomorrow.'

'The whisky baron who can't hold his liquor.'

'Pretty much sums it up.'

Dorothy returned to the room, straightening out her cornflower blue blouse. A frown grew as her focus shifted from Frank still talking to the waitress at the pay table to Gavin and Felicity. She beelined for them.

Gavin got to his feet and hugged her. 'Good to see you, Mum. Even if it was a bit of a shock.'

'Come with me a second. I want to show you something I saw in the foyer. Excuse us a minute, Felicity.' She tugged his arm and he followed her. The foyer was noticeably cooler. His mum kept walking until she was at the front door and out of earshot of the reception desk.

'What is it you want to show me?'

'Nothing. I just wanted a quick word without Felicity over-hearing. And I don't want to say it in front of your father either because he thinks the sun shines from that girl's every orifice.'

'What are you talking about?'

'Just be very careful with her.'

'In what way?'

'She's very ambitious. She plays the airhead by wearing all that make-up and nail polish.' His mum screwed up her face. 'Vile stuff. But you don't go from tour guide to chief exec's PA without ambition. And she can talk the talk. She convinced your father to let her have the job when she had no qualifications or experience in the role, so watch she doesn't do the same to you. I wouldn't want her sweet-talking you and the next thing we know, she's sitting in Julian's seat, or worse, yours.'

'There's nothing wrong with ambition, Mum.'

'True, but I don't like her methods. If she wants to move up the career ladder, it has to be on merit. Not on anything else.' She glanced around. 'And for heaven's sake, don't let her sleep her way to the top. People already say she had some hold over your father, though his soft spot for her is more like an affectionate uncle. Goodness knows what they'd think if she gets her claws into you. We'd never live it down if there was a scandal like that.'

'Seriously?' Gavin tugged at his cuffs. How laughable was this? 'Like she would ever do that? Like I would!'

'Just be very careful. She's clever and she knows how to play games. Make sure you don't enter into them.'

'Rest assured, I won't. There's nothing I hate more than games. I won't be playing any of them and I won't be "sweet-talked" into anything. Felicity is good at her job. Can't you just accept that?'

'Of course. I'm delighted to hear it.' His mum pushed up on tiptoes and kissed his cheek. He hugged her and sighed.

'Ah, there you are,' Dad said.

Gavin pulled away from his mum. Dad and Felicity had both arrived in the foyer.

'Time to go,' Mum said. 'Be sensible.' She patted Gavin's arm. 'And we'll send some pictures of Orkney. Goodbye, Felicity,' she added.

'Bye. Nice to see you again.'

'And you,' Dad said. 'Keep up the good work and keep my son on the straight and narrow.'

Gavin folded his arms and rolled his eyes. 'Excuse me? Why?' It wasn't like he was a rebellious teenager. Like the walking stuffed shirt could ever be anything other than sensible.

Dad chuckled. 'Good luck with the rest of the visits.'

Gavin leaned on the door frame and watched them leave. Felicity's fragrance drifted into his consciousness and he flicked his gaze to her.

'Was your mum ok?' she asked.

'Fine. She just worries, as all mums do, I suppose.'

Her hand touched his arm and he held his breath. 'It was kind of them to surprise you.'

He supposed it was but the touch of her fingertips had rendered him unable to talk.

'We should go to bed.' She moved her hand to stifle a yawn.

He glanced at her, trying not to imagine she'd said that as an invitation. His face must have given him away. She flapped and shook her head.

'I meant individually, obviously. I know that sounded like... Well... I—'

'It's ok.' He straightened up and rubbed the back of his neck. 'I know what you meant. Sleep well. I'll see you in the morning.' With a brief nod, he took the stairs two at a time and headed straight for his room without a backward glance.

Chapter Thirteen

Felicity

The scent of wood, pine, and wildflowers wafted towards Felicity as she made her way along the path beside the loch. Snuffling through the trees ahead were Briony's dogs. Becker, the older one, stopped frequently to sniff the air and gaze around. She couldn't blame him. The view was stunning.

Briony called to Rafa, the lolloping year-old puppy, who, like Becker, was of no particular breed but large, brown and hairy.

'It's hilarious that you called him after Rafael Nadal.' Felicity shook her head and chuckled, tossing her hair over her shoulders and drinking in the beauty of the landscape. The water was a vibrant blue, and the sun shone down, making the surface glitter and sparkle like thousands of diamonds were twinkling on it.

'Well, I can only assume Becker was called after Boris Becker, as my grandmother named him and I never had a chance to ask her, but I can't think of any other Beckers. So Zach and I thought we'd continue the tradition. Zach thought Rafa was a bit punchier than Roger or Novak.'

'Definitely, suits him.'

Bird song filled the air. Rafa chased off sparrows and thrushes and scattered some wood pigeons in a dappled glade. The distant rush of a waterfall and the gentle lap of water on the shore made everything feel peaceful.

'I miss all this.' Felicity's shoulders drooped.

'Aw.' Briony put her hand around her shoulder. 'I wish you hadn't left.'

'Sometimes I wish that too. But I really like this job. It's challenging and interesting, but...'

'It's in Edinburgh.'

'Exactly.'

They carried on along the path by the lochside until the rushing water got louder. A small waterfall cascaded down a rocky hillside, crashing into a stream and tumbling into the loch, creating a soft mist. A small wooden bridge crossed the stream and Felicity leaned on the rail and closed her eyes. She breathed in the fresh scent of the water, letting tranquillity wash over her.

'What happened yesterday evening?' Briony interrupted her reverie. 'I went home but I saw Frank Sinclair arriving with his wife. I wasn't expecting them or I would have set a table for four.'

'No one was expecting them.' Felicity huffed out a sigh.

'Do they meddle all the time? I guess them being in charge for so long makes it hard for them to step away.'

'No, actually they don't. Or not that I see anyway. I suppose they might annoy Gavin all the time, but then, he wouldn't exactly tell me that.'

'Hmm.' Briony leaned on the rail beside Felicity, bending forward to make room for the bump. 'Why did he take over?'

'Duty, I think. He said something yesterday about being under pressure to do it since he was a child. He rebelled by doing something completely different and not even visiting.'

'I googled him.' Briony grinned. 'Well, after you made me google Zach when we first met, it's only fair that I return the compliment.'

'Haha.' Felicity giggled at the memory and how she and Briony had discovered something completely unexpected about Zach. 'And was there anything shocking?'

'Nope. His credentials on LinkedIn make him look like some whizz kid in the IT sector.'

'Which he is.'

'Which just makes me wonder why he left, but I couldn't find any scandals or anything.'

Felicity was ninety-nine per cent certain there were no scandals. Gavin wasn't a scandal type guy. If he'd chosen to do what he believed was the right thing, he would do it. Though sadly, it seemed he'd sacrificed his own dreams and goals.

'I should get back. We're meeting all day before another site visit tomorrow.'

'At least he's easy on the eye.' Briony gave her a little nudge.

'Nope. That's not a good thing.'

'Isn't it?'

'Not really. It's kind of distracting.' She turned to walk back along the path, trying to ignore the tug in her heart about how much she'd love to call this place home again.

'Oh dear.' Briony pulled a face as they headed back towards the hotel. 'So, the hot boss thing.'

'Yeah. That.'

Briony patted Felicity's back. 'And do you want it to develop further?'

'Are you kidding? How can I? No, just no. Like I don't even know where to start. He's my boss, my actual boss and the CEO of the whole company. I don't even register on the lowest rung of the ladder of people he might ever date. Plus, he's thirty-six.' The words came out quietly in case the birds were listening and taking messages back to him. 'I'm only twenty-five. His mum does not like me because I wear nail polish and... Oh god.' She stopped and covered her face. 'Why am I saying all this?'

Briony chuckled. 'Because you like him?'

'I do like him.' Out loud, the words crashed over Felicity like water from the falls. 'I don't even get exactly why I like him, but I do.'

'Sometimes there is no explanation.'

'But it's not like we had an eyes-meet moment or anything like that. I just feel... I don't know how to explain it. Honestly, is this why so many films and books are about secretaries and their bosses? Is it just not possible to work for someone and not fall for them?'

Briony smiled. 'I don't know. Maybe you just get used to each other. I take it from your list of objections that he's not seeing anyone.'

'I don't think so. He doesn't really talk about personal stuff.' Her mind harped back to the few brief snippets of things she knew about him, which really just made it more obvious why she shouldn't be interested in him. She didn't know him at all.

'Well, he took you to dinner, so I suspect not,' Briony said.

'That was business.'

'Really?'

'Yes. When he started, someone told me he had a reputation for being a player, but he doesn't seem like that, though how do you tell?'

'But if he's thirty-six, it doesn't seem likely he's been a squeaky-clean bachelor up until now. Is he divorced?'

'I'm pretty sure he's not. But thirty-six is too old for me, right?'

Briony smirked. 'Don't think so. I'm five years older than Zach. Who cares about age really? When I met you, you were twenty-one, but you seemed a lot more mature and sensible. Plus, he looks pretty fit to me.'

'Not helping.' But she was right. He was in good shape and looked like he worked out. He'd mentioned healthy eating before. So had Frank. He'd teased him about drinking carrot juice, which sent Felicity's mind dancing back to Christmas and the secret Santa note. Coincidence? Gavin may like carrot juice but wild swimming? Surely not? Was that how he kept fit? But none of that fitted in with someone who'd been proposed to and lost the love of their life... Or did it? Maybe it worked perfectly. Could it explain why he was still single at thirty-six despite being a great catch? 'I need to tell you something else. I've just thought about it.'

She reeled off the story to Briony as they neared the little shoreline close to the hotel where she'd seen Gavin wading in to get the child's ball. For someone who always seemed so buttoned up, getting into the water hadn't bothered him.

'Ok, that's curious,' Briony agreed. 'And what was in the gift?'

Heat bloomed in Felicity's cheeks. 'Gloves. The exact ones I wanted. I'd mentioned them in the staffroom one morning... But...' She frowned and shook her head. 'I'm not sure if he was there. Or if he was, he must have been listening from a distance.' And that was plausible. He'd done that before and heard people calling him a stuffed shirt.

'I think it was him. I just have a feeling.' Briony pulled an almost sorrowful expression. 'I think it's safe to say he likes you too, but if he's an intelligent guy, he won't make any rash decisions.'

Felicity sighed. Yes. That was true and she would do the same. But a throb had started up in her chest and it spread outward. It hurt to know she liked someone, and he might like her too, only they couldn't do anything about it without breaking hundreds of rules.

'Come and chat later when your meeting's over. We can drown your sorrows if you like.'

'Yeah. I might. Probably best if I limit the verging-on-romantic dinners with him.'

'Yes, tread carefully. You've worked hard for this job.'

'I know.' Felicity gave her a hug and stayed in Briony's hold. She'd missed having her friend nearby.

Briony let them use a conference room off the main dining room for their meeting. Gavin was already there with his laptop, iPad and his phone all set around. He was typing something and his fingers raced across the keyboard.

'Good morning.' He didn't look up and his fingers didn't stop moving as he spoke. 'Take a seat. I just have something to finish.'

Felicity sat and opened her notes, trying not to be disarmed by the speed of his typing or the concentration in his eyes. But keeping busy was difficult when all she wanted to do was watch him. She checked her emails until he glanced up, taking a breath like he'd just been swimming. The thought gave her another sucker punch to the chest. What would he look like wild swimming with those muscles on show?

'Right.' He interlocked his fingers and flexed them outward. 'Let's get started.'

'Tell me something first.'

'What?' His gaze linked with hers, causing a swoop that she really needed to get used to and soon. Because Briony was right, she'd worked hard for this job and it wasn't worth risking it for a silly crush.

'What exactly did you do when you were a computer programmer and software developer?'

He smiled and shook his head. 'How can I explain it in a few minutes? I suppose it's a bit like building a house. A programmer is like the architect, and a software developer is the builder. We work together to design and develop software that makes computers and other devices work. I did both jobs at different points in my career. A lot of the work I did latterly was in the gaming industry. High end gaming that needed incredible realism.'

'Sounds mindboggling.'

'It was so interesting and complex but I could disappear down a rabbit hole and not surface for days. It could feel like living in a CGI world. I was involved more and more in the management side of things but IT people are different from... Well, distillery people.'

'Better?'

Gavin nodded. 'We all speak a common language. The language of computers. It forges a bond. People in other industries call it being geeky or nerdy or whatever, but it's not like that. It's just a methodical and fundamental understanding of how technology works and how to get it to work for you.'

'Ok. Here's something a bit controversial.'

'Ye-es.' His eyebrows raised slowly as he said the word.

'Imagine this business is a computer programme that's full of bugs. You have to find them all and fix them all but you have to do it without deleting any of the major features, such as places or people. If a system or something isn't working, you can update and improve it, but that's all.' She peered at him with a little smile.

'My mother said you were one to watch.'

'Did she?' *Scary thought.*

'Yes. And she was right. You're smart. That's a good analogy but the parameters are quite narrow.'

'But you like a challenge. You must do or you wouldn't be here.' She rested her elbows on the table, linked her fingers together and laid her chin on them, peering at him. Maybe she was pushing it, but he looked relaxed and was almost smiling.

He leaned forward. 'You're exactly right. As usual. So, let's do it. I'll let you know where I see issues for improvement and we can think of a plan to move forward.'

She was ready, her cup overflowing with ideas and possibilities. He had the tech knowhow and drew up spreadsheets and interactive plans before she could even think of them. She shuffled around to his side of the table and moved in close, her heart beating fast.

His fingers flew over the keyboard as he pulled up a program, and she admired the way he expertly navigated the software. As the program loaded, he turned to her and smiled, his eyes warm and inviting. A flutter agitated her stomach again.

'This,' he said, his voice low, almost a whisper, 'is something we can use throughout all the departments. Just a sec...' He pulled up another screen, then closed it off, but not before she caught a glimpse the complex system of codes and algorithms dancing in front of her. What did that all mean? 'It can be cloud stored so all changes and updates are live. It'll need some testing but if we can get it up and running, it'll mean I can keep my finger on the pulse all the time. Each distillery and department within them can see what's happening at a glance. So, say we identify a need to update the sales system in the main distillery, we could click here.' He touched the screen. 'Ignore the graphics. They're primitive just now, but I can easily remedy that at a later date.' His voice was a soothing murmur in her ear. The idea he might have bought her the gloves added another layer to their interaction. He'd noticed her, singled her out, discovered something about her and bought her exactly the right gift. Maybe that was his programming mind in action. He'd matched her with the perfect gift, but he hadn't used AI. It had come from his own mind... Maybe his heart. Felicity swallowed at the thought and a powerful surge of connection soared through her like they were partners in work and in life. In reality, they were neither, but at this moment, they were supporting and inspiring each other in a way she'd never done with anyone. Work was at the core, but if she felt nothing for him, she wouldn't feel the tug to put in so much effort, and she was sure he was doing the same for her.

She was almost leaning on his arm as he pointed out the features and even with her limited knowledge of technology, she could foresee benefits.

'If this was up and running, you could run the business from anywhere.'

He frowned. 'I could, I suppose, though Edinburgh is the main HQ.'

'Why is that? It seems like it would be more sensible to have the headquarters here.'

'My mother is from Edinburgh and she never wanted to live full time up here. This was like their holiday home.'

'So, your parents moved the HQ to Edinburgh?'

'They did. It was at a time when lots of businesses were pulling out of smaller towns and relocating to the city. Though with remote working, none of that seems to matter as much anymore. I can see benefits of having a management centre here as well. The Edinburgh office could specialise in advertising, marketing and global distribution. But a senior executive of some sort would be useful up here.'

'Or you could relocate.'

'Me?' He shook his head. 'I don't think I'm made for rural life.'

'I used to feel like that.' She caught his eye and realised how close their faces were. Just how beautiful were his eyes? An almost teal shade of blue. 'But I loved it so much. It was like a dream.' Her lips moved as the words came out and she wasn't sure if she was talking about her life here or this moment with him. He didn't look away but his pupils flickered slightly towards her mouth. She held her breath. The air between them was crackling with electricity and it shocked her nerve ends, making the tension unbearable. But nothing could happen here. One of them would have to look away. She wanted to be sensible and do just that but she couldn't. He obviously couldn't either – or didn't want to.

A knock on the door made them both jump and Felicity swallowed, smoothing out the folds of her ditsy dress.

'Come in.' Gavin's voice sounded rough. Her heart raced. He was as affected by this as her... This being what? An unspeakable attraction between them? Or a nightmare?

'Hi.' Briony poked her head around the door. 'Am I disturbing you? I've got something I'd like to run by you if you have a minute but I can come back at another time if it's more convenient.'

'Now is fine. Sit down, please.' Gavin gestured to a chair opposite, and Felicity rolled her seat away from him so it didn't look like she was about to leap into his lap.

Briony smiled but her eyes moved between them subtly, like she was trying to work out if their sitting so close was innocent or not. Felicity wasn't sure she could give a truthful answer, even if Briony asked outright. Gavin was a magnet tugging her to him even when she was trying to keep her distance – and right now, she wasn't trying too hard.

'How can we help?' Gavin asked and the word 'we' struck Felicity to the core. Her body and soul were oversensitive to the slightest thing. If he so much as accidentally brushed against her, she might faint or ignite into a flaming ball of lust.

'Well, Felicity knows that in the past, your father was a frequent sponsor of local events.' Briony said. 'We would often display banners advertising the distillery in return for sponsorship and we sell the whisky in the bar of course.'

'Reciprocity.' He raised his eyebrows.

'Exactly. Except I can't say that word for toffee; it always trips me up.'

He smiled. 'And would you like to start doing that again?'

'If you were up for it.'

He glanced at Felicity and she sat up straight, trying not to look too excited. This was exactly the direction she wanted to steer him in. 'I think it's a perfect idea. And I don't think it should stop here, even though I'll always have a soft spot for this hotel.' She winked at Briony.

'Then go ahead.' He rubbed his hands together. 'I'm happy to run with any suggestions. What did you have in mind?'

'Well, there's the Autumn Gold Festival and the Forest Light Show in the autumn,' Briony said.

Felicity opened her iPad. 'I'll put in the dates and we can get some banners made up.'

'We're having a ceilidh on Friday.' Briony pulled a side pout. 'But that might be too short notice to do anything for, though you're welcome to attend. I believe your parents attended ceilidhs here when my grandmother owned the hotel. They were big supporters of local events.'

'Attend?' Gavin's eyes darted to Felicity. 'I, er, don't know.'

'It sounds like great fun.' She tapped her iPad. Of course she wanted to support Briony, but, oh god, her heart was racing at the thought of stealing a dance with Gavin.

'I don't think it's my thing,' he said. 'But you go if you want to. I don't have anything to wear.'

'If you need a kilt, there's a shop in Glenbriar that hires them out. I'm sure they'd have something.' Briony beamed at him.

'No. Felicity can represent the company.' He cast her a brief glance. 'If you want to.'

'Sure, no problem.' But her heart sank a notch. He was being sensible but it wouldn't be anything like as fun without him.

Chapter Fourteen

Gavin

Gavin hauled off his t-shirt and cast it aside on a flat boulder by the shore. The problem with wild swimming was that very few places were completely private. But he wasn't skinny dipping, so even if anyone saw him, he wasn't doing any harm. It didn't wholly remove the awkwardness he always felt as he slowly made his way into the loch.

The cool water brushed over his feet. This was his first time in freshwater – definitely colder than the sea. Soon it was up to his knees, then his thighs; it lapped at the edge of his swim shorts. He took a deep breath, braced himself, then plunged forward, braving the thrill of the chill and gasping as it hit. As soon as his arms ploughed through the water, the shock dissipated and his skin acclimatised.

Even in the early morning light, he could tell it was going to be another beautiful day. With his second distillery visit on the agenda, he wanted to burn off some physical energy before the mental exertion started. And more than that, there was the emotional overload that walloped him every time he was close to Felicity. Working with her was both a joy and a torture. He couldn't remember anyone before – with the possible exception of Holly

– who he'd been able to work with so easily and so seamlessly. Ideas flowed between them as effortlessly as the water cascading from a nearby waterfall. Barriers fell away, opening possibilities rather than throwing out obstacles. Her suggestion of looking at the business like a programme that needed to be debugged was genius. The path seemed clearer already, and he'd spent the evening prepping reports and action plans for Julian and the other department heads. Some of the suggestions wouldn't be what Julian wanted but they were what the company needed. Gavin's confidence at the helm of Sinclair Brothers was at an all-time high and he owed that to Felicity. Unfortunately, he couldn't shake off the utterly inappropriate personal feelings he had for her. Why couldn't he have met her when he was online dating? Why did she have to be someone who worked for him? He sensed the connection wasn't one way either. The way she looked at him sometimes... Or was that just wishful thinking? Wishful and hopeless because he couldn't act on it.

He swam back to the shore, waded out and peered around. It was unlikely anyone was about this early, though people might be walking dogs before work. Hopefully, it was out of the way enough for no one to notice him. He quickly pulled off his wet swimming shorts and towelled himself down before putting on his joggers and a t-shirt. If Felicity or anyone else caught him with wet hair, hopefully it would just look like he was very sweaty from a run. What an image. He shook his head with a smirk, then ran his hand vigorously through his hair several times, fluffing it up and hoping he could dry it off just in case.

A receptionist he didn't recognise was at the desk and he made it back to his suite without anyone seeing him. Mission accomplished. He showered, dressed in his suit, and headed to breakfast. No one would know what he'd been doing. Had Felicity guessed he was the sender of the Secret Santa gift? The carrot juice might have put her onto it.

He sat at a small table by the window, overlooking the tranquil waters of Loch Briar where he'd swam earlier, though he'd been much further up where the trees provided plenty of cover. The sun shone brightly in a wall-to-wall blue sky.

As he perused the menu, a young server approached with a tray loaded with a pot of coffee, a plate of toast and a dish of condiments which, according to the menu, were all locally produced. There was something to be said for the small-town ethos with buy-local initiatives being all the rage. This was a lot more personal than the little plastic jam sachets in big hotel chains.

'Can I get you a cooked breakfast?' the server asked.

Gavin had been on a healthy eating drive for a while now but he'd always had a weakness for square sausages and black pudding. Just once wouldn't hurt.

'Yes, please.'

The server returned ten minutes later, with a plate piled high with a classic Scottish breakfast. Fried eggs, black pudding, square sausages, bacon, fried tomatoes and a heap of fluffy tattie scones. He half closed his eyes at the smell of the feast. He could see how people got addicted to food like this but he had faith in his discipline.

He was just about to take a bite of his black pudding when Felicity walked in. Hell. Would his discipline extend to this?

She approached the table, her hair pulled back in an updo with some loose tendrils coiling around her face. Whatever she wore, she always looked well-turned out and stylish. She had on her customary pencil skirt with a lightweight purple blouse, very similar to the Glenbriar Distillery trademark colour.

'Good morning. Can I sit here?' She indicated the seat across from him.

'Of course. I wasn't sure if you'd been in already.'

'No. I overslept. The beds are so comfy.' She perused the plate in front of him, her nose wrinkling slightly.

'Is my breakfast grossing you out?'

She laughed. 'No, sorry. You eat what you want.' She glanced at the menu.

He listened as she ordered her breakfast, noting the way she avoided the fried options. She was so like him. Normally, he was exactly the same.

'Do you ever give in?' he asked.

'To what?' She frowned at him.

'To food like this. I hardly ever do, but sometimes temptation gets the better of me.' Just so long as those temptations were only food and not... Well, the woman sitting opposite. 'It's become a bit of an obsession with me.'

'I know exactly how that feels.'

The server arrived with a tray of toast and jams.

'I...' Felicity stumbled over her words, which wasn't like her, and he eyed her.

'Are you ok?'

'I had an eating disorder growing up.'

He raised his eyebrows and opened his mouth. How to reply?

'I don't really talk about it. Some people aren't very sympathetic and think I did it for attention, but it's not like that.'

'I'm sure it isn't.'

'It's a mental disorder really. I was hospitalised for a while when it got out of control. I had to be fed by a tube. But I got therapy and that really helped, but I still can't eat a lot and some food just scares me.'

'Like my breakfast.' He cringed. 'Sorry, I didn't realise.'

'No, no. I don't mind if you eat it. I just couldn't eat that. Sometimes if I go out and I'm served a big portion, it freaks me out because I know I won't be able to finish it.'

'I'm sorry, I never knew any of this.'

She gave a little shrug. 'You wouldn't. I hardly ever tell anyone.'

But she'd told him.

'Sorry,' she added. 'I didn't mean to put a depressing spin on things.'

'You haven't. I'm honoured you chose to tell me.'

She cast him a little smile and spread some jam on her toast. 'Jam is a weakness of mine though. I'll concede that. Especially homemade jam.'

Without thinking, he put his hand out and placed it over hers. He held it firmly. 'Thank you.'

She stared at him. 'What for?'

'For confiding in me and trusting me. Not just trusting me but trusting *in* me. And for being here with me and helping me to see the light.' He brushed his thumb over the pale skin on the back of her hand. 'You've been a loyal friend to me this week and I feel so much more confident in my role. I just want you to know I appreciate the pivotal part you've played in that.'

'You're welcome. It's my p-pleasure.'

At the stutter in her word, he released her hand. It was his too. Just looking at her filled him with pleasure... and desire.

One of the hotel's resident dogs strolled into the dining room, wagging his tail and making a beeline for their table.

'Look out,' Gavin said. 'I met this dog the other day and he tried to jump all over me.'

'That's Becker.' Felicity laughed. 'He's a bit too old for jumping now. He used to bowl people over when he was younger.' She patted her knees and Becker sidled up to her. 'Hello, gorgeous.' She ruffled his head. 'Are you after Gavin's meat?'

A double entendre if ever he heard one. He cleared his throat and looked away.

'Hey, Becker,' an American voice called and Becker turned away from Felicity.

She got up. 'Zach!' Running to the man, she flung her arms around his neck. 'I've missed you.'

'Whoa.' He gave her a pat on the back, then stepped out of her grip.

Zach? He was the owner's partner, right? His mop of black hair was like Jon Snow from *Game of Thrones*.

Felicity returned to the table, still smiling.

'You really miss it up here with all your friends, don't you?' Gavin dabbed at his lips with his napkin.

She nodded.

'Would you ever move back?'

'I'd love to, but I like my job too.'

'Yeah, that's a conundrum alright.'

Gavin flicked through his emails, resting his phone on the steering wheel as he waited for Felicity, who was still inside the hotel. Was she gossiping to her friend again? Or maybe she'd run into some more old friends. He stopped scrolling and raised his eyebrow, spying a reply from Julian.

To: GWSinclair@Sinclairbros.com

From: JMorrison@Sinclairbros.com

Subject: RE: Upgrade and improvement visits

Thanks for the update. Sounds like there is lots to be done in the highland distilleries, which is not surprising. We'll need to balance the required improvements against costs and projected figures. It wouldn't be wise to invest in extensive upgrades if we won't get the return.

Look forward to further discussion on the matter when you return.

J

The corner of Gavin's lip twitched. Julian made a good point. He always did but he consistently missed something. Something Felicity saw as a top priority. And she was right again. The Edinburgh control centre was Julian's baby, and he thrived there, but he was short-sighted. The Perthshire distilleries were at the core of the business. Without them, what was Sinclair Brothers? Glenbriar on its own was a viable product but take away the two smaller distilleries and what was left? Glenbriar and one lowland distillery that satisfied the mass-production needs of the international market. But all the heart and soul would be gone.

'My job isn't to cut away the dead wood,' Gavin muttered at his phone. 'It's to encourage new growth in forgotten and neglected areas.' And they were going to start straight away with Torrindhu.

Felicity dashed out of the front door of the hotel and across to the car. 'Sorry about that. I had a phone call from Julian.'

Gavin frowned and started the engine. 'Why was he calling you? He's just emailed me.'

'I know.' She clicked her belt. 'He wanted to tell me a list of projected figures and said I should show them to you.'

He rolled the car out of the car park and shook his head. 'Why didn't he just tell me directly?'

'I get the feeling he thinks I'm causing trouble. It wasn't really you he wanted to know those figures. He wants me to see how badly the distillery is doing, so I'll give up trying to persuade you to keep it open.'

'And are you going to give up?'

'Nope.'

'I didn't think so.'

'He obviously thinks my persuasive powers are influential.'

'And he's right.' Gavin smiled, flicking his eyes her way, knowing he should keep them firmly on the road.

'Do you know where you're going today?' Her question didn't mask the smile in her voice.

'I checked Google maps before we left. Though it would be easier if you just let me use the Satnav.'

'I'm not stopping you from using it. I just thought it was silly to use it for Glenbriar, as it's just ten minutes away and easy to find.'

'Well, you can direct me in the good old-fashioned way.'

'If you're so old-fashioned, I'm surprised you want me directing you. Isn't it more manly just to get lost then blame everyone else?'

He chuckled. 'I suspect my dad would agree with you.'

'Mine definitely would.'

He'd kept his attention firmly on the road but he had the sense she was x-raying him. Years of being scrawny and too thin still gave him a shiver of uncertainty, but he knew he had the goods now. The muscular build so many women seemed to want. Wouldn't it be just his luck if she wasn't one of them? Maybe she was the woman who didn't care what he looked like and would settle for him just being himself – be happy he could provide stability and security. But wait... He couldn't do that for her. His pheromones had him sniffing her out as a partner and he couldn't stop wandering into the world of what if...

Sheep dotted the rolling hills as he wound along the quiet road. The Torrindhu distillery was nestled in a glen where it was visible from some distance as they approached from above. The romantic setting led to many photographs of it in their advertising literature.

'You wouldn't want to lose this, would you?' Felicity turned her head to him.

'No. It's stunning. I don't want any closures on my watch.'

'Wow. I call that a win.'

'You see. That's the power of your persuasion. You've convinced me and you don't need to convince anyone else.'

'What about Julian?'

'Leave him to me. I'm in charge, remember? It's his job to do what I want, not the other way round.'

From the corner of his eye, he caught her nipping her lip and giving him a wide-eyed appraisal. 'Love it. You've evolved already.'

'I just needed the motivation. And you provided it.'

'I think we make a pretty good team.'

He nodded as he turned in the driveway towards the small parking area outside the old stone wall. 'We're a great team, all things considered.' He stopped the car. 'And you deserve a medal for putting up with me and believing.'

'I believe because I like you.'

He blinked and caught her eye.

'I mean, nothing weird. I just think you're a good person and you deserve a chance.' She opened her door and got out rather quickly. Gavin took a minute to compose himself. *She likes me?* Nothing weird though; nothing that crossed boundaries then. Sensible. But he liked her too. A lot. An awful lot more than he should.

As they walked through the entrance gates, the potent scent of malt and barley hit him squarely on the nose. The familiar smell was one he associated with the Glenbriar Distillery, but here it seemed more raw. Perhaps it was ingrained in the fabric of the old stone buildings and intrinsically linked to the surrounding landscape. This distillery had a skeleton staff, no receptionist or guide anymore. Those jobs had already gone. Tours had to be booked in advance and a guide would travel from Glenbriar to carry them out.

Felicity beamed as she stepped up to the front door. 'I used to love coming here, but, oh my god, I think you might have trouble with Angus.'

'Why?'

'You'll see. I don't want to scare you. He's a sweetheart really, but he doesn't mince his words.'

'Great.' Gavin sighed. 'Let's go meet him.'

Angus had a grizzled air about him. On shaking his hand, Gavin had a fleeting memory of meeting him when he'd been about twelve. Considering that was a quarter of a century ago, it was surprising that Angus looked much as he remembered. Kind of ageless but maybe not in the kindest of ways.

'So, you've graced us with your presence at last.' Angus peered at him from under bushy brows.

'Indeed.'

'You look awfy like your dad.'

Gavin hoped that was a compliment.

'And young Flissy. You're back.'

'I am. How are you, Angus? It's been a long time.' She stepped up and put her arms around him.

Was there anyone she didn't hug? *Apart from me.* Which was ok, of course. Kind of.

'I'm not too bad. Well, at the moment. We'll see how I feel after this visit.'

She took a step back. 'This isn't going to hurt.'

'Really?' Angus frowned at Gavin, then threw open a side door. 'This is the warehouse. We still have some good stock.'

Gavin ducked inside, scanning over rows upon rows of oak casks, each one filled with the precious liquid that would become Torrindhu whisky.

'So, Mr Sinclair, I've heard some rumours going about. Why don't you just give it to me straight instead of putting on the niceties?'

'It's like Felicity said. This isn't going to be a painful visit. Far from it. The distillery isn't closing. My job is to keep it going and get the best out of it. Now, that might mean change but change for the better. If there are any issues that you have, problems that need solved, bugs that need fixing,' – he aimed a brief smile at Felicity – 'then this is the time to tell me. Or if you'd rather make a list and email me, that's fine. I'm here to find out how we can get this place running to full capacity again.'

Felicity gave him a supportive nod and patted Angus on the back. 'You work so hard here and I know it isn't easy when you're on your own most of the time.'

'I didn't use to be. We had eight workers at one point.'

'Then maybe we need to aim for that again.' Gavin ran his hand over his watch.

'But how can you afford that? I heard that the company was cutting back on smaller, less profitable distilleries.'

'But Torrindhu is unique.' Felicity stroked one of the oak casks. 'Its remote location is a selling point. The whisky produced here is high quality and very popular among locals, tourists, and whisky connoisseurs. We're working on ways to make it more profitable. Maybe we could increase tourism by offering tours and tastings more frequently.'

'Felicity is very good at thinking outside of the box.' Gavin gave her a little smile.

'Aye, she is that.' Angus put his hands in his pockets. 'She reminds me of your mother. The driving force behind the great man.'

Gavin knew what he meant but ideas flickered in his mind like someone was flipping the pages of a book. Visions whizzed before him, starting with him and Felicity as a married couple, stepping out at company functions and promoting the business worldwide. They were the public face of the company, as his parents had been. People invited them to charity openings and they attended community events. Their family home featured in Highland Home magazine and they posed with their beautiful children. His eyes suddenly clocked Felicity's. Her expression mirrored his, slightly perplexed, though not angry or upset, like she'd been looking at the same pages and liked what she saw.

'Yes.' Gavin blinked and refocused on Angus. 'Felicity and my mother are both very determined women. We're aware of the challenges facing the distillery, but we're also aware of the potential it holds. You can rest assured we'll do everything in our power to ensure the distillery's future.'

Angus let out a sigh and ruffled his straggly grey hair. 'I hope so. I believe in your sincerity anyway. You seem to have got a reputation that doesn't actually fit you.'

Gavin and Felicity exchanged a glance, both knowing that reputation had fitted him perfectly until the start of the week. Her pep talk had catapulted competent-boss-Gavin into the world.

They finished the tour with Angus, then sat in the quirky little area styled like an old-fashioned inn. This was a place they needed to capitalise on. Foreign tourists would go nuts for this kind of thing.

'I love the name.' Gavin read the sign above the small bar: *The Illicit Still.*

'Used to be quite the trysting point back in the day, from what I've heard,' Angus said. 'But that was when people lived and worked in the community. It's not the same now. Rich business folk buy up the houses and commute or use them for holidays.'

Gavin winced. That was exactly what his parents had done.

'And there's no public transport or anything out here,' Angus continued. 'We're too out of the way for people to bother with.'

'If getting here is an issue, maybe we should consider investing in a company mini-bus. We could transport tour groups here from Glenbriar, Aberfeldy, Pitlochry, Crieff or wherever they were heading from.' Gavin looked between Felicity and Angus, who both nodded.

'People always love doing the whisky tasting here and getting photographs,' Felicity said. 'Because it looks so olde-worlde.'

Gavin cast her an approving smile. So much to look into. His father had hammered these places into good shape only for external forces to set them right back. Economical uncertainties wouldn't go away but they could factor them into the solutions and be flexible.

As they were about to leave, Gavin stole another glance at Felicity. He couldn't keep his eyes off her. She said goodbye to Angus and gave him another hug.

'Take care of yourself, lass.' Angus ruffled her hair. 'And thank you, Mr Sinclair.'

'Honestly, Gavin is fine.' As he'd already told Angus several times. He didn't expect any change, but being called Mr Sinclair by someone of Angus's age and experience was strange.

They said their goodbyes and Felicity turned to Gavin, giving him a warm smile. As their eyes met, a jolt of electricity hurtled through him. The attraction to her was ridiculously intense. How long could he resist? *You must! Don't let it interfere with your professional relationship.*

He forced himself to look away and focus on the tasks ahead. They had a distillery chain to save and that was all he should be interested in.

CHAPTER FIFTEEN

Felicity

Felicity lay in bed, staring at the ceiling. The trip was going great. She'd won over Gavin and couldn't ask for better results. So why was she lying here feeling like she'd got nowhere and done nothing?

Inside her chest, a gnawing ache was growing, getting more and more painful every minute. Nothing would take it away. Well, nothing except the forbidden Gavin fruit. She wanted to cry and scream all at once. Her frustration was at boiling point, but she didn't move. Was this her life now? Resigned to dream about the sexy CEO like every bloody cliched PA should. How ridiculous had she got? But it didn't stop her from liking him. Maybe even more than like. He wasn't the grumpy sod he'd been when they met. He was calm, steady and... Oh god. She sat up. Thinking like this wasn't helping.

With the birds going crazy outside her window, she wasn't likely to get back to sleep but there were hours before she had to meet with Gavin. Maybe she should go for a run. Without giving it too much thought, she dressed in her black sport leggings and matching crop top, pulled her hair into a tight ponytail and headed off. The track was firm underfoot as she jogged along the side of the loch. In the bright blue sky, the sun was already high and bright, though it hadn't fully warmed up yet.

Her therapist had told her she would probably never be wholly satisfied with her figure. It wasn't just part of her condition but human nature. Although she was tall and slim, when she ran she thought her breasts felt too big, even though she knew for a fact they weren't. They were a perfectly normal size, possibly even on the small side for most, but no matter what sports bra she wore, they always seemed to jiggle. This crop top was supposed to keep her steady, but she wasn't convinced.

A splashing sound in the loch distracted her. Maybe it was a beaver. Since they'd been reintroduced, she'd never seen one, but knew people who had. One of her friends had apparently spotted one randomly crossing the road in Glenbriar. She slowed and moved to the edge of the path where there was a deer track down to the loch side. Then she saw it and her eyes flew wide. Not a beaver. Just a very, very, very hot Gavin. Holy guacamole. Her heart ignited and her mind raced onto fast forward.

He rose from the loch like Neptune, all golden skin covered in beads of water like little gems. His physique was incredible, broad-shouldered and muscular. With a shake of his head, he waded deeper, then pushed into an elegant breaststroke. A vision of his hands stroking her breasts made her tingle. *Hell*. This was getting worse.

He swam with grace and power, almost animal-like. His muscles rippled under his skin as he cut through the water. Felicity drank him all in. He was a wild swimmer, after all. Which only left the proposal from the riddle. She still couldn't quite get her head around the idea of that. Should she confess that she knew and ask him about it? Somehow it felt like crossing a line. Knowing he gave her those gloves opened the door to the possibility that he'd liked her more than he should have for some time now… And she felt exactly the same.

He was completely at ease, unaware of her watching him. Now would be a good time to creep back up the track. The birds in the tree above were making such a racket, nothing much could be heard over them, and she could run for it. The coo of a wood pigeon joined the twittering. She watched for a few more minutes, but really, she should move. Something warm and wet splattered on her face.

'What the…' She put her fingers to it. 'Ew!' She let out a small scream and jumped. But it was too late. The pigeon had aimed a bottom explosion from above and slimy green poo dripped down her face and over her crop top. Gross. So gross.

'Felicity, is that you?'

Noooooo! Could this get any worse? She'd yelped loud enough for Gavin to hear and there he was at the edge of the loch, peering into the trees.

Should she bolt before he recognised her? But she wanted to wash off the mess. Keeping her head down she moved out of the cover of the trees.

'Yes, it's me. I just stopped to see what was in the loch. I thought you were a beaver. Then this bloody bird.' She held out her hands. 'It's covered me. Yuck.'

A small smile quirked at the edge of his lips. 'Oops.'

'It's not funny.'

'I'm not laughing.' Except clearly, he was.

'I need to get this off me.'

'Use the loch water.'

'But it's on my top.' And even though the thought of taking it off in front of him had some appeal, she wasn't going to.

'Well, bend down, or something.' The smile was growing on his face.

'I can't believe you think this is funny.'

He put his hands to his lips, doing a terrible job of hiding his laugh. 'But you know it's meant to be good luck—'

'Do not even go there.' She marched to the side of the loch and tried to scoop up water and wash the mess from her hair. 'This is so gross.'

'Do you want some help?'

Again, the vision of his hands grazing her chest slipped into her mind. 'How can you help me?'

'Sorry.' He put up his hands and stepped back.

She frowned at him as he hovered uncertainly, then started sniggering. He smirked too, though it looked like he was battling to stop himself. Then they both burst like a pair of clowns. Only one of them was a very hot, topless clown with strong muscles and the other was a bird-poo-covered one. 'Can you actually believe this?' She looked at her top in despair.

'Just wear it back. It's not that far.'

'No, I can't. I need this mess off. Is it off my face?' She caught his eye and his smile slipped a little as he made a very obvious check.

'Not really. There's some there...' He pointed without touching her. 'And some in your hair.'

'Oh god.'

'Let me do it. I can see where it is.'

She held her breath. 'Ok,' she whispered.

He crouched by the water's edge. 'Come down. It'll be easier.'

She moved in beside him, tingles shooting all over her body as he shuffled to face her. He wet his hands and brought a scoop of water up in his palm.

'Close your eyes. I don't want it to go into them.'

She did. His left hand cupped her cheek, soft and warm, supporting her as he anointed her forehead gently. The water lapped as he captured some more. She kept her eyes shut, enhancing the tenderness of the moment. Softly, his hands trickled cool water over her and he gently brushed at her skin with the pad of his thumb before doing the same around her hairline. She gave in wholly to the moment, forgetting where she was and what he was actually doing. It was like a sensory massage. What she needed now was for his lips to touch hers. A little sigh escaped her. She was so relaxed her head would slump were it not for his hold.

'There you go. Good as new.' His voice was soft but enough to pull her back into the present.

She opened her eyes. He lifted his hand but she caught it and held it in place.

'Are you ok?' His lips barely moved as he spoke.

Very slowly, she shook her head, still holding his palm to her cheek. 'I feel like I want to...' She swallowed and dropped her gaze to his lips.

'Oh jeez.' He dropped his hand from her cheek, turned towards the water and submerged his hands rubbing them together.

Shit. Had she blown it? What was she thinking… or not thinking? She drew in a breath, her eyes leaping to her stained top, and worse. The bloody thing that was supposed to restrain her was too thin to hide her treacherous nipples. They'd jumped to attention at Gavin's touch. Hell, hell, hell. He'd probably noticed. With her eyes being shut, she couldn't see where he'd been looking, though the ugly poo blot might have put him off. And now he had his back resolutely to her. She'd mucked up big time.

'I'm sorry. I didn't mean anything.' The words tumbled out before she could stop them. 'I should get this mess off my top.'

He kept his eyes trained on his hands. 'You should probably do that yourself.'

'Of course. I didn't mean. I wasn't suggesting…' Though her desperate body and her runaway mouth had already told him the truth.

'It's ok. I understand. I'll go, then if you want to take it off…'

'Gavin, please. I'm sorry. I shouldn't have… I just…'

He glanced at her, his eyes wary. 'I told you I understand. But this is dangerous.'

'I know.' She swallowed. 'Listen, can we talk?'

'What about?' He shook the water off his hands.

'Two seconds.' She dipped her hands in the water, leaned forward and wiped off as much of the mess as she could. It left her in a very wet, very clingy top. The fabric gathered at her nipples, which were desperately trying to escape through it, betraying all the lust pumping around inside her. 'You wild swim,' she said, still crouching by the loch.

He let out a sigh and stared forward. 'Yup.'

She shifted onto her bottom – crouching this long was painful – and folded her arms, trying to cover her wet top.

He sat too, pushing his legs out in front of him, then raising one knee and draping his wrist over it. 'Is that what you want to talk about?'

'Partly. Do you also like carrot juice?'

'Maybe, I do.'

'I think you do. Which leaves me with two questions.'

He rolled his head around to face her, his jaw set like he was bracing himself. 'And what are they?'

'What happened to the love of your life and how did you know I wanted gloves like that?'

He didn't have to answer, of course, but an unspoken understanding had opened up. The dynamic had shifted. She'd almost stupidly asked for a kiss but he hadn't run away. Not yet.

'The love of my life was Holly.'

'And she proposed to you?'

'She did. When I was twenty-six.'

'Why did you turn her down?'

'Because I didn't realise what I had until it was too late. I thought I was too young and it was too soon. But life goes faster than you think. That day feels like yesterday but it was ten years ago. Even after we split, I thought I'd meet someone else, and I tried, but it never happened.' He gave a little shrug. 'And that's my sad story.'

She cocked her head and gave him a commiserating look. 'And the gloves?'

'I overheard you talking about them.'

'But how could you have?'

'I was listening from the other side of the room.'

'Why?'

'I always listen to you. Even when I try not to, I hear your voice.'

She stared at him and he held eye contact.

'I'm sorry.' He shook his head and looked away.

'Why?'

'Because I'm being highly inappropriate. I should be on that path walking as quickly as I can. Or you should be. Why are we sitting here, inviting danger?'

'Because we like each other?' She picked up a little stone and chucked it in the water. 'I think.'

He faced her again. 'Even if we do, it's irrelevant.'

'Is it? You just said life goes faster than you think. What if we waste a chance?' Her mouth was running faster than her brain again. But what did she expect from him?

'A chance of what?'

Trust him to bring the sensible questions to the party. 'Anything.' She could hardly look at him. 'I just know I like you.'

'I like you too,' he said, sounding almost desperate. 'But what can we really have? It's not like we can date or anything, is it? I'm your boss.'

'I know, and it hurts. Not you being my boss. Just knowing that nothing can ever happen.'

'Plenty can happen, Felicity. But my god it would mean playing with fire.'

'Are you suggesting... A fling?'

His brow furrowed and he shook his head. 'I'm not sure what I'm suggesting.'

'Maybe we need to get it out of our system while we're here. You know, what happens in Glenbriar stays in Glenbriar.'

'That's madness.'

'Yeah. I'm sorry. I should know better than to open my big mouth.' She shuffled, ready to get to her feet, but his hand landed on hers, holding it to the ground.

'My discipline has been out the window this week. I gave into that breakfast yesterday and now... Well, I want you a lot more than some fried eggs and bacon.'

She stared at him, hardly believing her ears. Her brain cells broke into clashing warfare with her hormones, battling to be sensible, but desperate for a physical release. Anything that would quench the burning desire. 'You want me?'

'Of course I do. You're... you're all I bloody think about, all the time.'

'I do too. I can't stop thinking about you.' She locked eyes with him and their lips drew close. A buzz of energy surged through the tiny gap between them. Then he leaned closer.

'You really want to do this?' he asked.

'More than anything. Do you?'

He pressed his lips to hers. A bolt hit her in the tummy, surging once, then twice, then a third time as she relaxed into the full divine pleasure. His hand raised to her cheek, gliding over it. His powerful arms supported her and he tilted his head slightly, deepening the kiss so gently. She groaned. This was an indulgent experience to explore and enjoy, like it was happening in slow motion but that didn't dampen the passion. It increased it. He was taking time getting to know her lips, then gradually her tongue. She moaned and more bolts fired through her stomach. Such bliss.

His free hand slid around the bare skin between her top and her leggings. 'Can I touch you?' he breathed in between dotted kisses on her cheek and neck.

'Please.' She was pretty sure no one had ever explicitly asked her before.

Like a feather brushing over her, he skimmed her top, finding her eager nipples, and applying gentle pressure as they carried on kissing. The warmth of his palms relieved the tension in her breasts, sending her spinning in a heavenly moment of fantasy to a world she no longer recognised. And she liked it. Really, really liked it.

The birds were still singing and even that dratted pigeon was cooing nearby. The sun was shining and she was making out with Gavin on the shore of a loch where anyone could see them. It was risky but the thought drifted off as she melted into his arms. Nothing else mattered. She felt safer and more alive than ever. She wanted to curl into him and let him take her away to a land of paradise.

'Felicity,' he whispered softly in her ear, while his cheek still gently grazed against hers. The hand that had been sending her into another dimension moved, resting on her waist. 'This is all… very nice. Beyond nice. Beyond anything really.'

She closed her eyes and let his words fall softly. He slipped his hand up her body and stroked her cheek, still supporting her fully. She felt weightless.

'But we have to stop. I know it's early, and this is a remote spot, but we're out in public and it's bad enough that the CEO is having his wicked way with his PA, never mind getting caught.'

Her eyes slowly opened and met directly with his. Everything she'd fantasised about seeing in them was there now. His pupils were wide, his expression kind.

'I don't want to stop.' Her voice sounded like a plaintive whine.

He stroked her cheek one way, then ran his fingertips back over the other. 'I don't want to either but it's not really a choice.'

'What happens now?'

'We go back to the hotel and we work.'

'Ok.' She forced herself to breathe. So this was just a quick fumble – though not one she'd easily forget.

He swallowed and looked around. 'I'm not giving you the brush off, though it would probably be sensible if I did. If you want to pick this up again later in a more private place, then we can.'

'Are you serious?'

'Only if you want to.' He pulled back a little.

'Yes. I do. I really do. I wasn't lying when I said I think about you all the time.'

He pressed a lingering kiss on her cheek, then pulled back and drew in a deep breath. 'But this is all on the understanding that what happens in Glenbriar stays in Glenbriar, yes?'

'Totally.'

'Ok. Then we should get back and do some work. Can you do that?'

'I can do anything.' She smiled at him.

'I believe it. That's why I like you.' He released her and she pulled her knees to her chest, huddling into them as he pulled on a t-shirt. 'Doesn't matter if anyone sees me dressed for swimming now. My secret's out.'

She looked up at him and nodded. 'Yup. You're busted.'

He put out his hand. She took it and he pulled her to her feet like she was as light as a rag doll. With a little squeeze of her fingers, he smiled. 'I know this isn't the sweetest outcome, but let's get through the work and then we can play.' He ran his hands down her cheek. 'Is that ok? You look sad.'

She smiled and ran her finger down his arm. 'I am a bit, but you're right, I just have to be patient.'

'Good things come to those who wait.' He held eye contact with her and she read beautiful promises in his shining irises. 'I'm going to run on ahead. I don't think we should go in together when I'm dressed like this.' He looked at his wet swim shorts. Her eyes followed and she smirked.

'Indeed. Well, I'll see you in the office at nine.'

'Or breakfast at eight. It's up to you.' He glanced around and blinked, then leaned in and kissed her cheek again. 'See you there.'

She watched him jog off, then took in several lungfuls of air. It was hard mastering her disappointment but what might happen later? *Good things come to those who wait.* Promises, promises. She ran her fingers along her lips. If the kisses of the last twenty minutes were anything to go by, she was in for a treat. She just had to keep a sensible head and get through the day. But right now, she needed to run, burn off the tension in her body and clear her head, because her mind had been blown out of the water and there was no scrambling it back into place.

Chapter Sixteen

Gavin adjusted his cuffs and peered out of the window of the meeting room in the Loch View Hotel. Felicity hadn't joined him for breakfast and that bothered him almost as much as what they'd done together by the loch. She'd confessed to having an eating disorder yesterday and now she'd skipped breakfast after their kiss. What if she got sick again, and he was the cause? He didn't want to hurt her.

He ruffled up his hair. Nothing could make this situation right. 'Aw, Christ.' What a mess this was, but the underlying issues were even bigger than the surface problem. If this really was just a fling with a pretty girl in a hotel for a week, then so be it. Once, he'd taken a woman he'd met while online dating to an IT conference and they'd spent the week having meaningless sex while saving him the ignominy of turning up alone. But nothing he did with Felicity was meaningless and he knew it. Because he liked her. Really liked her. Respected her. Valued her. Possibly even more. But how could he square that with what he wanted to be to her and still work with her?

The door opened and she sidled in, smiling and looking as well turned out as ever. Not a hair out of place to suggest anything unusual might have happened that morning.

'Hey. I—' His head bobbed like a nodding dog. Everything he wanted to say got jumbled before he opened his mouth, so he didn't speak.

'So...' She sat opposite where he'd set up his laptop. 'Business.'

'Yes. Business. I missed you at breakfast.' Was that a totally arsy thing to say? He didn't even want to think of all the ways it could be construed when he was really just hoping she wasn't off her food.

'Sorry, I couldn't face it.'

He tilted his head, aware his expression probably looked horribly patronising. 'It's not my place to interfere, but just for the record, I don't want to put you off food.' He facepalmed. 'That came out wrong. Hopefully, I'm not disgusting enough to put you off food.'

'You're not disgusting at all and I'm not going off food forever. I'm just, I don't know, unsettled.'

'Felicity.' He let out a sigh. 'That's exactly what I mean. I don't want you to feel like that.'

'It isn't all bad. Some of it's... excitement. I'm just a bit hyper. It's kind of bad but good, you know.'

'That's why we have the phrase naughty but nice.'

She grinned. 'It's exactly that.'

'Well, just so you know. I don't make a habit of kissing my PAs. I only did it because I really do like you.' The words were out before he'd thought them through. Was that a terrible thing to say when they'd agreed to a fling and nothing more? But it felt like the honourable thing to say at least.

'Good. Because I like you too and I can definitely say I've never kissed my boss before.'

'Excellent. So… Shall we crack on?' He quirked an eyebrow as he woke his laptop.

The strangeness of the moment evaporated once they started working through an action plan for Torrindhu. This boded well. They could pull out the professional guns when they needed to.

He flipped onto another spreadsheet. 'And we still have Inverbuie tomorrow.'

'It's completely different again.' Felicity pulled up a picture on her iPad. 'It's almost as big as Glenbriar but it's more modern and, you know, not in a good way.'

'No. That building is hideous.' He screwed his nose up at the picture. 'It looks like the worst of sixties architecture.'

'That's the first thing visitors see, so it sets the tone. The whisky is a good seller but it's missing something unique.'

'Then why don't we shake things right up? Let's produce gin or vodka or both. We have the infrastructure and this is an area full of farms that can supply potatoes and wheat as well as barley and whey products. We'd be supporting other local businesses as well as diversifying.'

Her eyes widened, a smile growing on her beautiful face. 'Oh my god, Gavin. That's an absolutely genius idea. I love it so much.'

He swallowed as the words left her mouth. Her eyes hadn't left his and it almost felt like she'd just said she loved *him*. He wanted to knock the table out of the way, pull her into his arms and tell her he loved her too. But that was madness. He just loved working with her, that was all. And kissing her... But that was separate, right?

'Teamwork makes the dream work.' He held up his hand across the table and she high-fived him. 'Now, we just have to break it to everyone else.'

'Let's get a plan first.' She tapped away at her iPad. 'And I might contact some local farms and get ballpark figures, so we have numbers to throw at Julian. He likes numbers.'

'That he does.'

She left to make the calls and Gavin carried on with the virtual system he was designing. Then he fired off some emails to Julian and the other department heads, explaining how the tour was going and letting them know changes were coming – good ones. Though Julian likely wouldn't see it like that.

The weather was so beautiful outside it seemed wasteful being stuck indoors, so he packed up his laptop and took a seat at one of the picnic tables outside. He'd been typing for a few minutes when Zach strolled by with Becker and another dog.

'Hey. Do you need a drink out here?' Zach asked.

'Actually, I wouldn't mind a sparkling water.'

'Sure. I'll fix that for you.'

As Zach opened the door, Gavin became aware of voices and laughing inside. Was that Felicity? She was probably with Briony. Hopefully they weren't talking about what happened this morning. But friends told friends stuff like that, didn't they? Well, women did. His friends liked to talk about sport, sometimes work and these days their families, but personal stuff, no thanks, and that suited him fine. He couldn't imagine offloading his thoughts to anyone. They were so conflicting and some of them were completely cringy. The only person he wanted to talk to was Felicity and that wasn't a good idea, not when most of the thoughts were about her.

Here sat Gavin Sinclair, chief exec of Sinclair Brothers' Whisky Co, outwardly respectable, but inwardly planning on taking his PA to bed that very night. What would anyone make of that?

'Oh, Jesus Christ.' He threw back his head. How bad did that sound?

'Your water.'

He jumped at the voice. 'Oh, thanks.'

Zach placed it on the table. 'Can I get you anything else?'

'Er, no, thank you.'

'No problem.' He turned to go inside.

'Is Felicity in there?'

'Yeah, she's talking to Briony.'

'If she's not too busy, could you ask her to come out here, please?'

'Sure.'

He sipped his water, staring at his screen until the door opened behind him and Felicity appeared.

'What's up? Zach said you were asking for me.'

'Did you tell Briony about us?'

Felicity shook her head. 'Of course I didn't. Why?'

'I'm just edgy about it.'

'Me too.'

'Let's take a break. In fact, let's go somewhere for lunch and have a change of scenery.'

'Where?'

'No idea. But I've got an awesome PA who's amazing at finding the best places.'

She shook her head and smiled. 'You are really naughty.'

'You ain't seen nothing yet.' He gave her an OTT wink.

She giggled and the sound tickled him, setting him off too.

'Let me look up some places.' She pulled out her phone.

'I'm officially giving us the afternoon off. We can't do too much in case tomorrow's visit changes things, so let's call it a day and get some lunch.'

Gavin left the car in the car park in the centre of Glenbriar and he and Felicity walked through the pretty streets. He gazed around, reading the names of the businesses and grinning like a big kid, which was what he'd been the last time he was here.

'It still looks the same as I remember. More modern though.' The shops and cafes were mostly on the ground floor of old Victorian buildings, making the main street a postcard-perfect Scottish tourist town.

Felicity beamed. 'Ooh, I love this shop.' She pointed in the window of a place called Wood 'n' Chic. Fancy upcycled furniture was displayed in the large windows. 'And I know the owner. She's lovely.' She peered in through the window. 'That's not her though. She seems to have someone else working in the shop.'

'There is some nice stuff in there.'

'Oh, my god, look at that.' Felicity pointed to a delicately wrought tea light holder in the shape of two swans, their necks forming a love heart. 'I love swans, because of my name I guess, but that is so beautiful. I wonder if Stella made it. It's so detailed and pretty. I bet it's expensive.'

'I suppose you pay for quality. Speaking of which, my mum needs that sideboard.' Gavin nodded at a gorgeous navy and teal piece with gold handles. 'The one she has is so dated, but she probably wouldn't like it. She's not into bright colours.'

'Your mum is a scary lady. And she does not like me.'

'Yeah. I think she's threatened by you. In fact, I think she feels that way about most women.' The back of his hand brushed hers. She glanced down at the contact point and looped her pointer finger around his.

He tightened the hold for a second, then let go. 'We should be careful, if anyone sees us...'

The streets were bustling with people even though the tourist season was in its early days. His fingers kept brushing hers as they walked. Maybe his subconscious was engineering any reason to make physical contact with her, or perhaps it was just a natural attraction. They didn't draw any attention from passers-by. His mind filled with images again of a future where they were partners, real ones, not just a CEO and a PA using a business trip for a quick fling. His life had turned into a cliché and he wasn't doing anything to shake it up.

They passed several coffee shops and cafes but Felicity pointed down a road that curved off to the side towards the River Briar.

'I remember this now,' Gavin said. 'There's a footbridge, isn't there? It shakes when you walk over it.'

'The wobbly bridge, or so called. That's the one.'

'I once jumped on it and Mum freaked. She just stood in the middle screaming until my dad came and rescued her.'

'Seriously? I never thought of you as a naughty kid.'

'I wasn't. I didn't mean to scare her; I just thought it would be fun to make it move.'

'Well, behave this time.'

They approached the bridge and stepped onto it. It sprung as they moved towards the middle. He looked down at the restaurant on the riverbank. 'Is that where we're going?'

'Do you like the look of it?'

'Stunning.' His eyes strayed back to her. 'Just beautiful.'

They gazed at each other for a long moment before he refocused on the old stone building. It had an outdoor seating area on a deck with a perfect view of the river.

'It's called The Cross Keys,' she said. 'It's been here since the 18th century. There used to be a small ferry that people would take to cross the river before the bridge was built.'

'You know everything about everything, don't you?'

'I learned it all when I was doing the distillery tours. People asked so many odd questions I had to have an answer.'

He took hold of her hand, pulling her to a stop and placed himself in front of her. 'I think you're amazing on so many levels.' He glanced around. Seeing no one, he cupped her cheek. 'Can I—'

She nodded and he leaned in and kissed her. Maybe it was his imagination but the bridge seemed to rock them gently as he tasted her lips again.

'You are just gorgeous.' He drew back, admiring the red maxi dress she had on. 'You always look perfect, but I don't normally get the chance to tell you.'

She smiled and ran her finger down his shirt. 'You look pretty handsome yourself.'

They crossed to the other side, making their way down a gentle incline to the restaurant. The sun reflected off the water as it flowed past, dancing over stones and boulders.

A waitress led them to their table on the deck with a perfect view of the River Briar. The small footbridge they'd just crossed and the lush greenery of the riverbank provided the backdrop.

'Did you only invite me to lunch so you could monitor my eating habits?' Felicity gave him a sly look.

'No. I just want to spend time with you. If you need anything from me, support, whatever, I'm happy to do it, but I don't want to interfere. You confided in me and I appreciate it. I get that you don't talk a lot about it. But I'd also like to think you told me because you know I care enough to want to make sure you're ok.'

She smiled but it looked almost like she was holding back tears. She nodded. 'Thank you.' Her hand moved to her mouth and she covered it.

'Hey. It's ok.' He shifted his seat, so he was closer to her and put his arm around her shoulder. 'You were right to tell me, but if I get annoying, just tell me to butt out.'

She giggled and lifted her menu. 'No, I'm glad you brought me here. I probably would have skipped food all day otherwise, even though I know it's not sensible. It's the way my mind works... or doesn't. I can usually manage it ok, but sometimes when I'm stressed or... Well... I'm not exactly stressed about this; it's just different.'

'Listen, your mind definitely works. There's no doubt about that. Now come on, let's feed you up.' With a quick side glance, he checked the coast was clear, then gave her a peck on the side of her forehead.

She smiled shyly and lifted her menu. 'Yes, let's do that.'

'We need to keep your energy levels up. I wouldn't want you falling asleep in the middle of an important meeting.'

'What meeting? I thought you decreed an afternoon off.'

He leaned in. 'It's a very close and intimate meeting and you and I are the only people invited.'

Chapter Seventeen

Felicity

Gavin smiled, lifted Felicity's hand and raised it to his lips. Something of a Jane Austen hero flickered in his eyes as he gently kissed the back of it. Her pulse sped up. What a romantic he was turning out to be. Just a pity he was also her boss. A boss she happened to like far too much.

Perhaps the conflict showed on her face because he frowned and lowered her hand. 'Sorry, I probably shouldn't have done that.'

She glanced around but the outdoor eating area was quiet. 'It's ok.'

'Is it?' He rubbed his hand over his jaw. 'Is any of this really ok?'

She took hold of his arm and leaned in closer. 'There's no getting away from who we are to each other. I love working with you but I can't deny how I feel about you either. Maybe it's unrealistic, but I want the best of both worlds.' However impractical that would be, especially if the relationship developed, which no doubt it would, one way or another, for bad or good. They'd already crossed a line and they couldn't retract their actions from the morning.

'I wish I knew how to make that work. But all the bright ideas have come from you this week.'

'Not all of them,' she said. 'Your diversification ideas are genius.'

Gavin stared out over the water. 'I have no idea how to make things work for you and me but something came into my head earlier about the business. Can I tell you? Or would you rather we didn't talk shop?'

'Tell me anything.'

'From all the suggestions you've made this week, I think the way forward is to have a dedicated project manager based in Glenbriar. Someone who can oversee all the new developments and ensure the three distilleries work in harmony.'

'That sounds like a great idea.'

'It would need to be a particular kind of person to take it on. Someone with ideas and enthusiasm as well as drive and experience.'

She grinned. 'Julian definitely has the last two qualities.'

He cocked his head. 'No way would he want to move up here and I wouldn't trust him with it either. We need fresh blood.'

'Or you could do it yourself.'

'No, I think I'd rather employ someone with a better matched skill set.'

'I'm sure lots of people would apply. If I was more qualified, I would. It sounds amazing.' She took a sip of her drink. A job like that was too far out of her reach to even enter her imagination.

Gavin sat back and rubbed his fingertips together. 'Actually, I think you should apply. I think subconsciously I had you in mind all along. It's got to be someone as dedicated as you. And on-paper qualifications aren't everything. You're in-tune with the distilleries and the workforce.'

Her chest was zinging and her head whizzing. Ideas flew around, both exciting and terrifying. How could she do anything like that? She was only twenty-five. But at the same time she saw clear paths she could lead the company down.

'But I have no experience in that kind of job.'

'Everyone has to start somewhere. I'll need to think more about it anyway and discuss it with Julian.'

Felicity forced down her lunch. She'd already skipped break-fast and although Gavin had said she could tell him to butt out if she felt he was interfering, she appreciated his support. It was harder to skip meals when someone was looking out for her. But her stomach was churning in a wheel of uncertainty. That job sounded ideal but how could she go for it when she wanted to go for him? Maybe she shouldn't do either.

What if they actually slept together? And she couldn't deny she wanted to. If she went for the position after that, what then? If the truth came out, everyone would think she'd slept her way to the top. Was that what she was doing?

'I don't know what to do.' The words tumbled out as they got into the car to return to the hotel. She'd barely spoken a word on the way back through the town. Gavin hadn't said much either.

'About what?'

'Anything.' She got into the passenger seat and covered her eyes.

'Talk to me,' he said.

'Don't you see what's going to happen?'

'What?'

'If we sleep together.' She tried to hold her emotions together but it was difficult. 'Then I can't go for that job.'

'I know, Felicity. Today was nice, but maybe we should leave it at that.'

She frowned and blinked, trying to work out what his expression meant but it was so flat and unreadable. Nice? Was that what he'd thought about their day? After all the intense passion of the morning? All he had to say for it was nice.

'I'm so confused.' She let out a long sigh and leaned back into the headrest.

'I am too. And I'm sorry if I've muddied the waters even more by mentioning that job. I've never...'

She caught his eye. 'Never what?'

'Never felt like this. I've had a relationship with a colleague before. I worked with Holly but we were a couple before we worked together. I don't know the rules here. I just know the politics seem all wrong, but the feelings seem all right.'

'Exactly. But how can we separate them?'

'I'm not sure we can.'

'Are you saying we should forget about us and go back to how we were before?'

He let out a long sigh. 'We both know that's the sensible course of action.'

'And we both know that's not what either of us really wants.' She stared at him, daring him to contradict her.

He rubbed his chin and turned away. 'Right again. I want you more than anything right now, but it's that feeling which is messing with my head.'

'Mine too.'

'But if we're going to do something about it, we'll have to be super discreet.'

'I wasn't exactly going to go shouting about it.'

'I know that. But we're staying in a hotel. It's a public place. Your friend works there. And while I'm sure she's trustworthy, it's not a given that she won't let something slip.'

Briony wouldn't snoop on purpose but she was observant and would probably notice if they decided to visit each other's rooms. 'I don't think she'll say anything to anyone.' But she wasn't so sure Briony wouldn't try to talk her out of it. Probably with good reason, though she wouldn't ever stop her seeing someone. Not if it was what Felicity really wanted and this yearning for Gavin wouldn't just evaporate. Every time her brain threw up an objection, her heart interjected.

He tapped the wheel. 'I know somewhere we could go where no one would see us, or know we'd been there.'

'Where?'

'My parents' house.'

'Oh. I'd forgotten about that. And can you get in?'

'Yes.'

'And they don't have security cameras?'

Gavin smirked. 'Not yet. They had new ones installed at their Gullane house but Mum doesn't like the fact she gets a message every time a delivery driver leaves a parcel. They're not up here enough to make it worth their while.'

'Can we go now?'

'If you're sure. I'm not going to push you into anything.'

'I'm sure, even though I know it's mad, but I don't think I can stand this much longer.'

'I can't either. But remember, what happens in Glenbriar…'

'Stays in Glenbriar. Like I could forget.'

He fired up the engine.

'Where is the house?' she asked.

'Not far. Up past the distillery and out of town at the top end, near the Lower Briar Woods.'

'Oh, I know those woods. It's where the light show was held.'

He drove up the main street and turned towards the distillery, following the hill road up and out of town. The woodland got thicker as they went on, then Gavin pulled on the indicator and turned into an entrance on the opposite side of the road from the forest. A heavy, black wrought-iron gate barred the way, suspended between two sandstone pillars. He opened the window, leaned over and keyed a number into a box. 'Let's hope they haven't changed this.'

For a few seconds, Felicity held her breath, sure they must have, as the gates stayed solemnly shut. Then, with a soft whir, they slowly spread before them. A short, tree-lined driveway led to a wide open driveway and a sprawling villa. Somehow she'd imagined an old house but this was modern, almost Mediterranean in its design. All whitewashed, with an elegant archway and a covered patio area at the door. On one side of the house was a turret, perhaps a nod to more traditional architecture.

Set amidst its own private woodland, the property shone proudly in the countryside. Hills and fields surrounded it, rolling into the distance.

'Wow, this place is very grand.'

'Isn't it?' Gavin gave her a little smile. 'My parents had it built about thirty years ago. We used to come for holidays. It has a pool house.' He pointed at a long low building next to the woodland area that was attached to the main house by a glassed panelled section. Inside, patio furniture was set around with a lot of potted plants. 'The front is all glass, so you can look out over the view as you swim, though there won't be any water in it today.'

'It's stunning.' Felicity so didn't belong here. She was from a rough estate that probably had about as much square milage as this place only shared between hundreds of people. If Dorothy Sinclair ever found out she'd been here, she'd flip her lid.

Gavin got out of the car first and raked around behind a small bush close to the long low steps up the entrance. 'There's a key box down here.'

Felicity grinned. 'I wondered what you were doing.'

'Here we go.' He dangled the key, then hopped up to the door and opened it. He held it open and she stepped inside, gazing around. Frank and Dorothy's Sinclair's highland home had always been a more traditional place in her imaginings. This was so much more contemporary, though perhaps not completely up to date. Some pieces looked a little dated but nothing to complain about.

'It's beautiful.'

'Would you like a tour?'

'Of course.' The hallway was on the chilly side and she shivered. Gavin moved closer and held out his arm, indicating for them to walk, but she deliberately misinterpreted it as an invitation to lean into him.

'Hey.' He gathered her to his chest and held her. 'Everything's ok. I'm not going to pressure you into anything. Whatever you choose to do about us or with your career, I promise I'll support your decision. I don't play games.'

'I just wish we could be like normal people,' she said, pulling back and gazing into his gleaming turquoise eyes.

'We are normal people. We just have a conflict between what we crave in our heart and what we know is sensible. But we're intelligent enough to be discreet, so if you want to indulge your heart for a little while, you'll find an equally indulgent heart right here.' He bumped his fist into his chest. 'But only if that's what you really want.'

'Get this out of our system, you mean?'

'That could be one way of looking at it.'

'And does that ever work?'

He brushed his palm over the small of her back. 'I'm not sure I can answer that. It's not something I've done before.'

'Neither have I.'

He led her through the various reception rooms on the ground floor. Each one had that same modern but slightly dated look. An underlying tone of wealth and quality permeated through each piece of furniture.

After looking around the huge country kitchen and dining area, they returned to the main hallway. Its stone tiled floor continued the Mediterranean theme and a large staircase wound up to a gallery-style upper floor.

'My parents have the tower bedroom.' He opened the door for her. 'It's pretty dramatic. My sister always wanted it because she thought it was a princess room.'

'I can imagine.' Felicity looked around, her eyes wide. Princess room was an understatement. It had a huge oak four-poster bed with twisted posts and a brown two-seater Chesterfield sofa at the end. 'And what does your room look like?'

'I'm not sure.' He gave a shrug, closed the door and stepped into the wide gallery corridor that ran around the upper floor. 'I haven't been here for years.'

'I forgot. How did you know how to open the gates and get the key?'

'Because my parents keep inviting me and, in every message, they leave instructions. But I kept away, so I could avoid the unavoidable.'

'You mean the job you're doing now?'

'Exactly. I never wanted it really. I caved to parental pressure.' He raised his brows. 'It's my weakness. Not always, but yeah, it happens.'

'It seems like quite a noble weakness, you know, making your parents proud.'

He shook his head. 'It doesn't feel like that to me. I feel like I was groomed for this job and even when I made it clear I didn't want it, they carried on acting as though it was my birthright and a gift I couldn't refuse. In the end, they were right. I know they didn't do it with ugly motives, but they've never understood that I might not feel exactly the same way they do. In fact, they think they own my feelings, especially my mum.'

'Is that why you turned down your ex when she proposed?'

'One of the reasons. I can't blame my parents wholly for it. My mum never liked her and subconsciously that influenced my decision but part of it was me. I didn't think I was ready. I was out of touch with my feelings as I have been for much of my life.'

'Even now?'

'Sometimes.' He ran his fingertips down her cheek. 'The only feeling I'm super certain of now is how strongly I feel about you, even though I know I shouldn't.'

'Same.' She reached out and held his face in her palms. 'I just want to be with you. I know how crazy it is and how difficult it'll make things. I'm not stupid.'

'You're definitely not that.'

'But I can't ignore this. I'll go mad.'

'Me too.' He placed his hands on her waist and drew her close to him. 'I really want you so badly.' Lowering his forehead, he rested it on hers. 'But I stand by my promise. Whatever you want to do, I'll support you.'

'I want to be with you. Right now.' Always. She tilted her head and raised her lips to him. The instant zing of raw passion brought all the sensations from the morning flooding back. The soft caress of his hands had her body writhing for more, eager to get into the right position to allow every desperate nerve end its moment to be satisfied. She ground against him in the most exquisite fashion.

'Come with me.' He pulled gently out of the kiss, took her hand, and opened the door to another room, spacious and bright. No four-poster bed but still large and pristine. It wasn't made up apart from a sheet. Bare pillows and a duvet without a cover were folded at the foot of the mattress. A long grey chaise was at the end of the bed. 'Hmm. Not exactly ready for our arrival.' He took off his watch, slipped his wallet out of his back pocket and placed them on the bedside cabinet. Then he got out his phone and, after tapping something on the screen, put it face down beside his watch.

His actions were so decisive. Felicity fiddled with the straps of her dress. He might be reserved and uncertain about his job, but something told her he wouldn't be an innocent bystander in whatever they did next.

'Sorry.' He pulled a face at the unmade bed. 'Maybe this isn't the best place.'

'It's fine. I don't really care where we are. You're the only thing I care about.'

He closed the gap between them, slipped his fingers under the straps of her dress and unhooked them over her shoulders. 'And I care about you too. Let me take care of you.'

Her eyes closed as he gently pressed kisses on her exposed neck, then moved along her collarbone. Slowly, he lowered the ruched bodice of her maxi dress. She hadn't bothered with a bra. This dress didn't need one, and her breasts burst free, ready to play.

His keyboard skills weren't the only thing his fingers were good at. The soft caresses he placed on her had such power she could do nothing but moan. He undid the top button of his shirt and she took charge of the next one, moving down until he wrestled it off and tossed it away. His chest was so ridiculously hot. Gavin Sinclair was a stuffed shirt all right. Stuffed with muscle power. She pressed up against it, enjoying the heated friction of skin on skin. He brought his lips to hers again, soothing away more tension.

'Take a seat.' He waved his hand towards the chaise. She did so, leaning on the arm with her elbow, aware that with her long dress, she must look like a shameless Regency belle. But was he a rake or an honourable hero? Kneeling on the floor at the end of the chaise, he slowly took off her flat pumps, then kissed her ankle. She lay back, breasts bared, her breathing rapid, as he kissed further up, lifting her dress higher so it draped over her tummy and onto the floor. His mouth was heading straight for her most intimate place and she could hardly bear the tension. His kissing had already reduced her to a whimpering mess but now... He slipped off her knickers and let his wicked lips and tongue play, knowing exactly what to do with them and where to put them for maximum impact. She let go of everything. All niggly thoughts vanished. Throwing back her head, she gasped for breath. He didn't stop, even as she fisted the folds of her dress. Wild sensations set her body on fire, more intense than anything she'd ever experienced before. She grabbed his hair and let out a scream of delight as the most powerful wave hit.

Her eyes were shut and she wasn't sure she could open them. Had any of that been real? If she peeked out, would she be back at the hotel in her own bed, dreaming?

'Are you ok?' A soft voice spoke in her ear and she was aware of warmth beside her. Her eyes opened and Gavin was crouched on the floor close to her.

'Did I faint?'

'I don't know. Did you? You suddenly went very quiet.'

'That was just incredible.' She swallowed. 'I thought maybe I'd dreamt it.'

He got to his feet and her face was level with his bulging crotch. She had a sudden urge to unfasten his trousers and return his favour, but before she could move, he leaned down and scooped her up like she weighed nothing.

'You didn't dream anything.' He carried her to the bed, stopping only to press a kiss to her lips; she responded with interest. 'I'm the one who must be dreaming.' He lowered her gently onto the mattress. 'But I don't think even in my dreams I could have conjured up someone as amazing as you.'

She let out a little laugh.

'I'm serious.' He sat beside her, stroking the hair from her face. 'You're everything and more.' His hand trailed down, skimming her breasts and thumbing her nipples. She smiled, still slightly dazed, vaguely aware they hadn't bothered to close the curtains and it was bright sunlight outside. He tugged her dress over her head, slipped it off fully, and cast it aside. Goosebumps rose on her as his eyes raked her fully naked body. 'You really are beautiful, stunning. Just perfect.'

He got to his feet and removed his remaining clothes. She didn't look away; she wanted to see everything. He was such a well put together man. His whole body was magnificent, perfectly shaped and proportioned. He didn't look nervous or embarrassed as he flipped open his wallet and took out a condom. She smiled, opening her arms to him as he lay down beside her. He tucked a strand of her hair behind her ear and gazed at her like she was truly the most wonderful person he'd ever seen. It made her weak all over. His strong arms tugged her close and held her. Although contentment oozed into her as he kissed her, bigger fires started within. He moved on top of her and spread her legs wide.

'Is this definitely ok?' he asked.

'Yes.' She braced her hands on his firm abs.

He lowered his lips to hers again for a moment, then, holding her gaze, he nudged gently inside. She wrapped her legs behind him, drawing him close, loving the heat.

She stared back at him, hyperaware of the new sensations and the intoxicating scent of their combined bodies.

They'd stepped out of the office and opened a door to bliss. The energy and friction drove her to another new level of pleasure as she answered his thrusting hips. She arched off the bed, clenching as he ground into her.

'Oh, this is too good,' he groaned.

'Oh god, it is. Please... Hold me, please,' she whimpered, her body starting to shake.

He wrapped his arms about her, drawing her to his hot slab of a chest, still moving divinely inside her. She closed her eyes, giving way to another spectacular and explosive sensation that set her whole world alight.

Chapter Eighteen

Gavin

Gavin dragged the uncovered duvet from the foot of the bed and lifted it over him and Felicity.

'You're a cuddler, aren't you?' he said, shuffling in close.

'With you, I definitely am.'

'You beautiful woman.' He nuzzled into her hair. 'There's something so wrong about being in bed in the sunshine at five o'clock on a weekday, but you know what, I don't really care.'

'Oh, god. We're so bad.'

He loved the way she was curled into him and he held her there, stroking his hand down her cheek. 'I get the feeling you've spent your life behaving yourself. I know I certainly have. It's time for our rebellion.'

'If this is rebellion, it's amazing.' A contented sigh escaped her.

He closed his eyes and half smiled, half kissed her forehead. 'I think *you're* amazing. I...' He stopped. *I love you so much. I adore you.* The words hovered in limbo between his brain and his mouth. 'I want you to enjoy this.'

'I'm loving it.'

'Me too.'

The warmth and overload of happy hormones made him drowsy and his body was so fully relaxed he had no desire to move. Holding her close and occasionally kissing her or exchanging a few soft words were all he could do. Lazily, she kissed him back and their tongues touched softly, further consummating their bond.

A bang from downstairs made him pull back and his eyes sprang open. 'Did you hear that?'

Felicity sat up. 'What was it?'

'Hello!' A woman's voice called out.

'Holy shit.' Gavin jumped out of the bed. 'Who the hell is that?'

Felicity crossed her hands over her chest and stared around wide eyed.

'Hello.' The voice said again. 'Is there anyone here?'

He grabbed his clothes and pulled them on as fast as he could. Footsteps on the tiled floor downstairs were getting louder.

'Gavin? Are you here?'

He pulled a face at Felicity as she grabbed her dress and dragged it over her head. The voice wasn't familiar but whoever it was knew his name. What was going on? He hastily tucked in his shirt, opened the door and crossed the corridor to look over the rail of the gallery. His gaze settled on the hallway below. A middle-aged woman stood there, her back to him as she peered up at the staircase.

He cleared his throat. 'Can I help you?'

The woman jumped, her hand leaping to her chest as she spotted him. He took in her round, friendly features. The cleaner? His mum had employed the same person for years but he couldn't for the life of him remember her name. And why was she here? What bloody bad timing if she'd showed up to clean, but it didn't explain how she knew he was there. His car was outside but she wouldn't know what car he drove.

She blinked. 'Gavin? Is that you?'

'Yes.' He strode along the gallery, descended the staircase, and met her at the bottom. 'What are you doing here?'

'Your mother sent me. She received an alert that there was activity in the house and tried to reach you, but when you didn't answer, she asked me to come and check things out.'

Seriously? They *had* installed an alarm system. He hadn't even checked. That was his first mistake.

'I must have missed her calls. My phone is... dead.' Well, switched off. He hadn't wanted random messages coming in during his time with Felicity. That was his second mistake.

'Oh, I see. Well, not to worry. It's no problem.' The woman glanced around. 'I was glad to help and your mum seemed very worried. She thought it was you but she said you were with someone else and when she couldn't get hold of you, she panicked.'

He kept his face impassive but his insides groaned. Mum panic? *As if.* She probably knew exactly who he was with and had sent this woman to find out why they were here.

'Well, she needn't have worried. I'm fine.'

'Is someone else with you?'

'Just a colleague. They're using the bathroom. I was giving them a tour of the house before we left. We had work to do and the place we've been using was busy. I didn't think Mum and Dad would mind if I came up here for the afternoon.'

'I'm sure they don't mind at all. I'll message your mum and let her know.' She peered at him. 'It's been far too long since I last saw you. You were just a boy. Do you remember me?'

'Of course. I'm sorry I don't recall your name but you've worked here for a long time, haven't you?'

'My name's June and, gosh, yes, I've worked here ever since they bought the place. Not that there's ever much to do. Your mother keeps it in such good condition. I usually just make up the beds if there are visitors and give it a quick hoover and a dust. But you're not staying over, are you?'

'No. We're leaving shortly.'

A floorboard creaked above and Gavin spun around but it must have come from the bedroom as no one was visible in the gallery.

'What bathroom is your colleague using?' June frowned. 'One of the en suites?'

'Er, yes, must be.'

'I hope it was clean. I mean, I'm sure it would be but I haven't been in since your parents were here at the beginning of the week.'

'Everything looks fine.'

June raised an eyebrow. 'Are you sure? I could give it a quick clean just now while I'm here.'

'Er, no thank you. If you don't mind, I'd like to finish things off with my colleague and we have confidential business, so we really can't have anyone else here. It's procedure, you understand.

We won't leave a mess, I promise.' In fact, every bit of evidence would be bagged and binned several miles away. He wouldn't put it past his mother to check all the bins.

June nodded. 'Of course, if you're sure. And if you need any-thing, just call. My number is in the book by the door. I'll head off and message your mother.' Her eyes darted around. 'I hope your colleague is all right. She's been in the bathroom for a long time.'

She. Dammit. June knew which meant his mother did too.

'I'm sure she's fine.' He watched as June made her way to the door. He followed, standing in the doorway as she headed to her car, her phone in her hand. With a sigh, he stepped back inside. What now? When June's car crunched down the driveway, he looked out and spotted the sensor cam at the side of the door. *Ugh.*

A heavy sense of dread weighed on his shoulders as he climbed the stairs. His phone would be too red hot to touch. And poor Felicity. He pushed open the bedroom door and she jumped back.

'Oh my god,' she said. 'What was that all about?'

'Could you hear what she was saying?'

'Bits of it. Your parents have a sensor cam or something that alerts them when the gate opens?'

'A new sensor cam. I can't believe I didn't check. And it caught us coming in. My mother has apparently been phoning and mes-saging me ever since to check it was me.'

'But I didn't hear any messages.'

'I switched off my phone. I didn't want to be disturbed.'

She smiled. 'Aw. That's actually sweet.'

'Maybe. But also bloody stupid. If I'd left it on, I could have replied and told her we were just having a quick look around. Now, she knows I've been here for ages. June will tell her I came downstairs from the bedroom, and she heard the floor creaking, so she knows you were up here too. Honestly, my mother will put it all together in seconds.' He sank onto the bed, rested his elbows on his knees and dropped his face into his hands. 'I'm so done for. She probably suspected already, which is why she sent someone over. Oh god.'

The bed dipped as Felicity sat beside him. Her slender arm looped around his back. 'I'm sorry.'

'It's not your fault.'

'Well, she can't prove anything, not unless she has spy cameras up here too.'

He looked up. 'Don't even go there.'

'I'm sure she doesn't. And if she does, well, what a show.'

'That's not even funny.'

She giggled and rubbed his back. 'Did you tell her we were working?'

'Yes. But I doubt she'll buy it. The fact we were upstairs and it took me so long to get down. Oh boy.' He let out a long sigh.

'Maybe you should check your phone.'

'I really don't want to. If I do, I can't reply for a while yet. I told June my phone was dead. Because really, who turns their phone off these days?'

'Considerate men like you.'

Her smile was irresistible. He put his arm around her shoulder. 'I just value time with you more than electronics. And that's saying something, coming from the man who has a house with approximately twelve monitors, three top-of-the-line gaming laptops, a brand-new sound system, and a VR setup that would turn most gamers green.'

Felicity giggled and the soft touch tickled his neck. 'I often wondered what your home looked like.'

'Teenage boys would wet themselves over it.' He glanced at her. That was another reason he'd finally decided to take on this job. He'd got too obsessed with technology and craved something real. He'd definitely had that this afternoon and now the real world was catching up with him. Unfortunately, it didn't have a reset button or an off-switch.

Felicity leaned in and kissed his cheek. 'I really like you,' she whispered.

'I like you too, an awful lot.'

'And I like what you do to me. That was quite an experience.'

'I enjoyed every second of it until June showed up.' He pressed his lips to hers and kissed her softly. It comforted him but set off more alarm bells. Sleeping with her hadn't put out the fires or even dampened the longing. If anything, it made him crave more. *I love you so much.* He broke away before things got heated again. So much for his big idea that this would be more private than the hotel. 'Maybe I should check my phone.'

'You said you wanted to wait.' A smile played at the corner of her lips.

'I did.'

'Let's give it half an hour. I think I know something we can do while we wait.' She pushed him further back on the bed, hitched up her dress and straddled him.

'Just how much trouble do you want to get me into?'

'Lots.' She pulled down her straps.

'Ok. Trouble it is.' He leaned close and kissed one of her perky, soft breasts. She moaned and tossed her head back.

This definitely beat freaking out for half an hour. Passion built quickly, like it had only been put on hold before and now it was back and needed an immediate outlet. Her body fitted his so perfectly and she arched and flexed on top of him like she was performing a sensual dance just for him. If the security system had a sound monitor, anyone listening would be treated to her squeals of delight and his rough groaning as she rode him to another explosive climax.

'Oh. God. Felicity. You. Are. Incredible.' The words came out in fits as he desperately fought for air. If the world was still spinning, it had left him behind. He was dazed and covered in a faint sheen of sweat. She lolled on top of him, kissing the over-sensitive skin at his Adam's apple and stroking him. He splayed his fingers on her back, holding her close. They'd reverted to the place they'd been when June had interrupted them earlier. Another cuddle-coma.

Every second that ticked by while he was in this house would fuel his mother's wrath. But he wanted to hold Felicity as long as possible in this blissful embrace.

When they finally dragged themselves out of bed, washed, dressed and made sure the room looked like no one had ever set foot in it, they left. He kept his back covering the camera as Felicity went down the step. If there was the off chance his mum hadn't recognised the second person, he might be ok. But his mum knew Felicity was in Glenbriar and after what she'd said to him after their dinner the other night, it was enough to make his insides squirm.

Finally, they were on their way back to the hotel.

No one was about on the first floor and he let Felicity into his room. His phone was burning a hole in his pocket now and he couldn't delay looking at it anymore. He pulled it out and switched it on. Felicity sat on a little sofa by the window, watching with raised eyebrows and a helpless expression.

He slumped down beside her as the message thread loaded and it buzzed with numerous missed calls. All from Mum. At least there had been no business disasters while he was offline.

'Your mum is very concerned for you.' Felicity glanced over at his screen.

'She doesn't want me seeing you in anything other than a professional capacity.'

'But...' She frowned. 'She can't know anything, can she?'

'She took me aside after our meal the other night to tell me she thought you were trying to sleep your way to the top.'

'What? I'm not doing that. I—'

'I know you're not.' He settled his hand on her thigh. 'My mother doesn't know you like I do.'

'But I wear nail polish, so I'm doomed.'

'She doesn't like you because she didn't choose you. She only wants me to date women she picks or deems acceptable.' He sighed.

'Oh dear.'

'But I'm thirty-six years old. I can flipping well choose for myself. And if I want you and you want me, then I'll find a way to make it work.'

'You are?'

'Yes, I am.' He had no idea how, but why should his mother dictate his future? He glanced down and his phone and the messages displayed one after the other.

MUM: Are you at the Glenbriar house? I just had a notification saying someone was there and the person in the film looked like you. Just wanted to check.

MUM: Is Felicity there too? It looked like her.

MUM: Are you still there? I tried calling.

MUM: Gavin. Is that you at the house? Now, I'm getting worried. Dad thinks it's you but why aren't you answering?

MUM: What are you doing at the house? There is no film of you leaving. Are you still there? Have you left by another door? Did you lock up?

MUM: If you don't answer, I'll have to send June around to check everything's ok. It might be inconvenient for her, but I don't get why you're not answering.

MUM: Have called June. She's on her way.

MUM: June just messaged and says you're there with a colleague who was in the toilet for a very long time. I don't mind you using the house for business but please let me know in future. June said she hadn't even had a chance to clean. I hope Felicity is well and that she hasn't come down with food poisoning. Dad wants to know what confidential business you were working on.

Gavin rolled his eyes. 'For fuck's sake.'

Felicity smirked at him. 'I think that's only the second time I've ever heard you swear.'

'I just can't believe my mother.'

He typed out a very quick message.

Sorry can't discuss business here, nothing for Dad to worry about. The house seemed a quieter place to work than the hotel. I didn't think you'd mind and I didn't notice the security camera, otherwise I would have let you know. Didn't want to disturb you. The house was perfectly clean and I've left it as I found it. Felicity is fine.

He hit send but he hadn't heard the end of this. In fact, switching his phone off for the rest of the week was looking very appealing, only somewhere down the line he was going to have to face the very loud music.

Chapter Nineteen

Felicity

Smells of coffee and bacon hit Felicity as she entered the dining room on Friday morning. Sometimes it was enough to put her off going in but her stomach groaned and she felt quite peckish. Her meal with Gavin yesterday seemed so long ago and neither of them had been very hungry in the evening. It was catching up on her now. They had their last visit of the week to Inverbuie to get through before the ceilidh that evening. Gavin had already said he didn't want to attend and, after the developments from the day before, it was probably better if he didn't. How could she hide her feelings when all she'd want to do would be to dance the night away in his arms?

He was already at a table by the window and gave her a little smile of acknowledgement. This was the professional track – a working breakfast – and that was fine. What happened in Glenbriar after all… Or maybe it should be what happened in their private life stayed in their private life. He'd said he'd find a way to make things work if she wanted and she did, though how he would do that, she had no idea.

'Morning.' She took the seat opposite him.

'Good morning.' He glanced at her and the warmth in his eyes betrayed everything without him saying a word. Hopefully, no one else could discern it. Had he always looked at her like that? Maybe she was just more keenly aware of it now. 'Ready for today?'

'Indeed.' She smoothed her skirt. 'Are you going to suggest the diversification plans today or save it until everyone gets together next week?'

'Save it, I think. Let's just get a feel of the place first. Then you and I can work on the plan together on Monday and Tuesday and we can put it to them on Wednesday when we meet. I'm not even going to alert Julian to the plans as he'd have too much time to think up objections and probably tell my dad, who might freak out and try to take charge.' Gavin sighed and rolled his eyes. 'Sometimes I'm not sure why he gave up in the first place.'

'It'll be fine. And' – she gave him a cheeky smirk – 'leave your dad to me. He's always liked me.'

'I know. Which is another reason my mum doesn't.'

'It was never like that.' She glared at him, torn between shock and amusement.

'Just as well.' He raised an eyebrow.

'I've always liked older guys but not *that* much older.'

They grinned at each other.

Once they were safely in the car, she turned to Gavin and let out a slow whistle. 'Are we doing ok?'

'Let's hope so.'

'Was your mum still messaging you last night?'

'Oh yes. I don't think she dares ask me outright if you and I were... well, doing what we were doing. But she suspects. I can tell from the passive aggressive tone of her messages and the underlying sense of disappointment filtering in.' He pulled the car into a small layby beside the woods and Felicity checked around, frowning.

'What's wrong?'

'Nothing.' He pulled on the handbrake. 'I'd just really like to give you a good morning kiss.'

She smiled. 'Then go ahead.'

He leaned over, cradled her face in his hands, then gently pressed his lips to hers. She soaked it in, loving being reunited with him. His minty taste zinged against her tongue and she let out a contented sigh.

He broke off with a wink, then cruised onto the road again. 'That's better. Now I can be professional.'

'Me too, and yes, it's much better.' She pulled down the mirror and reapplied her lippy.

When they arrived at Inverbuie, Gavin spent a few minutes replying to an urgent email but didn't elaborate on what it was. Hopefully not his parents again. Her chest flickered with unease as he pocketed his phone. It wasn't like him not to tell her everything but it seemed this was something he didn't want to share. His smile suggested it was nothing to worry about however. She led the way across a little red iron bridge to the front door of the somewhat ugly building that housed the distillery. Someone had attempted to spruce it up with potted plants and hanging baskets at the door.

'It could do with a bit of a facelift,' Gavin said. 'But it looks serviceable enough.'

The foyer was much more up to standard, with modern fittings and the staff dressed neatly in the company purple. Felicity beamed and greeted them like the long-lost friends they were.

'It's been so long.' She hugged Fee MacKenzie, the receptionist, and shook hands with the manager, Alistair Turner. 'This is Gavin Sinclair, our chief exec. I think you met at Frank's retiral dinner.'

'Yes, yes, we did.' Alistair shook Gavin's hand.

'Everything's looking great.' Gavin's eyes roamed around the room. The confidence he'd been lacking on Monday now radiated from him and Felicity gave him a quick smile. Why should she hide how thrilled she was? He maybe hadn't wanted this job but he could definitely do it. No one meeting him for the first time today would think he was anything but the in-control CEO he should be.

The distinctive malty distillery scent filled the air, flooding her with a stream of memories. Happy days in a happy place.

She'd spent so much of yesterday enjoying Gavin's company she'd almost forgotten his suggestion of creating a new management role. Could she do it? How amazing would it be to have some say in the business she'd grown so attached to? It was the opportunity of a lifetime but what did it mean for their budding relationship? Did they really have a relationship? What happens in Glenbriar... Except now, it felt much bigger than that, or potentially much bigger. What would they have to do to make it work? Would one of them have to stand down and leave the company? Gavin made no secret of his not loving the role or even wanting it in the first place, but he wasn't a quitter. Would he go that far to make things work?

'Well, Mr Sinclair, Miss Swan,' Alistair said. 'Let me officially welcome you to Inverbuie. Of course, Miss Swan has been here before and knows the workings very well.'

'Indeed,' Gavin said. 'And please, Gavin is fine.'

'And so's Felicity.' She gave Alistair a smile, and he nodded.

'Excellent. So, Gavin and Felicity, shall we get started?'

'Absolutely.' Gavin indicated for him to lead the way.

'Felicity could probably do a better job of this than me. You always had a way with the punters.'

'Thanks, Alistair. I loved doing the tours. I miss it.'

He led the way towards the production area. 'It's quite a spacious area we have here, thanks to the modern building. The stills are in great working order, and we use only the finest locally sourced barley and spring water from the Buie Burn. I don't know if you're aware that the name Buie Burn actually means yellow stream in Gaelic.'

Felicity smirked. She knew the story but Gavin shook his head.

'The concept of yellow water isn't always a pleasant one,' Alistair continued. 'It's the peat that gives it the yellowish colour. The story goes that the water is so perfect, the locals used to believe it was almost whisky already, hence the colour. They would probably have translated it as golden water, which sounds a lot better.'

Gavin smiled and his whole demeanour seemed more relaxed and open. 'I love the way you keep the local stories going.'

'The punters lap it up,' Alistair said. 'There's a long history. Although this building is modern, it was built over an existing still, and more than likely one that started off illegally, as most of them did. Now, if you'll look over here, we have the mash tun.' He indicated the large copper tank. 'And through here, we have our maturation warehouse.' He opened a door to reveal rows upon rows of oak barrels. 'This is where the magic happens.'

Gavin walked over to a barrel and ran a fingertip along the smooth wood. Those hands were so strong, but gentle. A pleasure-memory tremored through Felicity.

'Each barrel holds a unique blend of whisky,' Alistair said. 'Time and patience are the key ingredients. I think the issue we have is that this whisky isn't currently as popular as the others.'

'Yes, we're aware of that,' Gavin said.

Alistair rubbed his chin and glanced at Felicity. 'I know you're here to assess the efficiency of our distillery. I run a tight ship, but the popularity of one whisky over another isn't something within my control.'

'We understand.' Felicity gave him what she hoped was a reassuring smile.

He frowned slightly, looking from her to Gavin. 'I'm fully aware this is the most likely place to be axed if the rumours of cutbacks and closures are to be believed.'

Gavin held up his hand. 'Please, don't worry. This trip isn't a mission to shut down anywhere. The opposite in fact. No decisions have been made and they won't be until we've had a full consultation. We're here to gather information and get a better understanding of the operations of all the distilleries in the group. And we're open to exploring new opportunities and ways to diversify our portfolio because closures are the last thing we want.'

'I see.' Alistair's frown deepened.

'If you have any thoughts or opinions on potential diversification ideas, feel free to let me know, either now or in an email. I'm open to any ideas.'

Alistair ran his hand through his thick, dark hair. 'Whatever we do, I think it's important to stay true to our roots. But I see the value in exploring new ventures, such as expanding our product line or adding further tours and tastings. There's space here that could even be used for dining facilities. I believe some distilleries are opening cafes or restaurants alongside and there's potential for that here, though of course it would mean investment.'

'It's a great idea,' Felicity said.

'I'm not averse to investment,' Gavin added. 'We just need to make sure we have robust plans in place to justify the expenditure.'

'I'm glad you're looking for long-term solutions and not closures.' Alistair headed for the exit door.

'Closure is not something I want, and it would be an absolute last resort once we'd explored all other avenues.' Gavin followed him out. 'We'll definitely keep your suggestions in mind as we continue our assessment.'

'I'd like to make sure Inverbuie remains a thriving part of the Glenbriar Group for years to come.' Alistair held the door for them.

Felicity smiled as she went through.

After talking to the other staff, she and Gavin headed back to the hotel. Her mind was whirring.

Gavin tapped the steering wheel, looking pensive. 'So, do you think Alistair's restaurant idea is viable?'

'Sure, why not? Especially if we were to include gin production. Gin is so popular at the moment. It's one of the most ordered drinks in restaurants.'

'A smart move to stay ahead in the market then. But I have no idea how to go about producing it. It's a whole new thing to investigate.'

'I did a quick google of it and I think we could convert one of the warehouses into a gin still room, though we'd need to purchase the equipment. We could source the botanicals locally to make the gin unique to the area.' She pulled out her phone and brought up her emails. 'I sent out some feelers to local farmers and I've had a few responses from places that could fulfil the supply if given notice of the timeframe. I also looked into the cost of the equipment. It's not cheap, but I think it would be a worthwhile investment.'

He raised an eyebrow. 'Wow, you're right on top of this, aren't you?'

She smiled; she'd rather be on top of him. 'I want to make this a success. I believe in you and I believe in this idea.'

'You're such a wonderful person. I don't know how I ever got by without you. You have such a way with people. And I appreciate the way you always make me feel like my best self.'

She patted his thigh. 'Anytime.'

He took one hand off the wheel and laid it over hers. 'So, what did you find out about the cost?'

'A new still plus fermentation tanks and other supplies will come to around a hundred and fifty thousand. But as we already have bottling facilities, it significantly reduces the outlay. If we were starting from scratch, it would be a lot more.'

He took up the wheel with both hands again. 'In the grand scheme of things, that's not actually as much as I thought and if it brings in more revenue, it'll definitely be worth it.'

'I agree. Shall we start putting together a business plan this afternoon and see if we can make this a reality?'

He squeezed her hand again. 'Absolutely.'

Briony brought out a plate of sandwiches, and Felicity and Gavin worked through the afternoon. Felicity smiled to herself. The growing feelings for Gavin weren't putting her off work or making their professional discussions fall to pieces. The opposite. It was enjoyable and they thought and acted like one. With him much more relaxed, the ideas flowed. He typed everything into boxes and put it into the right places on his new system design.

He checked his watch. 'It's four fifteen. Listen, would you mind if we called it a day? It's Friday afternoon after all, and I need to nip into town and get a few things.'

'Oh. Sure.' An odd sensation fluttered through her again, similar to the one she'd had that morning when he'd replied to his email without giving her details. Not that she needed to know but it was like he was excluding her.

'We can reconvene on Monday morning.' He closed the lid of his laptop and smiled. 'Do you have plans for the weekend?'

'Well, I thought maybe you and me... If you wanted to. Or is that too risky?'

'Of course I want to be with you, but I don't want to get in the way if you already have something on.'

'Nothing. I'd much rather spend time with you.'

'That's settled then. Maybe you'd like to do some wild swimming?'

She raised an eyebrow. 'I like kayaking and paddleboarding, but I've never actually been wild swimming. I wouldn't mind watching you though.'

He smirked. 'That sounds highly unfair.'

'I'm going to the ceilidh tonight. Are you sure I can't persuade you to come?'

He got to his feet and lifted his case. 'I might look in.'

'That would be good. In fact, I should go and see Briony. She's got a dress I can wear.' She gathered everything together and put it in her briefcase.

'Great. Well, I'll probably see you later.' He glanced briefly at the door, then leaned over and placed a quick kiss on her cheek. 'You've done an amazing job this week. I've enjoyed everything we've done together. I'm so glad I've got you.' With another quick peck, he left.

She blinked and touched her cheek. He wouldn't be stealing kisses like that once they were back in Edinburgh.

Briony was in the private quarters at the back of the hotel. It had been nicely renovated since Felicity had last been and now looked modern and open plan, unlike the shabby and retro tiredness of before.

'These dresses will all be a bit loose on you.' Briony opened the door to her bedroom. It was also much fresher and airier. 'You're so thin but I'm not likely to fit them again for some time.'

'I'm sure they'll be fine. Who's going to notice?'

'Um, only that hot boss of yours.' Briony put her hands on her hips. 'I know, don't tell me, you're just colleagues.'

'Hmm.' Felicity let out a sigh and slumped onto the bed.

'What does that mean?'

'Things have moved on a bit.'

Briony sat beside her and put her arm around her shoulder. 'Hey. What's up?'

She hung her head. 'It's so complicated. I really like him but, well, there's this new job he wants to create and it's like my dream job. But there's no way I can apply for a position like that if he and I are... together.'

'And is that a possibility?'

She shrugged. 'Maybe.'

'Have you and him been sharing rooms?' Briony cocked an eyebrow.

'Kind of.' She hid her face. 'I really care about him and I'm sure he feels the same about me, which makes the work situation so freaking impossible.'

Briony rubbed her back. 'Just take your time. If you want to apply for that job, do it. If he stops you, then he's not worth it. I don't think you should let an opportunity like that slip by for a man you don't know that well.'

Felicity peered at her and cast her a look. 'Says the woman who's having a baby with the man she met when he was on holiday for a week.'

Briony laughed, got to her feet and lifted two dresses on hangers from the wardrobe door. 'So true. The value of hindsight. Not that I'd change anything that happened with Zach.' She rubbed her hand over her tummy. 'But just take care. I wouldn't want you to throw away a job only to find he's not the commitment type.'

Good point. Gavin had said himself he'd turned down a proposal because he wasn't ready for commitment. Was he now? What if, in the initial rush of love, he thought it was a good idea, but as time went by, his resolve faded? Maybe he didn't want to give up a cyber apartment for a partner, possibly children. She may be running ahead of herself.

She tried on both the dresses and wasn't sure which one she preferred. They were both lovely.

'Which one do you think Gavin will prefer?' Briony raised her eyebrows.

'That doesn't really matter. He's not going to be there anyway.'

'Isn't he? Surely he'll change his mind now the two of you are more friendly.'

'He said he might drop in for a little while, but I don't think it's really his thing. I doubt he wants local people approaching him and comparing him to his dad. It's not easy for him.'

'That's a pity. I'll be on and off working, but I'll make sure you get a table with some of the old crew. Hayley's going. You could sit with her.'

'Oh brilliant. I'd love to see her again. I'll message her, but I wish you would just rest. You look weary.'

'I know, but Zach's on duty too, so if I need to rest for a bit, he'll take over.'

'Good.'

With the prospect of seeing some old friends, the evening without Gavin didn't look so bleak. Felicity made her way to the dining room just after seven to find it all beautifully set up. She was almost immediately engulfed by arms and a tight hug.

'You're back.' Hayley jumped up and down.

'For a few days anyway. Look at you, you look great.'

Hayley was nicely tanned and wearing a long black sequined dress, her chestnut hair in an immaculate up-do, as was to be expected from a hairdresser. 'Come and get a table. You remember Stella who owns Wood 'n' Chic? She's coming with her husband, George. She's always good fun.'

'Yes. I remember her.'

'And I can introduce you to Cha. She's a new friend of mine. We met when I was doing her hair. It's blue and so stunning.'

'You seem to meet a lot of friends doing hair. That's how we met.'

'I remember. It's great. I just wish I could meet some nice men too. I have hundreds of friends but never a date.'

'Aw.' Felicity cocked her head. 'That's a shame.'

'It's fine. Come to the table and meet my darling little cousin, Willow. She's such a wee beauty, you'll love her.'

'What age is she?'

'Twenty-five.'

'I thought you were talking about a child.'

'Oh, no, sorry.' Hayley giggled. 'I shouldn't call her little, but she'll always be my baby cousin. She has cerebral palsy, but she's such a trooper, she never lets it stop her. Come and meet her.'

Felicity followed Hayley to one of the round tables at the edge of the dance floor. A pretty young woman with extremely long dark blonde hair smiled up at them. Her eyes were large and framed by thick lashes, and her cheeks were rosy, giving her a youthful look that seemed to warrant Hayley's calling her 'baby cousin'.

'Willow, this is Felicity.'

'Hi.' Willow gave her a little wave.

'This is so cute,' Hayley said. 'Two of my favourite people in the whole world are about to meet.'

Felicity took a seat. 'Nice to meet you, Willow. What do you do?'

'Oh... I work at the Old Schoolhouse. It's a retreat and a home for young adults with learning needs.'

'That's great. I think I know the place. It's near that village with the unpronounceable name.'

'Clachnabronnachan,' Willow said.

'Exactly. I—' Felicity's eyes landed on the person who'd just come through the door. Gavin. And not just normal Gavin in his work suit, but Gavin fully togged in a kilt suit, looking like a model in a wedding magazine. 'Oh my god.'

'What's wrong?' Hayley said, and she and Willow followed her sightline. 'Is that your date?'

'Er... no. He's boss, I mean my Gavin – my boss, Gavin.' Bloody hell. What was going on with her? 'I didn't think he was coming.' She swallowed and raised her hand to him. 'I hope you don't mind if he joins us.'

'Of course not.' Hayley beamed. 'This is all very intriguing.'

Hayley's gossip radar seemed set to bounce off the scale but Felicity couldn't drag her eyes from Gavin. How and where had he got that outfit? Her cheeks coloured as he moved closer and, without any explanation, she suddenly knew that was what the email and the sneaking off were about. He'd done it to surprise her... And succeeded. She needed to talk to him before he reached her because when he sat down, Hayley would be listening to every word.

'Excuse me, two seconds.' She jumped to her feet and darted towards him.

CHAPTER TWENTY

Gavin

G avin adjusted his bowtie and froze. Felicity was beelining for him. What was she going to do?

'Hi.' She stopped just before him, smiling. 'I didn't think you were coming.'

'I wanted to surprise you and to make sure I had the right out-fit, especially if we're still meant to be representing the business.'

'You look awesome.'

'So do you. Very beautiful.' His eyes flickered to the table she'd just left, where two young women were watching everything.

She swallowed. 'I didn't know you were coming, so I've arranged to sit with some people.'

Ah, he should have thought about that. 'We don't have to sit together.' Though the idea of sitting alone was excruciating. He'd wait ten minutes, then sneak back to his room. 'I'm happy to leave you with your friends.'

'I don't want you to leave me. I want you to sit with us too, but, well, we'll have to be sensible.'

'Understood. I can definitely be sensible. It's my middle name. Usually.' Though she had a knack for changing that. 'It's a bit too much of a public place to be anything else.'

'True. Well, come over and I'll introduce you.' She made to walk, then stopped again, and he almost collided with her, the beautiful Felicity scent attacking his senses. 'By the way, thank you. I'm so thrilled you came.'

'Anything for you.'

A pretty young woman with glossy brown hair and matching eyes looked up and beamed as Felicity took a seat next to her. On her other side was an even younger woman with very long hair.

'This is Gavin Sinclair. We work together and we're on a business trip.'

'Pleased to meet you.' The dark-haired woman threw out her hand and Gavin shook it. 'I'm Hayley. I'm a hairdresser and this is Willow, my wee beauty of a cousin.'

'Hi.' Gavin shook her hand too.

'You're a Sinclair?' Hayley continued.

'Yes.' Gavin took a seat beside Felicity.

'You must be the new owner of the distillery.'

'That's right.'

'And Dorothy is your mum.'

'Yes. Do you know her?'

'I do her hair sometimes when she's up here. She was in just the other day. Monday, I think, though I can't remember exactly. The days all blend into one. She said you were on a business trip here.'

Gavin smiled but it was fake. What else might his mum have 'let slip' to her hairdresser? Hopefully Hayley was professional enough not to repeat it, especially if it was something rude about Felicity.

'Oh, here's Stella and George.' Hayley waved at two more people and Gavin caught Felicity glancing at him.

She scrunched up her face and mouthed 'sorry'.

He smiled and leaned closer. 'It's fine. I can't be a hermit forever. Might as well get out and show the face of the distillery. I was supposed to be writing blog posts and all sorts about this kind of thing, wasn't I?'

'Yes. You still should. This is the perfect opportunity.' Felicity beamed.

'This is Stella and this is George,' Hayley said and Gavin shook their hands. 'This is Gavin Sinclair, you know, the whisky man.'

Stella smiled. 'You're famous around here.'

'Am I?' More like infamous if the rumours were to be believed.

'Well, the Sinclair family is.'

'You run the furniture shop, don't you?'

'Yes. I do.'

'I saw a sideboard in there that I think my mum should have.'

Stella sat up. 'Shall I reserve it for you?'

'I'll see if I can call in next week and arrange something,' he said.

'Were the kiddies good?' Hayley asked.

'Not too bad. They love George's mum and she dotes on them, so they're quite happy.' Stella fluffed out her curly hair. 'Alex is always a bit clingier, but Ava has second child syndrome and basically shoves us out of the door. She acts more like eighteen than ten months.'

Gavin let the chat wash over him, joining in if he needed to, but mostly watching people coming in. Would any of the distillery staff attend? That might be slightly awkward. It wasn't an enormous room but it was surprising how many people fitted in. A band warmed up in one corner and a man swaggered across the room to chat to them. He flicked his longish hair out of his face. Gavin raised an eyebrow. *What was the point of me going to all the fuss of emailing a hire shop and getting an expensive outfit when guys like him are strutting around?* Celtic tattoos covered his muscly arms. He had on a kilt, but he'd paired it with a tight t-shirt and thick boots.

'There's Brann the builder,' Hayley said with a little giggle.

Maybe he heard her because he looked their way, scanned over the table and sent them a very pronounced wink. Felicity laughed. Gavin's blood hit boiling point and he clenched his fists.

'Ooh,' Hayley said to Felicity. 'You've got an admirer.'

Yes, she does, and it's me. He had to force his jaw shut to stop him from saying the words aloud.

'Stop it.' Felicity's cheeks had gone very red. 'He wasn't winking at me. Maybe it's you he's after.'

Hayley chuckled. 'I don't think so. It was just a joke. I think someone told me he was married.'

'Seriously?'

'Yeah, I'll need to investigate further,' Hayley said.

'He said something about having kids, so maybe he is.'

Gavin watched him cross the room and march up behind a young couple. He pushed his way between them and flung his arms over both their shoulders. If someone had butted in on him like that he wouldn't have found it funny, though the young couple didn't seem to care.

Leaning further back in his chair, he moved his head close to Felicity so he could whisper as the conversation carried on around them. 'Are you sure he's not an admirer?'

'I'm sure.'

'And he's not one of those bad boys girls normally love?'

'He may well be, but I'm not one of them,' she said.

'Good.'

'Are you jealous?'

'Very.'

She giggled and shook her head. 'No need to be.'

He sat up straight again. 'Would anybody like a drink?'

'Sure.' Stella fished in her bag for her wallet.

'I'll get them.' Gavin put up his hand.

'Does that mean we all have to drink the whisky?' George asked with a smile.

'Well... Maybe.' Gavin grinned. 'No, really, have whatever you like.'

'I'll come with you,' Felicity said. 'And give you a hand.'

'It's fine. You enjoy the chat with your friends. I've got this.'

Of course having his PA on hand to remember everything was useful but he managed, carefully avoiding Brann the builder in case the jealous beast rose in him again.

After a few drinks, the dancefloor filled. George and Stella left to join in, but Gavin didn't dare ask Felicity.

'Want to dance with your big cousin?' Hayley grinned at Willow. 'I need to take to the floor and find out what my brother is doing with Elyse Reid. And I see Cha and Nick. I need to introduce her to Felicity.'

Willow got to her feet. She had a crutch propped on the chair but didn't take it. Hayley took her hand and led her onto the floor.

'She's such a busybody,' Felicity said, sipping her drink.

'Does she know everyone?'

'Pretty much. She loves people and she's always kind even if she is a gossip.' She turned to Gavin. 'Should we dance? Or is it not allowed?'

'Not allowed.' He glanced at her, then raised an eyebrow. 'But will anyone notice? It makes me look unchivalrous sitting here and refusing to dance with you. And I don't want Brann the builder stealing you away.'

'I would say there's no danger, but he might ask me. Who knows?'

'Come on then.' Gavin put out his hand and Felicity took it. He led her to the floor and soon they were spinning and laughing with the others.

Felicity blew her hair out of her face at the end of the dance. 'That was a bit energetic.'

'Try doing it in this outfit.' Gavin loosened his collar. 'It's hot in here.'

'You're not wrong.' She arched an eyebrow with a wicked smile.

'Careful.' He glanced around. 'Though we could get together for a "meeting" later.'

'One of our very intimate ones?' she whispered.

'Exactly.'

'Sounds perfect and I'm dying to know if you're a true Scotsman.' Her focus roamed to his sporran.

'Born and bred.'

Her smile grew.

'Are we dancing another or sitting this one out?' he asked.

'Whatever you fancy.'

'Well, there's only one thing in this room I fancy.' He took her hand.

Her long eyelashes fluttered over her inky black pupils.

The music struck up a slower number but with some specific moves that neither he nor Felicity were great at following. He laughed as she ducked under his arm while everyone else was waltzing. 'We got that bit wrong.'

'I'm English,' she said. 'It's expected.'

'What's my excuse?'

'I'm leading you astray.'

'Sounds about right.'

At the end of the dance, they returned to the table. Hayley was still dancing with random people but Willow was back with Stella and George, looking at pictures on Stella's phone.

'George's mum has sent photos of the kiddies fast asleep.' Stella beamed and turned the phone for them to see.

'Aw.' Felicity smiled at them. 'So cute. And your son has really inherited your hair.'

Gavin glanced back to see the sleeping toddler had a curly blonde mop, very like Stella. A strange thought wandered into his head. If he had children, would they look like him or... Felicity?

Yes, here he was planning their future again, when really, there might not be a future for them.

Felicity pulled out her own phone and skimmed through some messages. Her finger froze over the screen and she nudged Gavin with her foot under the table. He frowned at her and she handed him the phone. He read the message from Fee MacKenzie, the receptionist at Inverbuie.

*FEE MACKENZIE: Hey! Was so good to see you today. It's been such a long time. I wish we'd had more time to catch up. Maybe if you're still here next week, we could sort something one afternoon. Oh, and do you want to hear something funny? One of our guides told me he thought you and Mr Sinclair were married *laughing emoji*. He didn't realise you were his PA. He said he heard Mr S saying, 'we this, we that,' and he assumed you were a couple!! How funny is that!! Let me know about next week. X*

'Oh great.' Gavin half closed his eyes and returned the phone. 'Let's get another drink.'

As soon as they were away from the table, she said, 'We didn't even do anything and I feel like we've been rumbled.'

'Maybe not. Everyone should have known who you were. It said in the emails.'

'Yeah, but maybe he missed that info. Guides don't get a lot of time to read the emails. And also, your mum was like a PA to your dad sometimes. Maybe he thought we were like that.'

'Maybe. And there's nothing much we can do about it. We chose to play with fire.' He shook his head. 'We've been burned.'

'But this is just the surface.' Felicity let out a sigh. 'It's only going to get worse, isn't it?'

'Probably. Maybe we should stop.'

'Do you want to?'

'No. You know I don't.'

'What can we do about it?'

'That's what I don't know.' He took a long, hard look at her. 'And it's getting more and more complicated by the second.' How they were going to get around it was impossible to see. But he was sure no matter what else happened, he didn't want to give up on her. If she couldn't handle the pressure and wanted to stop, he'd respect that, even if it broke him. But if he could just find a way to make it work.

Later that night, they lay in bed, deep in an embrace, and Gavin kissed her like his life depended on it. He held her close, pouring all the love he had into her, wanting her to know just how special she was to him.

He had to come up with a solution, and fast.

CHAPTER TWENTY-ONE

Felicity

Felicity trudged across the purple moorland, swatting flies away from her face with one hand, the other interlocked with Gavin's. Out here, it was safe enough, with nothing but rolling hills to spy on them.

The sun shone on Felicity's bare arms and shoulders, warming them gently. Gavin was sensibly dressed in shorts and a polo shirt, along with hiking boots. Felicity was making do in her running shorts, crop top and trainers, plus factor-fifty, just in case. She didn't want to burn. Like the gallant man he was, Gavin carried everything in his rucksack while she walked free, savouring the feel of her hand in his. How natural it felt, like they were just an average couple enjoying a weekend walk. Not the boss and his PA sneaking away so no one would see what they were up to.

'Do you know where you're going?' She smiled at him, not really concerned if this tramp through the purple and pink heather led nowhere. His company was the best bit.

'Kind of. The map said to follow the path but it's so overgrown. I think this is it. Just as well it's not boggy underfoot.'

'Definitely. I only have these trainers.' She shielded her eyes and scanned around. 'It is stunning up here. When I lived here, I did a lot of walks, but I've never been this way.'

'I think my dad brought us when we were children, but it all kind of blends in my mind these days. God, I was such a grumpy kid. I was well behaved but my moods must have driven my parents mad.'

'I think kids are hardwired to do that to their parents.'

'Possibly. Then the tables turn when you grow up and your parents are the ones to drive you mad. It's true for me anyway.'

She squeezed his hand and chuckled. 'Your mum just likes to know what you're up to.'

'Don't I know it. How is your family these days? Everyone doing ok? I bet they miss you being about.'

She let out a sigh. 'I did the best I could. My life is here now and they know that. But that was so kind of you to let me go to them.'

'I told you, anything for you.' He smiled at her.

'I think it really helped my mum. I used to try to help her as much as I could, but then I got sick and everything was foggy. I know that sounds silly, but it was like I could never finish anything. I couldn't focus or study, so I didn't do well in exams. The house was so overcrowded and it was always chaotic. They thought I wouldn't last a week when I told them I was leaving to work in Scotland.'

'Why on earth did you choose to do it?'

'I was looking at lots of different things and something about the ad caught my eye. It was a picture of a landscape a bit like this.

I remember thinking about how I'd never really been anywhere interesting. It was only for six months originally, so it seemed like the perfect opportunity to travel somewhere new and do a job that provided accommodation too. I did a phone interview with Jerry and he told me to come up and do a trial for a month. I ended up being there for three years.'

'You were brave to take that first step.'

'It's always the hardest one.'

'Yup. But why did you go for the promotion if you liked it here so much?'

'Your dad said I should. He said I'd be ideal. I thought he was joking, then I decided to go for it but never thought I'd get picked.'

'I'm glad you did.' He smiled at her. 'I always had a soft spot for you, even though I know I shouldn't have.'

She nuzzled her cheek on his shoulder. 'I always liked you too, even if I did think you were a bit stuffy.'

'Charming.'

She giggled. 'When you let me go home to my family in January, I saw what a good guy you really were. I hope I don't have to do it again though. I told my mum it was a one off and she gets it. Doesn't take away the guilt though.'

'If you need to do it again, we'll work something out. I'll make sure it's ok.'

Her heart hiccupped. He was just the best. Of course he would make sure it was ok. He always did the right thing. Even when they were doing the wrong thing, he did it in an honourable way... Like this fling.

'I had a whole lot of messages from Hayley. She thinks you fancy me.'

'She's right.'

Felicity giggled. 'But we're supposed to be keeping it secret.'

'Yeah. We're doing a really crap job at that, though I am trying.'

'Because, like I said, you're a good guy and an honourable one.'

'I don't feel it right now.'

'You are though. I know you wouldn't give us away on purpose.'

'My body is more likely to give me away than my mouth.' He stopped and ran his thumb down her cheek, skimming his gaze over her face, then tucking a lock of hair behind her ear. 'I just wish we could be open about this, but I know that's not a sensible move.'

She looped her arm around his neck and pulled him close. They kissed long and deep, bodies moulding together, with only blue skies and a few wisps of cloud to see them. Would she ever get enough of him? These days were surely numbered. If this was a Glenbriar fling, then in a few too short days, it would all be over.

She pulled away, frowning.

'Are you ok?'

'I don't know.' She started walking again.

'Come on, talk to me.' He grasped her hand. 'You can say anything you want.'

'I just can't bear how soon this will end.' Why had tears chosen this moment to make an appearance? She looked away, pushing back the evidence with the heel of her hand.

He slipped his fingers around her shoulder and drew her close again. 'Listen, I know we agreed this should be a fling while we're here, but I also said if you wanted to make it a longer arrangement, then I'd do what I could to bring it about. And I will. I'm not going to shut you out of my life as soon as we're back in Edinburgh. My feelings won't change. So let's not worry that what we're doing here has a shelf life. If we need more time, we'll give ourselves more time. We just need to be a lot better at keeping things discreet in the office than we have been up here. And I have to think of how we can make it work without jeopardising either of our jobs.' He pressed a slow kiss onto her forehead and Felicity breathed slowly, taking in his words.

'Ok.' She let out a long, shuddering sigh. 'That's good, because I was really scared.'

'Don't be.' He held her for a few more moments, stroking her back firmly and filling her with reassurance. Finally, she broke away and took his hand.

They carried on towards the lochan. 'Time for your induction into wild swimming,' he said.

'I've paddled in the sea in Brighton.'

'Call that a taster session.'

'What got you into wild swimming? You're the least likely person I can imagine who would actually enjoy it.'

'I always enjoyed swimming but I'm not a big fan of pools. The smell, the bodies, you know?'

She giggled. 'Oh dear, that's funny. Too much flesh on show for you?'

'Yup. Some of the more exclusive pools are ok, but when they're open to everyone and you can't move, then it's not really my scene. Even the changing rooms gross me out a bit. After a few tough years on the dating scene, I decided I had to do something different.' He ran his hand through his hair.

'Why?'

'I was a bit scrawny and this woman once, well, she burst out laughing when she saw me... like undressed. It was so awkward. I mean hookups often are. But this was like one of those night-mares that you're sitting on the toilet and you suddenly realise you're not in a bathroom but on a stage and thousands of people are watching you.'

'Oh, Gavin. That's so horrible. And I understand. I had a truly awful boyfriend once who made me feel so crap about myself. It cuts so deep and the hurt never leaves you.'

'Yup. Exactly. But it made me think if I was a bit fitter, then I might have more luck. You know that my body wouldn't get in the way of making that special connection. And I enjoyed swimming, so I started going to some of the quieter beaches and swimming there instead of in pools. I joined a swimming club too, so I can use the pool if it's too cold or dark to be outside, though I still feel I come out smelling of chlorine.'

'Well, it's done the job in the muscle department. But Gavin, that's not the reason you're attractive. Not for me anyway. I mean, it looks good and it feels good, no lie, but I fancied you way before I knew what was under that shirt.'

He grinned and pulled her in for a side hug. 'Yay. My brains have finally won after all the years of training.'

She prodded him. 'I told you I'm not complaining about the six-pack.'

'Thanks.' He let out a little laugh. 'I think that's the lochan down there.' He pointed and the glimmering surface of the water was clear in the midst of the heather moor.

'Wow, this is so pretty.' Her eyes drank everything in as they reached the bank. 'I think I'd prefer to kayak on it, but I'd never get it up here.'

'You'll enjoy this too.' He opened the rucksack, pulled out a rolled-up picnic blanket and spread it on a grassy patch of ground close to the gleaming water.

'This is very organised.' She beamed.

'Sometimes I can manage without a PA holding my life together, though not often.' He lazed back on the blanket, propping himself up with his elbow and patted for her to join him. She mirrored his pose, facing him and smiling.

Bees buzzed around the heather and a few ducks swished past, breaking the peace with an echoing quack, but otherwise, silence prevailed.

'So, picnic or swim first?' Gavin rubbed the tip of his nose against hers as he spoke.

'Isn't it a rule not to eat before you swim?'

'We're not entering a competition or anything, so I don't think it'll matter. We'll just do whatever feels right.'

'I think I'd like to try the water first. I don't know if I'll even manage to swim. It might be too cold.'

'It should be ok in this weather, but we'll do whatever you want. I've got microfibre towels in the bag. They're great for drying fast and they roll up super small.'

'You really are an expert.'

'Aren't I just.' He sat up, crossed his arms over his chest and tugged off his shirt.

Felicity watched him. *Tasty.* He was an expert at many things. How he'd had such an unsuccessful time dating was a mystery because he was the whole package. His bedroom skills were better than anything she'd encountered so far.

Next, his shorts and boxers came off and on went his swim shorts. 'Your turn.'

'Ok.' Slowly, Felicity removed her crop top. Now he was watching her. She sat up tall and flicked her hair over her shoulder, like a mermaid, making sure he got the best view, then she slipped her bikini over her head.

'Should I tie it for you?'

'I thought you'd rather help take it off than put it on.' She wriggled out of her jogging shorts and knickers and pulled on her bikini bottoms as Gavin knelt behind her. He kissed the back of her neck before tying her bikini. She leaned back into him. 'We could just stay like this.'

'You're not getting away with that.' He gently massaged her shoulders. 'Come on, you'll enjoy it. I'll keep you safe. Then we can warm up after.'

It sounded utterly delightful, though it didn't take away the fact she had to set foot in the water first.

He strolled in like he was doing nothing more interesting than stepping into a bath. 'It's not too cold. It's pretty exposed to the sun.'

She took baby steps, dipping her toes at the edges. 'You think this isn't cold?'

'Just go for it. It's worse if you go slow.' He waded a little further, then sank down so only his head and neck were visible. 'It's actually really nice.'

She glanced from side to side. What was in here with them? When she had the safety of a kayak and a wetsuit, she never cared, but actually putting bare feet into the depths was a different matter.

Gavin swam towards her, his broad strokes cutting through the water. He straightened up and walked closer, his skin glistening with droplets. 'Come on, it's ok.'

'What lives in here? Fish? Frogs? Loch monsters?'

He chuckled. 'You're the one who knows all the local legends, you tell me.'

'Ha. You should ask Zach about that. He's written books about it.'

'Has he?'

'Yes. A fantasy book series called *Legends of the Loch*. I've read one of them even though it isn't my usual thing and it's actually really good. Both he and Briony write. Briony's written some kids' books, and she illustrates them too. They're so cute.'

'Wow. Talented people.' Gavin took her hand. 'I'll look out for that legend one. It sounds right up my street. I used to design games for stories like that.'

'I bet he'd love it if you did that for him.'

'I'm not sure I have the time these days. Now, come on. I promise there's nothing monstrous in here. Just some plants and maybe a few fish, though I'm not sure how the fish get all the way up here.'

'The eggs get caught in osprey feathers.'

'Do they?' He arched an eyebrow.

'Yeah. Someone asked me on a tour once, so I investigated.'

'Wow. You're full of information.'

'Well, I'm good at googling stuff.'

'And remembering it.'

She let him lead her deeper, trying not to gasp as the water got higher up her body. He'd obviously conditioned himself for this, as he didn't seem in the least perturbed by any of it.

'You're doing great. Once you relax, you'll enjoy it. It's so refreshing.'

Her body slowly became accustomed to the temperature and when her chest was finally under, she breathed. 'I kind of get what you mean.' She was a reasonably confident swimmer and Gavin stuck close as she ventured in a few metres, checking she could still feel pebbles beneath her feet.

'Wow. I never thought I'd like this, but actually it's fun.' She pushed out and swam with Gavin beside her. With nature all around, this had a raw appeal.

He reached out and pulled her towards him. 'I'm just glad we're here together.'

They looked at each other for a moment, their eyes meeting in a silent understanding, then he kissed her. She relaxed into the sublime perfection of the moment. He held her close, pressing against her, his hands clamped around her bottom. After a minute or two, he let go, smiled and led her out. On the bank, he unfurled a towel. It seemed to open up to a much bigger size than the rolled-up bundle had suggested. He draped it around her and although it was lightweight and soft, it dried her quickly and she kept it wrapped around herself as she sat back on the blanket.

'Enjoy that?' Gavin towelled himself down, flipped the towel over his shoulder and resumed his position from earlier, propping himself up on his elbow.

'I did.'

'Would you like lunch now?'

'Yeah. I think so.'

He sat up and unpacked the bag. 'Courtesy of the hotel.'

'I guessed that. I didn't think you'd snuck all the ingredients into your room and made it yourself.'

He grinned and opened the paper bag that was stuffed full of goodies. Felicity's appetite, which was usually pretty crappy, was fully functioning after the swim. Everything in the bag looked delicious, from baguettes to fruit pots and even some little cupcakes in a fancy box.

They ate their way through lunch, watching the sparkling surface on the lochan.

'You know I said Hayley was asking a million questions on messenger about us? I had to deflect her. Let's just hope your mum isn't in the salon any time soon. I can see Hayley blabbing without meaning to.'

'My mum isn't responsible for my choices.' He brushed some crumbs from the picnic blanket. 'But she could make things difficult, I concede that.' He let out a sigh. 'Let's make sure she has no further reason to put her nose in until we're sure where we're going.'

Felicity twirled a lock of her hair around her index finger, gazing over the sparkling lochan. They hadn't discussed the job since he'd first mentioned it and now didn't feel like the right time but it was there, hanging in the background along with the knowledge that if she applied, their relationship would surely have to end.

He dusted off his hands and cleared some crumbs from the blanket. 'Cuddle up and get warm?' He plonked the bag behind them like a pillow and opened his arms.

She shook the towel off her shoulder and curled into him, resting her head on the bag. He draped the soft towels across them like blankets and she closed her eyes with a sigh. This was bliss. Gavin softly kissed her brow, holding her close as the sun warmed them. He slipped a hand to her bikini top, slowly untied the string and freed her breasts. She moaned as he brushed his fingertips across them.

Could this get much better? Maybe. If she just had some assurance it wouldn't end horribly and that this dreamy moment wasn't lulling her into a false sense of security.

Chapter Twenty-Two

Gavin

Gavin swept a stray lock of hair off Felicity's forehead and gently slipped it behind her ear. Her eyes were still closed and her cheeks were rosy against the soft white pillow in his bed. Waking up next to her was something he could get used to. After spending hours cuddled up and enjoying each other's company by the lochan the day before, they'd come back to the hotel and spent several more hours 'cuddling' and enjoying more intimate time together. As it was Sunday morning, he didn't feel the need to break away from that. He touched his forehead against hers and closed his eyes again, hoping to block out the annoying thoughts that were tapping at his brain like someone chucking stones at a window.

She wasn't his girlfriend, even though she was the most special person he'd ever met. Why couldn't she be someone he'd met on online dating? Someone who had her own job, doing what she did, only for a different company, so they could be free to date as they pleased. And he would. No hesitation. He'd do everything to win her and keep her because he wanted her. Really wanted her. Not just to wake up beside for a week or two, but to wake up beside every day of his life. To have her at his side and to be at her side for whatever life threw at them. *Because I love her.* Pure and simple. He loved her so much it was tearing him apart. The uncertainty of their future was eating him and these beautiful moments together were the only thing keeping him going.

With a moan, she rolled into him and he pulled her close.

'I like a morning cuddle,' she said.

'Me too. In fact, I like an anytime-of-day cuddle with you.'

There was no rush to get up. And after a quick bathroom break each, neither had any desire to leave the bed for some time. All the desires they had were fully indulged beneath the covers.

It was almost eleven when Gavin flopped onto the end of the bed to pull on his socks, finally dressed. The shower was still running in the en suite; Felicity was washing her hair and singing. He smirked.

His phone buzzed from atop the bed and he spotted the caller ID straight away. His sister, Emily. Ok, that was weird. She rarely ever called him. They often sent messages back and forward but a call... Something serious must have happened.

'Hello?' He couldn't keep the concern out of his voice. 'What's up?'

'Hey Gav, how are you doing?'

He frowned. 'Me?'

'Yes, you.'

'I'm perfectly well, thanks.' He kept his voice low. 'Why are you calling? Is everything ok?'

'Oh gosh, yes.' She laughed and it seemed unnaturally high. 'I didn't mean to scare you. I just thought talking might be easier than messaging.'

'About what exactly?'

'Well, I heard from Mum that you and your PA had gone up to the house and she'd sent June to find out what was going on, as you wouldn't answer your phone.'

His heart sank and he balled his fists. His family loved meddling so much. But heat rose up his neck when he thought about the truth of what he'd been doing there. God, if they knew. He shuddered like he'd been caught in the act and was being punished by having a jar of maggots emptied over his skin. 'I already explained it to Mum and to June. What's the big deal? It was work stuff.'

'Hmm.' The noise sounded sceptical. 'Are you sure that's all it was? June told Mum you came out of a bedroom and your colleague was still in it. Mum also informs me that she's a particularly young and attractive colleague.'

'Oh, for god's sake.' His voice rose and he winced, hoping the shower was drowning him out. 'Mum and June are... Being sensationalist.'

'Are they?'

'Felicity is young, pretty, yes, I'm not denying it, but I'm her boss, remember?'

'I do. I remember very well.'

Her tone implied she didn't think *he* was remembering, which he was. The circumstances had made him break over that line which should not be crossed, but he wasn't going to explain himself. 'Look, my life is absolutely none of your business.'

Emily didn't reply for a few moments and her silence spoke volumes. She was interpreting his refusal to speak as a confession, which it might as well have been. He was guilty as hell.

Eventually, she sighed. 'I just don't want you to get hurt. None of us do.'

'And I—'

'We all know' – Emily cut in – 'that you want to meet someone but this isn't the right way to do it. Mum says this woman is very skilled at charming her way to the top. She started as a tour guide but managed to sweet talk Dad into letting her be your PA when she had zero qualifications for the job and no experience either. Mum says Dad always had a soft spot for her and she discouraged him from promoting her but it was the one time in his career he refused her. And now she's worried this woman is playing the same game with you.'

'I can assure you she's not.'

'Can you? Do you honestly know that for a fact?'

How could he? Only time would tell if she was sincere or not. His heart told him she was true but hearts often made mistakes, especially when they were in love. *There's that word again.* But surely Felicity wouldn't keep playing if all she wanted was a promotion. She'd said she'd like to be considered for the new position but that wasn't her motive. Was it? How could it be? No one was that good an actress, were they? The seed of doubt was in place and it unsettled him for a moment, almost as much as knowing what he was doing was wrong anyway. But he trusted her too much to let doubt win.

'Please, just let me live my life.'

'Oh, Gav. Don't play with fire. If you and her are having some kind of fling, how will that work out? Or are you planning on a long-term relationship?'

'We're colleagues. That's all I'm planning right now.'

Emily sighed audibly. 'If you say so, and I hope you'll keep it that way.'

'Felicity is a talented woman. If she gets promoted, it'll be on merit. I'm sure Dad saw that too and that's why he gave her the job as PA. She's demonstrated first-rate abilities and there's no reason she can't go far in the business but that's nothing to do with any personal feelings I may or may not have for her.'

'But that sounds like... I mean, are you in a relationship?'

He didn't answer.

'You can't go sleeping with her, then promoting her. You'll be strung up. No one will respect you ever again. This is exactly what Mum feared.'

'Who said I was sleeping with her or promoting her? Mum just doesn't like Felicity,' he muttered as the shower stopped. 'Because she wears nail polish.'

'What? Mum's not that shallow.'

'Isn't she? Sometimes it seems like it. And she definitely sees Felicity as a threat. She likes to handpick everybody and they all have to conform to a certain ideal but Felicity doesn't. Her figure, hairstyle, dress sense and everything about her are wrong.'

'Gavin, this is bad, you know that. Deep down, you must.'

'No, everything is fine. Just fine. Now, I need to go.' No point asking her not to mention this conversation to anyone. The second he hung up, she and his mum would be gossiping about it for the rest of the day.

'Just be careful,' she said. 'I'd hate you to get hurt.'

He ended the call with a sigh, dropped the phone onto the bed and put his head in his hands. Shit was about to hit the fan... Maybe it already had.

The bathroom door clicked open and Felicity came out with her hair wrapped high on top of her head with a white towel. Another large bath sheet was wrapped around her and she held it close. She looked at him with a slight frown.

'Who were you talking to?'

'My sister.'

'Oh. Well, I heard what you said.' She turned away and unwrapped the towel from her head, letting her damp hair loose over her bare shoulders.

'What did I say?' It was his turn to frown. He hadn't said anything bad, had he? Except denying he was sleeping with her, but he couldn't exactly confess to that.

'Something about me not conforming. My hair and body and everything.' She sat at the dressing table, her voice sounding choked like she had a cold, and when he caught her reflection, she blinked like she was holding back tears.

'Oh, god, Felicity. It was nothing like that.' He moved behind her, put his hands on her shoulders, leaned down and kissed her cheek. 'It's not me that thinks that. I was trying to explain what was happening here without actually telling her.'

'What *did* you tell her? That you didn't really like me because I'm every degree wrong.'

'No, you're every degree perfect, as far as I'm concerned. It's my mother who thinks otherwise.'

Felicity wiped her eyes and he perched himself on the edge of the stool beside her and pulled her in close.

'I would never say you're anything but perfect.' He stroked her bare shoulder. 'I'm so sorry.'

'It just makes me see how ridiculous this is. Everything we're doing here is mad. I was an idiot to think I could make this work for a week and then go back to normal.'

'If you were, then I was too. But let's not abandon hope yet.'

'Why not? Because you want to sleep with me some more before we call it a day?'

'Oh, come on, that's not fair. You know that's not what I'm saying.'

'Then what are you saying?'

'That I love you.'

'What?' She stared at him.

'I know. It's too soon to say that but it's how I feel.'

She put her hand on his knee, almost like she was bracing herself. 'I don't think it's too soon. I just didn't expect it. Christ, Gavin. I love you too but where the hell does that leave us?'

He cupped her face in his hands and gently kissed her brow. 'I don't know. Let's not think too hard about it. Let's just exist in the here and now.'

'Ok.' She sighed as she relaxed into him.

But they could only keep putting off the inevitable for so long. One day soon was going to be make or break day and at least one big decision would have to be made. Felicity shouldn't have to sacrifice her career for him. She'd proved how good she was at business and as her boss, it was his job to nurture that. His love couldn't be allowed to get in the way of her dreams. No woman in the modern world should have to give up her career for a man. If it came to the crunch, he would be the one to go, but something told him she wouldn't want that either.

She was the most important person in his life and he had to make sure she got the best deal possible.

CHAPTER TWENTY-THREE

Felicity stared at her bulging inbox and the sudden influx of messages on her phone, trying to make sense of the words swimming before her.

Monday morning was never going to be easy, not after the weekend of ups and downs they'd had. Saturday had put them on such a high but yesterday afternoon had been bittersweet. Gavin's call from his sister had damped things down and Felicity saw just what she was up against with his family. But he'd told her he loved her. *He actually loves me.* How could she go for the dream job now? What would people think if she got it? Everyone would think she'd slept her way to the top.

'I've got hundreds of messages asking me about my presentation to the board,' she said, glancing at Gavin. 'What presentation?'

Gavin pinched the bridge of his nose. 'Seriously? All I did was inform Julian I was considering creating a new role as project manager of the Highland Distilleries. And that you and I would pitch it to them at the meeting and that you'd also talk more about the developments. I thought it would sound good coming directly from you, as a lot of the ideas were yours. I should have asked you first, sorry.'

'I don't mind.' She'd done presentations on his behalf before but never her own ideas. Her stomach tensed and she felt a little sick. 'The tone of these messages is really odd.'

'How do you mean?'

'They're kind of teasing me. Look at this.' She held out her phone to show him the various messages, including ones that read: *are you about to become one of the execs?* And *ooh, look at you, the boss's pet!*

He slumped into a seat and sighed. 'Good god. How bloody annoying. What spin has Julian put on this? Sometimes I don't get him at all.'

'Gavin... What if...? Well, you said I could apply for that job but if I do...' She pressed her lips together and shook her head. 'Won't it look like I've slept my way into it... Not that I'm expecting to get it. Or to tell anyone... But if we're to have a future, we can't keep it secret forever.'

He rubbed at his clean-shaven jaw, watching her intently. 'Yes. I've thought about all of that too and I don't see an easy way out. I need to consider how to work it for the best. You are absolutely entitled to go for that job and don't let anything between us stop you.'

Did he mean that? He looked sincere. *And I would love that job.* But was she effectively signing the death warrant for their relationship?

'So, would you mind presenting your ideas at the meeting?' he asked.

Her heart and mind raced with jumbled thoughts, ideas, and worries. 'What if I screw up?'

He cocked his head. 'I suppose it's possible but I have faith in you. Just talk to them the way you've talked to me all week. Let your passion shine through.'

She let out a sigh, then took a deep inhale, trying to steady her breathing. 'Will you help me?'

'Of course I will. Just like you helped me.'

'If I practise what I'm going to say to you, that'll help.'

'Let's talk about the action plan first. That'll give us the best idea for the content of your speech. But when you're talking to the others, just act like you're telling me. Let all the Felicity fervour shine through.'

She chuckled. 'Felicity fervour?'

'That's going to be my new nickname for you. Fervent Felicity.' He smiled and her heart skipped a beat. He always made her feel special. She adored her place beside him, sharing his energy, relaxed and safe. If it were just the two of them and they could sweep away the crazy world of work and overbearing families, everything would be perfect. They could sort out the distilleries and be happy together. With their combined force, they could rule the world without too much difficultly. Except they couldn't. As they discussed the action plans, the paths cleared before them – the professional ones anyway. She knew the following day would be very different when Julian and the highland managers would be listening.

Before long, she had pages of notes, and her head was swimming. She could do this, couldn't she? If she was applying for the project management job, she'd have to get used to this.

'Right, let me practise.'

Gavin closed the lid of his laptop and steepled his fingers. She focused on him and took a deep breath.

'Start with The Glenbriar Distillery,' he said. 'It's the one with the fewest issues, so you can get some positive momentum going.'

'Ok.' She inhaled again, then blurted, 'The Glenbriar Distillery has a strong production foundation and it's important to maintain the quality of the products we're known for. Ugh...' She tossed her head back.

'Slow down. It's not a race. Just take it easy. You can do it. Remember how you once presented my skeleton notes at a meeting and everyone thought it was fantastic and it was? I gave you barely anything to work on and what you came up with was amazing. This is exactly the same.'

'Ok.' She took some more calming breaths. 'So, we'd like to implement a robust strategy for improvement and expansion with a range of planned upgrades, mainly for Inverbuie and Torrindhu. But the facilities at Glenbriar will be part of this. For example, the bottling facility will be used to support production at the other distilleries. We need to build the team ethos and work together.'

He nodded encouragingly and she went on. 'It's my vision to extend the chain into the community. It's imperative we source as many of the raw materials as we can from nearby suppliers.

This will help to reduce our carbon footprint and strengthen local links.'

'Excellent.' He smiled. 'I should invite Geoff Harrington to this. He'll love your green thinking.'

She beamed. 'Should I go on?'

'Sure. Talk me through the other plans.'

Suddenly he was the hot boss again, commanding the meeting of invisible people with his cool demeanour. Her heart swelled and she wanted to go to him and feel his arms around her. So much love was inside her but she had to focus. If they were to give themselves a fighting chance of their relationship ever being more than a fling, she must be able to separate work from pleasure.

'Right. Let's jump to Torrindhu. Our smallest and oldest distillery is a bit of a diamond in the rough and it's been neglected for too long. It has so much potential and we can start by improving the hospitality side of things. The tours need to start up again, either in conjunction with Glenbriar or possibly as dedicated tours with the addition of a shuttle bus. Currently, staffing issues are a problem and a priority would be ensuring it's properly staffed to continue efficiently. There might be opportunities for part time work or full-time jobs that overlap with some days in one of the other distilleries. In the spirit of staying local, we could also work with hotels and restaurants to offer package deals for visitors.'

'This is all great. I can't guarantee the audience tomorrow will be as receptive and they'll probably interrupt quite a bit.'

'That's ok. I know Julian will have plenty to say.'

'Yeah, leave him to me. I'm going to talk to him after this and give him a forum, so he doesn't feel the need to air everything during the meeting tomorrow.'

'Thanks.'

'And you don't have to say all of this. I'll be there too but I think it's only fair everyone knows how much of this idea was yours.'

'Thank you. I appreciate that.'

'Now, go on. Explain the plans for Inverbuie.'

'Inverbuie has the potential to be a real game-changer for us. It's in a modern building that might not be the most aesthetically pleasing, but it has the space for a café or restaurant. This gives us the opportunity to add fine dining to the whisky tasting session, possibly even cookery classes or cocktail workshops. The biggest change would be the exciting possibility of diversifying our production and adding a range of local gins to our portfolio. As the Inverbuie range is a consistent underachiever as far as our whiskies go, this would give it a whole new lease of life.' Now she was talking, the words flowed, and she forgot to be nervous, but would it be the same when Gavin wasn't the only person in the room? He already knew and approved of everything. His encouragement poured from every little smile and nod.

'That was great.'

Her shoulders sagged as the tension left them. 'I don't think I ever imagined having an opportunity like this.'

'I'm only doing what's right.' He pushed his seat closer. 'Before this week I was lost.' With a quick glance at the door, he added, 'In many ways.'

She swallowed. She'd helped him because she cared for him... loved him. *Why do I have to love him?* Their eyes met and she saw herself reflected in his irises. Her future was there, in his eyes, in his life, with him at her side, but it didn't seem possible to bring it about.

He raised his hand and pushed a strand of hair behind her ear. She loved it when he did that, like he was opening a curtain to see her better. Sometimes, she wondered if he could see right into her soul.

'Felicity, I—'

His phone buzzed on the desk and her heart froze as he looked away. What had he been about to say?

'I need to take this. It's Julian. Why don't you take a break? I'll come find you later.'

He leaned over as if to peck her cheek but she shifted and returned his kiss full on. He always tasted so good, clean and fresh. The phone stopped buzzing but she'd only just started. Her nerve ends humming.

'Later, Felicity, I need to call Julian.'

'Ok.' She left, watching him staring at his phone as she closed the door.

She headed straight to Briony's private quarters and knocked. No one replied. With a sigh, she went outside and sat on a bench overlooking the loch. Such tranquil beauty. If only her heart and mind could channel it, but her phone was bursting with messages from her work chat group. She opened it and sighed.

ELLA: what is actually going on? You're making a speech to the board? Does that mean you're an exec now? There are rumours flying around the office that you and Gavin are an item and he's promoting you!

WINNIE: to his wife

ELLA: or at least his PAHLF

LORAH: his what????

*ELLA: PA he likes to f**k (can't swear, Winnie doesn't approve)*

WINNIE: true. And hopefully, that acronym is not accurate in this case. I sincerely hope that is not what's been going on this week.

LORAH: @Felicity, do you even like him? Isn't he a sour face bleep bleep bleep?

ELLA: speaking objectively, he is nice looking, but I so wouldn't. Not that he'd look at me. Where are you, Felicity?

WINNIE: I'm more concerned about the other rumours that you must have slept with him to get into some promoted role. It's very disconcerting and I only mention it because I don't want you to get hurt. But honestly, the gossip mill is working overtime today.

Wasn't it just? Felicity's insides squirmed. This was just the start. Who was she kidding if she thought it was going to get any better?

Chapter Twenty-Four

Gavin

Gavin sat back in his chair, toying with his phone and staring at it. With a deep breath, he pressed the speaker button and called Julian.

'Ah, there you are,' Julian said. 'I thought I'd missed you.'

'I was in the middle of something.'

'We need to talk.' Julian's tone was snappy and business like. Of course he was the consummate professional who would never dream of having a relationship with an employee. *Why can't I be like that?* Just like he had been all his life... until now.

'Then shoot,' he said.

'Tell me about this promoted position you've invented.'

'I already outlined it to you in my email. I haven't written a detailed job description yet.'

'Right. And now explain why Felicity is making a speech tomorrow.'

'I told you that too. A lot of the development ideas are hers. It's only fair she has the chance to talk about them herself.'

'Diversifying and expanding the business is all well and good, but it comes with a lot of risks. I'd rather sell Inverbuie and

Torrindhu and focus solely on the expansion of Glenbriar, which was our original plan.'

Gavin ground his teeth but steadied himself. It had always been Julian's plan but they'd never agreed on it. 'Inverbuie and Torrindhu have a lot of potential, they just need investment.'

'Investment?'

'Yes. We need to create a more sustainable business model.' Gavin tapped his finger on the table, waiting for the objection.

'Sounds great in principle, but it's not realistic. You can't just snap your fingers and make these things happen.'

'Hence the need for the role of project manager. This is a long-term objective for the company. Selling distilleries should be a last resort.'

'And you don't see a problem here?'

'Should I?'

'Yes, Gavin, you should.'

'I don't know what you're talking about.'

'None of Felicity's ideas are necessary. She's come up with a bunch of hare-brained schemes to get you to invent a pointless role that she presumably thinks she'll walk into.'

'I haven't at any point suggested she walk into the role.' His insides squirmed because he knew she wanted it and honestly, he'd love her to have it.

'Good, because her management experience is zero.'

'As was mine.'

Julian let out a dry laugh. 'Not entirely. You'd managed plenty of teams and departments.'

'True, but everyone has to start somewhere.'

'So, you are considering it then?'

'That's my job. To consider every option.'

'What hold does she have over you?'

'Pardon?' Gavin balled his fists and swallowed. He should be grateful he had someone as ballsy as Julian, who was prepared to tackle the tough questions head on. It had worked in their favour before. He'd shone at the acquisition's meetings, adding some substantial names to their overseas portfolio, though some of that now seemed pointless. Why were they wasting so much time overseas when their roots and everything they stood for were right here?

'You heard me. Felicity has always been one to watch. She had your father wrapped around her little finger and now it seems like she's got to you too.'

'Let's stop this conversation. We aren't going to agree with each other on this but please come to the meeting tomorrow with an open mind.'

For a moment, silence prevailed, then Julian said, 'Sure. No problem.'

Gavin sighed and leaned back in his chair, massaging his forehead. If Julian showed up with an open mind, it would be the first of several minor miracles he needed. And Julian was right to be sceptical. All his concerns were valid. Felicity had every right to apply for the position when it came up, but how could Gavin promote her? If he did, he would have to step away from her for good.

He got to his feet and left the room that led through the dining room. It was quiet and only a few people were dotted around having a Monday lunch. He looked out of the large glass-fronted window wall towards the loch. Its surface glittered in the bright May sunlight. They'd been so blessed with beautiful weather. He blinked, doing a doubletake.

Close to the water's edge was Felicity and next to her was Briony with her two dogs. Standing in front of them was Brann the builder. Both women were laughing at him. He pulled up a bicep with a wide grin and Felicity reached out and squeezed it.

Gavin gritted his teeth. It was just innocent fooling around but his blood boiled seeing her put her fingers on another man. Brann was edgy with his tattoos, hair long enough to look cool and rough around the edges, a tight-fitting t-shirt and a toolbelt that was a metaphorical show of manhood if ever there was one. Gavin was ready to bet no one had ever laughed at him for being scrawny, but what did it matter?

Wasn't seeing her smile better than the heartbreak of having her upset at the thought of their fling ending? Because fling it must remain and it must end, and soon. Every indicator was pointing that way. With Julian so decided that Felicity was attempting to sleep her way to the top, how could it be any better? If the truth got out, it would look like that was exactly what she'd done and he couldn't allow that.

He sat at a table and lifted a menu, scanning it over briefly, then pulled out his phone.

GAVIN: Just about to have lunch. Want to join me? x

Crap. There went the kiss. Hopefully, no one from work ever saw it. Though people made mistakes like that all the time these days. Winnie George had once sent him a message saying 'love you lots' that was actually meant for one of her children. Her beetroot face had appeared at his office door later, apologising profusely.

Felicity must have read the message. She spun around and waved, excused herself from Briony and Brann and made her way to the dining room. Her soft ditsy dress fluttered around her as she headed up the path.

'Hey.' She stepped in through the French doors and sat opposite. 'How was the call?'

'As expected.'

'Julian hates me?'

'Hmm. Something like that.'

'Oh dear.' She bit into her lip.

'I asked him to keep an open mind tomorrow.'

'Oh god.' She pushed her hair behind her ears. 'I'm starting to panic every time I think about the presentation.'

'I know you can do it.'

She smiled. 'I'll do my best. I want to try.'

'And do you still want to apply for the new job?'

'I'd like to, but I don't think I'm qualified and... Well, what about us?'

'If you want to go for it, put us out of your mind.' His chest hurt but he forced a smile. She needed this opportunity more than she needed him. He had to stop his selfish heart from wanting her. She had a life to lead and if he gave her the best opportunity to shine, surely that was what was required. It would mean she could live her dream back in the town she loved. She didn't require his love to get by. If he still loved her from afar, that would be his business, but he couldn't jeopardise her future by making it seem like she'd slept her way into it.

'But Gavin, I don't want you to think I used you because I—'

'I don't think that. I know you wouldn't.' His gaze wandered outside and he spied Brann and Briony walking back up the path towards the hotel. 'What was Brann saying to you earlier when he was flexing his muscles?'

'Something about one of his kids measuring his biceps, then strapping a potato onto it. I'm not sure what he was on about.'

Why were they talking about this? Once Felicity was back up here in her new role, Gavin wouldn't be around to see if Brann pursued her or not. His insides burned at the thought. No one else should have her. But if he really cared, he had to give her this chance. 'Let's order,' he said. 'Then we should get back to work.'

'Yes, boss.'

He let out a little laugh, but that summed up exactly who he was.

Gavin woke early the next morning and found Felicity wide awake by his side. They just couldn't keep away from each other. 'Can't sleep?'

'Too nervous, or maybe I'm hyper.'

'I'd usually go for a swim before work when I feel like that, but I'm not sure if it's your thing.'

'Oh, why not?'

'You want to?'

'We've got plenty time, so yeah.'

Outside, it was a little cooler than it had been on previous mornings and a low mist rose from the loch, making it look eerie. Felicity's hand wound into his and he clutched it, clinging to these moments because who knew how many more of them they'd have?

He was so used to swimming wild in all weathers he took off his t-shirt without thinking. He only bothered with a wetsuit in winter. Normally, he could bear the temperatures once he got in and started moving. Felicity shivered as she took off her top and wriggled out of her jeans. Seeing her in that skimpy bikini started the usual chain reaction in his body and he knew he had to get into the water sharply to cool things down. Or should he take advantage of the quiet spot and make love to her right there and then? That was his body's preferred reaction, though not the sensible one.

'Come on, let's get in.' He wrapped his arm around her and led her to the water. Sense prevailing. For now. First time all week.

She let him lead her, squealing as the water got higher. 'This is freezing.'

'It's good for you.' He smiled. 'Seriously, it is. There are proven benefits. An increase in blood circulation, boosting the immune system, and it's also great for toning muscles.' He pulled a bicep. 'That's why I have muscles almost as big as Brann the builder and his potatoes.'

Felicity giggled. 'Gavin, I don't fancy Brann if that's what's bothering you. I only fancy you.' She slipped her arms around his neck, reached up and kissed him. The water may be cold but a roaring fire started inside him and he returned her kiss like there was no tomorrow. And maybe there wouldn't be.

By the time they got back to the hotel, they'd had a full workout and all their pent-up energy was relieved. Gavin dressed in his suit, sorted his cufflinks and made sure he looked the part. Felicity had returned to her own room to make sure she was immaculate too. How empty this beautiful suite was without her, but he had to get used to it. No point imagining how homely and wonderful it was with her by his side. Those fantasies couldn't have any more airtime.

The phone by the bed rang, taking him by surprise. Who would call him on that?

'Hello?'

'Good morning, Mr Sinclair, it's Janey from reception. You have a couple of people waiting in the foyer for you for this morning's meeting. They wanted me to let you know so you can come down.'

He frowned at his watch. Who had arrived this early and couldn't they just wait in the conference room? With an internal sigh, he said, 'Ok. I'll be down in a second.'

His brain had decided it was Angus Gibson from the Torrind-hu Distillery. He didn't seem used to things like this, though who was with him? Gavin would reassure him and maybe buy him a coffee before the meeting started. When he reached the bottom of the stairs and came face to face with his parents, he almost fell off the bottom step.

'What are you doing here?'

'Good morning to you too.' His mum stepped forward, took his face in her hands and kissed his cheek. 'We're here to give you moral support.'

'What?' He extricated himself from her and looked at his dad.

Dad threw out his hands like he'd just come along for the ride. 'You seem to have made some big inroads since last week, but we want you to know we're here if you need us.'

'I thought you were in Orkney?'

'We were, but we came back. We got to the house late last night.'

'Honestly, this is not necessary.' Gavin fiddled with his cuf-flinks.

'That's what I said.' Dad winked at him.

'Yes, it is absolutely necessary.' His mother narrowed her eyes. 'We need to be here to make sure you don't do anything that will jeopardise the reputation and future of the company.'

'Why would you think that, Mum? You were the one desper-ate for me to take over. I've done that and now I'm in charge. I'm doing everything I can to make sure the future is good for this company and its reputation is solid.'

'Then why are you letting a girl with no qualifications who was nothing but a tour guide until a year or so ago make an important speech to the board?'

He ground his teeth. 'Because she's given me the most robust and usable business solution of anyone. Everyone else is defeatist and wants to sell off Inverbuie and reduce Torrindhu to nothing but a name. Felicity's plans would mean a future for them both and with the money from the new acquisitions, we can easily afford to put funding in place for the schemes.'

'I think it sounds great.' His dad patted him on the shoulder.

Dorothy eyeballed her husband. 'Don't be so sentimental. The plans themselves are fine and I'm not knocking them. But from what I hear, she's sweet-talked you into creating some new position and she obviously fancies herself in it.'

'Mum, that is a completely unacceptable way to talk about Felicity.'

'What did I tell you?' His mum glared at his dad. 'He's completely smitten. She's ensnared him as I knew she would.

Dad eyed Gavin. 'This is all above board, isn't it?'

'Of course it is. I don't know where these rumours have come from. She's making a speech because this is something she's passionate about but at no point have I said she's going to get a promoted job. She's my PA and that's that.'

'Really? I know her game and I can guess what she's done to get you to give in to her.'

'No, that's—'

A little cough from behind interrupted him. He spun around to see Felicity standing a few steps up. Without looking at his mother, he cleared his throat, the tension rising to choking point. This was not what he needed half an hour before one of the most important business meetings of his life.

Chapter Twenty-Five

'Good morning, Felicity.' Frank Sinclair beamed almost too wide. Maybe he thought if his smile was bright enough he could dazzle them all and veil the awkwardness of the situation.

'Good morning.' Felicity's pulse drummed in her ears. It wasn't enough that she was about to make the biggest presentation of her life – oh no. She needed the added complication of Frank and Dorothy Sinclair. She'd rushed downstairs to look for Briony. Not this. Her mum had just got off the phone, saying her gran had taken a tumble and all Felicity's thoughts were jumbling around making a big mess. A quick chat with Briony might have sorted things out in the interim, but not now.

She'd overheard Gavin saying she'd never be anything more than his PA. Did that mean he didn't really want her to get this job? Was this how he was going to solve things? Perhaps expect her to sacrifice her career for them? She was almost willing to do it, except he'd given her hope. But had that been real?

Her eyes locked with Dorothy Sinclair's. Dorothy already suspected her of sleeping her way to the top. How could she prove that wasn't true if she got the job and she continued seeing

Gavin? No matter how she spun it, she couldn't make it work. Did she really want a future with him when this woman would always be there pulling the strings? Or was she big enough to handle it? Was he? Would he ever have the nerve to stand up to his mother? He'd missed out on a life he wanted before because his mother had hated his ex. *And here she is hating me.*

'Have you already had breakfast?' Frank smiled at Gavin and Felicity.

'Yes,' Gavin replied.

Felicity's tummy clenched at the thought and she was glad she hadn't eaten. Surely it would come back to visit if these nerves had their way.

'Then let's head for the meeting room,' Frank said.

'Actually, Dad, if you and Mum would wait in the lounge, I'd like to set up the room with Felicity. In fact, I'm not convinced the two of you being present is a good idea. It could seriously undermine me and my position.'

'I absolutely agree. And if you would feel happier, we won't come in.'

Dorothy glared at Frank. 'I'm not sure—'

'Yes, thank you,' Gavin said. 'That would be better. Once the meeting's over, I'll update you.'

'Very good.' Frank slapped his upper arm but Dorothy threw them all slaying looks.

Felicity heard her muttering but she didn't look back and followed Gavin towards the meeting room.

'I'm so sorry,' he said. 'I had no idea they were going to do anything like that.'

She sighed. 'I'm glad you told them not to come to the meeting. I think I might have thrown up with your mum staring at me like that.'

He held the door for her and as soon as she was in, he closed it and put his hand on her shoulder. 'I want you to shine today. Let everyone hear your ideas.'

'But... You just said...' She swallowed and the words wouldn't come.

'What did I say?'

'That I'd never be anything more than your PA. I wanted to apply for that job and this would have been a great start, but—'

'No buts. You're right. This is the perfect forum to practise in. I only said that because my mum put me on the spot. If you want to go for that job, I'll support you in any way I can.' His shoulders drooped a little, though his expression was determined.

She looked into his bright blue eyes. Where she'd imagined she saw a future for them both, she now saw a steely manager. The man his parents had raised him to be. He'd arrived. She'd helped him find his feet and now he was proving himself. Not only that, but he also believed in her. She had to do him proud, though she knew with every step she took closer to the dream job, she got further away from the man she loved.

He set up the room for Julian and Winnie to join on the video call and before Felicity had time to breathe, people were arriving. As the door shut behind Jerry Faulkner, Felicity caught a glimpse of Dorothy Sinclair sipping tea through very pursed lips. Her eyes were narrowed and her expression sour. This wasn't over by a long stretch. More was coming but Felicity had to put it out of her mind until this meeting was done.

Gavin closed the door fully and took his seat next to her. The expensive scent she'd grown to associate with so much intimacy and love swirled around, calming her just as his words and his embrace would do.

'Good morning, everyone.' He looked around the table, smiling. Yes, smiling. The grim expression he'd worn to cover his insecurities was gone. He was chilled and in control. 'I'd like to welcome you all here today. Just in case any of you aren't familiar with anyone else, I'll do a brief introduction. We have Julian Morrison, our senior exec, and Winnie George, head of advertising and marketing via video-link.' He pointed at the screen and Felicity was very glad Julian wasn't present in person. He may well be staring at her on camera but from here, she couldn't tell.

'Good morning,' Julian said.

Felicity smiled at Winnie, though Winnie obviously couldn't see who she was looking at either. Her expression remained flat as she said good morning.

'And in the room with us, we have Alistair Turner, manager of Inverbuie.' Gavin nodded at everyone as he spoke. 'Angus Gibson, chief distiller at Torrindhu. Jerry Faulkner, manager of the Glenbriar Distillery. And Victoria Bowley, who'll be taking minutes for us today.' Everyone said their good mornings before Gavin turned to Felicity. 'And of course, we have Felicity Swan, my PA. This week she's come up with some extremely exciting plans for the future of the chain and she'll be presenting these to you shortly.'

Jerry steepled his fingers and smiled at Felicity, though he was frowning slightly.

'As we all know,' Gavin went on, 'the distillery industry, as with all industries, is constantly evolving. On my visits last week, I saw for myself the areas that were performing well and those which are suffering due to lack of staffing or investment. In order to stay ahead of the game, we have to embrace change and innovation. That's why I've decided to appoint a dedicated project manager to coordinate upgrades and improvements to our distilleries. This person will be responsible for overseeing the implementation of new technologies, ensuring all projects are completed on time and within budget. The roles you do at present will remain unchanged and the command line will remain the same. This post is to allow someone to work with you but not take time away from your busy schedules.' He took a sip of water. 'Our Highland distilleries are the backbone of our company, and it's critical that we have a dedicated person who's responsible for them.'

'Has someone been appointed to the role?' Jerry asked.

'Not yet,' Gavin said. 'Once I have the full job description, we can advertise the post.'

'Wouldn't it be better to make it an in-house promotion and use someone who knows how the distilleries work?'

'Are you wanting it?' Alistair grinned at Jerry.

'No, I'm fine where I am. It just seems counterintuitive employing an outsider at this point.' He looked at Felicity and flicked up his eyebrow so briefly she thought she might have imagined it.

'The role itself is somewhat dubious,' Julian said.

Gavin ignored him and carried on. 'These are points for future discussion. Right now, I'd like to hand over to Felicity, who's going to talk through some of the development plans.'

Felicity's throat was so dry she was sure when she spoke it would be nothing but a croak that came out. All eyes were on her, some more encouraging than others. On the video-link, Winnie looked uncertain.

'So...' Felicity cleared her throat. 'Well, thank you, Gavin, for the welcome. I'd like to start by saying how honoured I am to have the opportunity to present these ideas. All week, and if I'm honest, for a long time before that, I've had so many ideas bouncing around my head for how we could move forward to ensure the rural Distilleries stay current and, most importantly, stay open. So, let me get started and if you have any questions, feel free to ask.'

She caught Gavin's eye and he leaned back and smiled. Alistair and Jerry nodded at each other.

Angus narrowed his eyes and frowned. 'While I appreciate the enthusiasm,' he said. 'I have some concerns about changing the way things have always been done. Change isn't always easy.'

'We fully understand that,' Gavin said. 'But at this juncture we have to embrace change, as staying put may lead to the only other alternative, which is unfortunately closure.'

Angus pulled a face and looked away.

'These proposals focus on investing in new technologies, expanding our production range, and diversifying. I believe that with these changes, we can increase profitability while still maintaining the quality and integrity of our products,' Felicity said. She tried not to make prolonged eye contact with anyone but was still keenly aware of the mixed bag of expressions.

'I think it all sounds great.' Jerry nodded his head with an approving smile. 'You were a top guide at Glenbriar when you worked there and I knew you'd go far. These ideas have great potential. I only hope whoever gets the job sees them through properly.'

'We'll make sure we employ a dedicated and driven individual,' Gavin said.

'I think you've got the very person right here.' Jerry pointed at Felicity. 'If these ideas were mostly hers, then she should be the one with the chance to follow them through.'

A warm flush flooded her cheeks and neck.

'I'm not sure about that idea,' Julian said. 'I have several issues regarding Felicity's suitability for such a role. Ideas are one thing but carrying them out entirely another.'

Gavin opened his mouth but Felicity spoke first. 'I don't expect to walk into a role like that. I'll make no secret of the fact I'd like to apply for it but if there's someone better qualified than me, then that's fine. What I've put to you here are ways I envisage the future for Sinclair Brothers. And I've always had the best interests of the company at heart. I know you do too, Julian, but your solution doesn't benefit everyone in this room. In fact, it would lead to job cuts and lose a huge part of the company's identity. These proposals not only mean everyone's job is secure but it could bring even more jobs and therefore benefit not just the company but also the area.'

'Indeed.' The snap in Julian's voice wasn't lost on her. 'I know your views on the community but as I've said before, our role isn't to benefit the community. While I accept that may be an outcome of any expansion, we shouldn't look on it as something we're honour bound to do. Because if job cuts come in the future, which they may, we can't afford to look at it sentimentally.'

'No one's looking at it sentimentally,' Gavin said. 'We're simply looking at the wider benefits, just as we'd have to assess the wider downfalls if we chose to sell.'

'Felicity, can I ask,' Winnie piped up. 'If you feel ready to take on a management role? It's a big step up. I know you're more than capable when it comes to the ideas and planning, but where's the support mechanism? Has there been adequate training?'

While kindness was in those words, some scepticism was there too.

'Whoever gets this job,' Gavin said, 'will have full support from the other managers, plus Julian and myself. We can set up a mentoring programme if necessary.'

'Or you could make sure you employ someone who knows what they're doing and doesn't need one,' Julian said.

'There's never any harm in showing compassion to employees in new jobs, Julian. Wherever they may be in their careers.' Gavin stared hard at the screen where Julian's cheeks coloured slightly.

Felicity caught Gavin's eye and almost laughed. He was a different man. This boardroom style Gavin was very sexy. Not that she was supposed to be thinking about things like that just now.

Even when he'd been grumping his way through meetings to hide his failings, he'd been hot, but now he was king of the room.

'Does anyone have anything they'd like to say before we move on?' Gavin looked around.

Felicity held her breath. She'd done it, but it wasn't over yet.

'Then let's move on to the more specific changes we'd like to implement and perhaps have a brainstorm about timeframes and resources.'

Alistair and Jerry had several ideas and jollied Angus along. Gavin opened his action plan on the smart board and collected their ideas and suggestions in an aesthetically pleasing way. He dragged items from place to place, moved timeframes and arranged actions.

'I think that's everything looking solid,' he said. 'Let's break there for lunch and we'll reconvene at one thirty. Julian and Winnie, you're welcome to join us again, but if you'd rather work together in the office and come back to us with your suggestions later, that would be fine.'

They agreed to come back later. Gavin leaned over on the pretext of putting something in his briefcase and whispered to Felicity, 'You did great. Well done. I'll head for lunch with Mum and Dad. Are you ok on your own?'

'Of course. I'll grab something with Victoria.'

Victoria was delighted when Felicity approached her. 'I'd be a spare part otherwise.'

They shared a table with Jerry, Alistair, and Angus, and the conversation strayed to work. Felicity didn't really mind. It was easier that way. From where she was sitting, she saw Gavin talking to his parents. Two minutes later, the three of them appeared at the table and joined them.

Felicity caught Gavin's eye as the conversation moved to Frank and Dorothy and how their retirement was going.

'Why are you here?' Jerry asked them. 'Don't you trust the lad?' He winked at Gavin.

It wouldn't have surprised Felicity if Dorothy said no.

'Of course we do.' Dorothy smiled. 'We were just passing and thought we'd pop in and say hello.'

Gavin raised his eyebrow and Felicity grinned. Dorothy wouldn't have accepted an excuse like that from them but here she was reeling them off herself.

Frank and Dorothy headed off for a walk after lunch and Felicity and the others worked through the afternoon until a robust plan had taken shape. They all left with smiles and lots of chatter. Even Angus seemed quite buoyant and excited.

Felicity checked her phone and saw a new message from Winnie. Her mind flickered as she registered it was a DM and not on the group chat.

WINNIE G: loved all your ideas today. Well done, you're a talented lady. Everything seemed very professional and thank goodness after so many people insinuating you and the boss were in cahoots (so to speak – you get my drift). I'm so glad that's not the case, though he's clearly very impressed – you should have seen his face when you were talking. He looked in awe! Speaking of which, what a difference in him. Seemed like he'd had a personality transplant. First time I've ever thought him remotely human but at the same time quite in control of the room. Obvs this trip has done the world for you both! See you soon! X

Felicity let out a sigh, not wanting to imagine how things would be if it ever got out that she and Gavin had been 'in cahoots' many times that week.

'Thank goodness that's done.'

She looked up to see Gavin packing away the conferencing hardware.

'It went ok, didn't it?'

'More than, Felicity. It was brilliant. You were perfect. You are perfect... For the job. If it was just up to me and Jerry, you'd have it. He was all for handing it to you there and then.'

She quirked a little smile, hoping he'd return it, maybe even give her a hug but he looked back at what he was doing. A wave of emotion overcame her for a second, almost knocking her sideways. Then she remembered Frank and Dorothy were still about, so it was sensible not to do anything silly.

'Mum and Dad want me to go to the house tonight and talk more about business.' He still didn't look at her. 'I really don't want to but I can't exactly say no without it looking, well, you know...'

'Yes. I do. That's fine. You should go.' Yes, he should. Though a piece of her heart broke off, making her insides sting.

'I'll message you.' He glanced at her. 'And truly, you were wonderful.'

'Thank you.'

They smiled at each other for a few seconds but it felt weird. After they'd been so close, it was like they were back to how they'd been at the start of the week, just looking, but not daring to get too close. Felicity backed out of the door with saggy shoulders.

As she crossed the dining room, she heard someone calling her name. She whirled around, hoping to see Briony, but Dorothy Sinclair was sitting at a small round table for two by the window. She waved Felicity over with a saccharine smile etched onto her face.

'Congratulations,' she said. 'Sit down. I'll order you a drink if you like.'

'I'm too exhausted for a drink.'

'Of course, completely understandable. Have a seat anyway, just for five minutes. I'm waiting for Frank. We walked around the loch this afternoon and he bumped into some golf club friends. He's still talking to them. I needed a cup of tea, so I abandoned them.'

No getting out of this then. Felicity took the seat opposite.

Dorothy poured herself a cup of tea and sipped it. 'So, you gave quite a wonderful presentation by all accounts.'

'Indeed.' Felicity tried to smile but she had a funny feeling this conversation was about to nosedive.

'Julian called and said you'd made a somewhat impassioned speech. I think you redeemed yourself in his eyes, so that's good, isn't it?'

'Um, yes. Very good.' Almost a miracle. Julian had never openly disliked her, but she'd always had the impression he disapproved of her.

'And apparently now you're after this promoted position. Frank and I will fully support your application, of course.'

Would she? 'Um, thank you.'

'Though, in the nicest possible way, I hope you understand the role is purely professional from here on in.'

Felicity's cheeks scalded her. She must look like a tomato. 'Of course I do. I mean, it was always—'

'Please.' Dorothy's voice was stern but still somehow sickly sweet. 'No need to embarrass either of us. Whatever you may have done to persuade my son to invent this role, you'll have to get it on your own merit. If you are successful, there should be no possible way for anyone to suggest you got it in a nefarious fashion. My son is, of course, a very eligible bachelor. It's not hard to see. But he's never been good at choosing for himself. Honestly, even as a child, we had to pick out his clothes, as he could never decide. I picked his subjects for him in High School otherwise he'd still have been puzzling out what to take. I haven't found his ideal life partner yet but I'm working on it. If in the interim he chooses to carry out short-term flings with women who throw themselves at him, that's his business. But be assured once they've run their course, he's not silly enough to let them continue, especially when the reputation of the business is at stake. Now, I fully admit, I was wrong to think you weren't suitable for the job of PA – you've shown yourself vastly overqualified. And for a while I thought Gavin had been drawn in but I should have given him more credit. He took this job on knowing all the responsibilities that go with it and after talking to him today, I know he'll always put the business first.'

Felicity nodded. What else could she do? He'd said he would work things out but they'd also agreed what happened in Glenbriar would stay in Glenbriar and that stay was drawing to a close.

'I wonder if you'll excuse me. I could do with a rest. It's been a busy day,' Felicity said.

'But of course.'

Felicity headed for her room. The rollercoaster of the day was about to crash, and she needed to be out of sight when it came off the rails completely.

CHAPTER TWENTY-SIX

'I had a wonderful chat with Felicity this afternoon.' Dorothy leaned back in her armchair in the living area back home.

Gavin had mixed feelings about showing face here again after being caught earlier in the week, almost like he was returning to the scene of a crime. Not to mention the thought of Felicity back at the hotel on her own, though he had to stop thoughts like that and make them none of his business. 'Did you?' No doubt his mother would tell him whether he wanted to hear or not, though he highly doubted it was wonderful. For Felicity anyway.

'Yes. I congratulated her on her ambition. Julian said he was pleasantly surprised by her.'

'Why is Julian still contacting the two of you about business matters?'

'We're friends.'

Gavin cocked his head. Was this any better than him seeing Felicity on non-work-related business? His parents were getting business info from an insider they were calling a friend. 'Well, I don't like it.'

'Oh, don't be silly. He had nothing but kind words to say. And when I spoke to her, she was delighted. I just wish she hadn't reduced herself to seduction techniques to get her own way. The good thing is, now we all know what she's been up to, she'll have to take the next step by herself and not use her dubious charms to get what she wants next.'

'Mother!' Gavin glared at her. 'She didn't.'

His mother held up her hand. 'If she didn't, she didn't, but I'm not stupid. I'm sure she understands the position now however. That'll make her see if she wants a promotion, she'll have to use the talents she showed in the meeting room and not... Well, whatever other methods she used before.'

Gavin knocked back a shot glass of their finest Torrindhu. 'This needs to stop. Right now. No more of this. How dare you speak about her like that? What right do you have?'

'Gavin. Please, don't shout. I think you've had too much to drink.'

'I haven't had nearly enough. But I don't need a drink in me to tell you that I won't accept this anymore.'

His dad opened the door and glanced between them. 'What's going on?'

'I was telling Gavin how impressed Julian was with Felicity, and well—'

'No, Mum. That is not what you were doing. You were insulting a very intelligent employee and trying to drag her down.'

'I... Well—'

'Julian said she was inspired,' Dad said, seemingly oblivious to the tension, or perhaps hoping he could diffuse it by ignoring it. 'I always believed she'd go far, but you saw the potential and acted on it.'

'Yeah.' Gavin poured another whisky. He didn't even like it that much but it numbed his brain. He downed it in one. 'I'm going to bed. I've had a long day.'

Her attitude towards Felicity was too hurtful.

He went to the kitchen and poured a large glass of water. Drinking so much whisky had been stupid and he wanted to cleanse it from his system.

As he passed the living room door on the way to the stairs, he caught his mum's voice.

'I suppose at least if she does get this promoted job, she'll be working up here and away from temptation.'

'Oh, Dorothy, don't be silly. Felicity is a very professional young woman. She can't help it if she turns a few heads.'

'Indeed. It's who turns her head I'm more worried about.'

Gavin rubbed at his neck. It felt itchy. In fact, his whole body felt like his skin was crawling. Should he walk on by and pretend he hadn't heard? Felicity deserved the right to move on in her career and he didn't want anyone looking at her and thinking she'd got it in disreputable circumstances. He'd crossed the line with her because he'd fallen in love with her. Now he had to fall back and let her move on.

'Mum.' He stepped inside the room. 'This obsession with Felicity is vitriolic. Please stop. I can't make you, but I'm asking you. Do it for me. And stop acting like she's some whore trying to sleep her way to the top. Accept that she's intelligent enough to do a good job and just because she happens to dress nicely, wear nail polish and look attractive doesn't mean she's using that as a means to get ahead.'

He didn't wait for an answer. He knew his mum well enough to know she wouldn't take his words well and she might digest them over time.

Felicity was deserving of her position, and she would have got there without him. Maybe he'd sped things up for her but she already had the skills. He'd said he'd support her in whatever choice she made and he stood by that. But how to break that news? Definitely not in a text, though he wasn't sure he could get the words out and look her in the eye at the same time. He could hardly bear even thinking them.

It wasn't like a breakup speech because they'd never been a couple, not really. What they'd had hardly constituted a relationship but he couldn't shake that feeling he had every time they were together that they were meant to be. How well they fitted. They adapted for each other, tried new things and thrived in each other's company. Now they had to restrict that to the workplace.

The stripped bed he'd shared so beautifully with her earlier in the week had been made up and now had a pretty floral duvet on it. The pattern reminded him of her ditsy dresses. He tossed off his shirt and threw it onto the chaise, smacking away the memories of her laid out for him like a beautiful nymph, falling apart at his touch. But so what? Good sex didn't equal a good relationship. He sat on the bed, gripping the mattress and breathing slowly. Convincing himself their relationship was shallow just wasn't working, because he knew there was more to it. So much more.

If the work connection didn't exist, they'd be perfect together. But it did.

He toed off his shoes, breathing slowly in and out, holding back an emotional dam that wanted to open. If he let go, he might scream, shout, smash things or even cry like a baby. Ten years ago, he'd walked away from a woman he wished he'd hung onto. Finally, he'd found someone else. Someone even better for him and he was going to do exactly the same thing again. What choice did he have?

He stripped off his trousers and lay back on the bed, scrolling through his phone, wanting to go straight to the message thread with Felicity but at the same time dreading it. He wasn't going to say anything there. That much he owed her, at the very least.

Finally, he pulled open messenger and saw a green dot next to her name. That didn't mean much these days. People left their devices logged in all over the place but for some reason it felt like she was lying in much the same position as him back in her hotel room. Maybe she was wondering what to say to him. A weird sense of an alternate reality hit him, like he was in a movie and the viewers could see both him and Felicity on a split screen; their positions mirrored each other but looked almost like they were lying side by side, only divided by that thin diagonal line. He glanced at the empty space beside him and he could almost see her there. And it would be so natural. In years to come, they could be like this, companionably reading or chatting before bed, children asleep in other rooms of the house – because they had children. They could be good parents; they were good people and had lots to offer. They would take holidays by the sea and teach the kids to wild swim and kayak, climb hills at the weekend and be a family.

Why was he still thinking like this? It was like dieting. Every time he told himself to do one thing, his brain did the other.

He typed out a message and as he did, three dots appeared. Surely not? She wasn't really doing exactly the same as him, was she?

GAVIN: you did great today. I'm so glad you're going to apply for the new job. Hope you're ok. Sorry, we didn't have more time to chat. X

Miss you, love you and all the other things he wanted to say, he kept back, conceding only the one kiss. He hit send and barely a second later, a message pinged in.

FELICITY: Can't thank you enough for the opportunity you gave me today. I was petrified but it was such a good experience. Hope you're having a great evening with your parents. Speak soon x

He let out a mirthless laugh. They'd sent each other the same meaningless messages at almost the exact same times. Because they both knew the game was up.

GAVIN: You always make me proud. Sleep well. X

If she was feeling anything like him, she wouldn't close her eyes all night.

CHAPTER TWENTY-SEVEN

Felicity

'Hi, Mum.' Felicity wanted to give her mum the best news and sound excited about it but as she perched on the end of her bed, her heart was heavy and her eyes raw. Without Gavin beside her, she'd hardly slept. How had she got so used to him being there after so short a time?

'Oh, hello, darling. How are you? Is everything alright?'

'It's more than alright, Mum.' Felicity pushed out her happiest tone. 'I'm on a once in a lifetime business trip and yesterday I got to make a really important speech.'

'Oh, wow!' Her mother exclaimed. 'That's great.'

'I know. And there's a chance for me to apply for a new job that would make me a project manager and would mean I could move back to Glenbriar.'

Which was exactly where she'd love to be. Only without Gavin, it felt like the second prize.

'I'm so happy for you, sweetie. Wait until I tell Dad and the others. Everyone will be so chuffed.'

The smile in Mum's voice shone through, warming Felicity's cold heart. 'Thanks, Mum. How's granny doing? Is she still in the hospital?'

'No, she's back at the care home and getting up to her usual trouble.'

'Oh? What's she done now?'

'Nothing serious but, oh my, she's been talking a lot about you.'

'Me?'

'Yes, she made a prediction about you.'

'Really? I dread to think.' Granny had claimed to have 'the gift' and sometimes she had a scarily accurate knack of knowing too much. Since the dementia had kicked in, Felicity wasn't sure what to make of her ramblings. 'What did she say?'

'She said you're going to marry a rich and handsome young man.'

Felicity couldn't help but smile. 'Really? She didn't happen to say when and give you his name and address, did she?'

Mum chuckled. 'No, she didn't. But is there anything I should know about?'

'Not really.' Nothing she could tell anyway.

'That's not an out and out no then.'

'It's as good as. And definitely no need to buy any hats.'

'Ah, pity. You're so beautiful, you'd be the perfect bride.'

'Thanks, Mum.'

'Well, who knows what the future holds? Granny might just turn out to be right.'

'Maybe she will.' Felicity's mind rushed back to Gavin. How could it not? He was handsome for sure and he was definitely well off. Did granny's prediction mean there was hope for their relationship yet? Or was it madness pinning her hopes on the ramblings of a wonderful old lady who could no longer remember her own name? But as Felicity said goodbye to her mum and ended the call, an odd flicker sparked in her chest. Maybe all wasn't lost yet.

Just face Gavin and ask him. Their messages last night had teetered about not going too close to anything contentious. How weird had it been for them both to message at the same time? But it wasn't really a surprise. Her connection to him often felt like it was on a higher plane. Their souls had that invisible bond and their physical connection reinforced it.

Breakfast was a complete no. She couldn't face it, so she held off leaving her room until just before nine, then headed for the conference room. She half hoped Briony would be at the desk and could give her a hug, but her friend had been so tired the last few days. Felicity wouldn't blame her if she was still in bed, especially when she'd kept her up late last night chatting about the job. Briony had insisted on feeding her champagne even though the poor woman could hardly walk now her pelvic pain was so bad.

Felicity opened the conference room door. Gavin was at the table with his laptop out next to two mugs and a plate of croissants and pains au chocolat.

'Gavin.' She tilted her head, torn between annoyance and gratitude.

'I'm not forcing you to eat them. They're just there in case you get peckish.'

She didn't need anyone looking after her but knowing someone cared was just what she needed. Sitting, she lifted the coffee, then took a corner from one of the croissants.

He looked at her and sighed. 'We need to talk about logistics today. I know it's not the most exciting subject, but we should get things moving.'

'Before you even appoint the project manager?'

'That's partly what I mean. I need to consider what their exact role will be and what tasks the current managers can carry out.'

'I need to ask you something.'

Gavin got to his feet, sighed and moved to the window. Leaning on the sill, he looked out. 'Sure, shoot. Ask me anything.'

Her heart raced. 'What will happen to us if I apply for that job?'

The back of his hairline was perfectly trimmed and sat along the sharp edge of his collar. He raised a hand and ran in over the back of his neck before turning to face her. 'No matter how I say this, it's not going to be easy for either of us. But we both know it's not appropriate for us to continue seeing each other.' He held eye contact and she tried to as well. 'I can't be involved in the interview process. I'll have to delegate it to Julian and someone from HR. I could possibly invite one of the distillery managers to be on the panel, but it can't be me. You'll have to earn the job yourself. And I believe you can do it.'

'But…' She swallowed. 'Does that mean you're going to tell people about us?'

He shook his head. 'No. I don't want to compromise your career. If you get the job, I want everyone to know you've earned it. I probably should declare our personal connection, but that could jeopardise your chances, so instead I'll say I don't think it's right me being on the panel as you and I have worked closely together for some time now and it could put both of us at a disadvantage.'

'And us?'

'Sorry, Felicity.' He looked away again. 'There can be no us.'

Tears pricked at the corners of her eyes. She knew this was coming, but it still felt like a punch in the gut. 'I understand.' She tried to keep her voice from shaking. 'I think.' Though she didn't have to like it and she couldn't stop herself wishing he would find a better solution, even if she knew in her heart there wasn't one.

'I care about you so much and your career is so important. You have an amazing future ahead,' he said. 'I want you to succeed and you can't do that if we're together. We'll never be able to stop people saying you slept your way into the job, even if we know it's not true.'

She nodded, covering her mouth with her hand. How could she stop *herself* thinking that was exactly what she'd done without meaning to? She might achieve a career goal she'd not even dreamed of before this week, but at what cost? Her personal dream of a future with Gavin was over.

'I know it's the right thing to do.' She could barely hold back the tears. 'If I apply for the job, I'll be professional, I swear.'

He moved around the table, sat beside her, and took her hand, his eyes glistening. 'I know you will. You're a wonderful woman. And you must go for the job. You're the perfect candidate and I know it's everything you've dreamed of.'

She stood abruptly. 'I need a moment. I'll be back shortly and we can talk about work.'

'Take as long as you need. I completely understand.'

She hurried from the room, up the stairs and into her bedroom, letting the tears flow, making sure no one saw her. Who needed unnecessary drama? These feelings were hers alone and she had to deal with them. Her heart was going to split in two and she wasn't sure it would fit back together ever again.

CHAPTER TWENTY-EIGHT

Gavin

July

Gavin straightened his tie, checking his reflection in the office restroom. Who was this man staring back at him? A man who, for the second time in his life, had walked away from the love of his life. And this time was even worse than the first.

What is wrong with me? Maybe he was spineless as well as being a stuffed shirt. And a stuffed shirt was all he was once again. The Edinburgh office was like a mystery place where he didn't quite get what was going on. When he'd been in Glenbriar with Felicity, everything had made sense. Now his life had lost direction and purpose.

He grabbed his suit jacket from his office and left for Princes Street. Every day he walked this street when arriving and leaving and every day he thought of that day at Christmas when he and Felicity had gone to The Espresso Lounge, and she'd almost walked out in front of a bicycle. But he wasn't a superhero, as she'd suggested. *I'm nothing but a coward, too afraid to chase what I want or decide for myself what's really important.* If he was brave, he would have chosen a life with Felicity and damn the company, his parents, and anyone else who tried to get in the way. He could walk into a job in programming tomorrow, but if he did, the name Sinclair Brothers would die with him. If he left, would it still be looked at as a family-run business? Did these things really matter? He didn't want them to, but that ever-gnawing guilt was there. He didn't want to let anyone down, but in trying to do the right thing, he'd let himself down.

Maybe there was irony in the fact his parents had chosen to meet him at The Espresso Lounge. Felicity had sat in almost the same place as his mum was sitting. She'd been dazzling in her reindeer jumper.

'There you are, darling.' Dorothy waved him over.

Gavin slung his jacket over the back of the chair and sat beside her. 'It's so muggy out there. Feels a bit thunderous.'

His mum fanned herself. 'I hate it when it's like this. We should have met at the house and walked to the beach.'

She was alluding to the Gullane house, of course. He usually liked visiting them there as it afforded good swimming opportunities but something had kept him away. His own bachelor pad in Leith was all levels of chic but completely soulless. Just like his life, it was empty without Felicity.

'So, how's it all going?' His dad grinned and rubbed his hands together.

Whatever else happened in his life, Gavin had to accept there was no taking the company away from his father. Dad just couldn't help being interested in all the goings on. Instead of resisting it, Gavin needed to embrace it. His dad had shown him he was sensible enough to keep out of the big decisions and had kept out of the meeting about upgrades and diversification in May.

He let out a sigh. 'I'd like to say everything is going great, but I'm not sure it is.'

'Why is that?' His dad looked puzzled and his mum sat back and blinked like she couldn't believe her ears.

'Some of the changes aren't working for me the way I'd hoped.'

His dad frowned. 'Dear, dear. I was delighted to hear Felicity got the new project management job. That was a fantastic appointment. That's going well, isn't it?'

His mum pursed her lips and fiddled with her wedding ring. 'Quite remarkable the power she holds over men. I was surprised at Julian.' Her words were little more than a murmur but Gavin heard them loud as a klaxon.

'Change the record, Mum. I told you before I don't want that kind of talk about my employees. It's totally unacceptable. No one can say Felicity hasn't earned that job on merit. Julian is her severest critic, but even he conceded that her interview coupled with her on-the-ground experience made her the best candidate.'

Dorothy put her hand to her chest. 'I meant nothing by it.'

Like he believed that.

'Why didn't you do the interviews yourself?' His dad asked.

Gavin had deliberately kept out of it as much as he could and kept his congratulations to a professional minimum. The day she'd cleared her stuff from the office before she moved to Glenbriar, he'd worked from home. How could he face seeing her leave his office one last time? He couldn't even bring himself to appoint a new PA.

'Let's order, then I'll explain.' Though he wasn't exactly sure how. Even though he knew what he wanted to say, he wasn't sure it made any sense. Or if it only made sense to his one-track mind.

Once he had his hands wrapped around a skinny latte, he looked between his parents. 'Business is going great. Julian does a great job running the Edinburgh office, so much so I'm almost obsolete.'

'He's very efficient indeed.' Dad sipped his tea.

'But that's hardly a problem,' His mum said. 'Or is something wrong elsewhere?'

She didn't mention Felicity, but Gavin was certain she was hinting at her being the source of the problem.

'The problem is my job. It feels like a waste of time. My role isn't to wander about the office like a figurehead.' *Or a stuffed shirt, a plank in a suit, or a spineless twat.* 'I feel like I'm in the wrong place. The heart of the company is in Glenbriar, close to the Highland distilleries. When I was there, I had a meaningful role. The job Felicity is doing is great but I should be there too. It should be as much my baby as hers.'

His mother blinked, then gaped – probably because of his word choice. 'I'm not sure I see what you're getting at.'

'The Highland Distilleries are the backbone of this company, but we've got complacent, thinking they'll run themselves. Now things are changing, I should be there, overseeing every part of it.'

'I quite agree.' Dad nodded. 'I always wanted to make the HQ in Glenbriar, but your mother liked living in Edinburgh. That's why we divided our time between the two.'

'Because Edinburgh is the best place to be when it comes to business.' Mum folded her arms. 'We agreed that long ago. I know this is a topic we've discussed before, but I truly believe the company's HQ is better suited to Edinburgh than Glenbriar. Glenbriar simply doesn't have the level of infrastructure or access to resources that Edinburgh does.'

'I'm aware of that, Mum. But technology has moved on apace since you and Dad took over.'

'But we can't just go relocating the staff, not when they're based here and have family here. Moving the headquarters would cause disruption to their lives. We don't want that kind of issue arising. It'll be a nightmare.'

'I'm not suggesting relocating anyone other than myself.'

'But if you're in Glenbriar, how will you keep up with developments and trends? Being based in Edinburgh put us at the forefront.'

'It's not the nineteen eighties, Mum. I can be on video calls anywhere in the world. If I need to be in Edinburgh in person, it's an hour and a half on a train. How is that a big deal?'

She shook her head and raised her finger. 'I perfectly understand the appeal of Glenbriar and its proximity to the rural distilleries, but other than that, I see no need for such an upheaval. Like you said, you can video call anywhere, so why not just video-call Glenbriar? That's the simplest solution.'

Gavin sighed and took a sip of his latte. Mother had spoken. She threw his dad a curt smile like she'd just had to diffuse a petty squabble between preschool children and risen victorious – as usual.

But this time, he was going to choose for himself.

'It's my decision, Mum. That's what I'm doing. I'm moving to Glenbriar.'

Her mouth fell open. 'I would urge you to think very carefully about that, son.'

'It sounds like he has.' Dad smiled and patted her hand. 'And I support the decision. I often felt we would be better placed close to the distilleries that are the backbone of the company. In fact, I think our being so much in Edinburgh has been some-what detrimental. We let things slip at Inverbuie and Torrindhu. What you're proposing, son, sounds like a workable plan and I'm pleased.'

'Thanks, Dad. I feel like I'm not making the impact I want to make. I want to be closer to the operations. The move won't affect the operations of the Edinburgh office. Julian will continue in his role and I'll be available to handle any necessary business there. But my primary focus will be on Highland Perthshire.'

His dad looked at him, his eyes a little misty. 'Follow your heart, son, and the rest will fall into place.'

'I'm not at all convinced.' His mother narrowed her eyes and stared at her coffee cup. 'Why do I get the feeling there's more to this than you're letting on?'

Gavin glanced away and shook his head. Why indeed? Because she had an uncanny knack of sniffing things out. Her nose for church gossip was famous but when it came to her children, it was a miracle she hadn't fitted him with a tracking device.

'Actually, there is something else weighing on my mind.'

'Oh? And what's that?' Dad frowned.

His mum slowly blinked in a very *I knew it* kind of way.

'I met someone and she's changed me. I want to be with her.'

'Aha!' Dad clapped his hands together. 'This is wonderful.'

Mum held up a hand to silence him. 'Let's not celebrate just yet. Gavin?' Her tone didn't conceal the warning note in her voice. 'It's not Felicity, is it?'

'Felicity?' Dad grinned. 'Is that likely?'

'Yes, it is Felicity.'

'Good gracious.' His dad almost choked on his coffee but he was grinning.

His mum's eyes widened and she shook her head. 'But Gavin, you can't act on any feelings you might have for her. It's out of the question.'

'Why should it be? Aside from her business skills, I love her.'

Dad brought his hands together. 'This is perfect. I can't imagine anyone better suited to you.'

His mum glared at him. 'Frank, he knows the rules. Gavin, you can't get involved with someone from work. It's unprofessional, especially as you just promoted her. You clearly have had some kind of relationship to get to this stage. I think we should investigate her promotion directly. I always suspected she was sleeping her way to a top job, and I was right. Disgusting behaviour. She needs to be removed from post immediately.'

'No, Mum. Felicity never asked for anything. Our personal relationship was always separate from work and as soon as she wanted to apply for that job, I walked away. I had nothing to do with her getting it. I didn't read her application or attend her interview.'

'That may be so,' his mum blustered. 'But you still can't take up with her like that.'

'Is there actually a rule that says I can't?'

His dad put his hand on her arm. 'Dorothy, have you forgotten? When we first met, I was in the same position as Gavin and you were my secretary. We fell in love, and now, years later, we're still together.'

Gavin looked between the two of them and his mouth fell open. 'Really? Are you serious? I had no idea.'

'It was completely different,' Mum said, her cheeks reddening. 'I gave up working for the company so we could be together. I don't see Felicity doing that. She's very ambitious.'

'And so were you,' Dad said. 'Just in a different way.'

'Felicity is ambitious, and I wouldn't expect her to give up anything for me,' Gavin said. 'That's why I walked away. Her career is just as important as mine.'

'Unbelievable,' Mum muttered. 'The modern world has gone mad.'

'But, Mum, you might have officially given up on your secretarial job, but everyone knew you were as much a driving force in the company as Dad. Is there any reason why it can't be like that for Felicity and me? Only I don't want her doing it from the sidelines.'

'Well said.' Dad smiled. 'Perhaps I should have done the same for you, Dorothy.'

'Oh fiddlesticks, I wouldn't have taken the job. It wouldn't have been right. I was a wife and a mother, not a working woman. It would have undermined your position.'

Gavin exchanged a look with his dad.

'I'm not saying it will be easy,' Dad said, 'but if you love her, you should go for it.'

'I'm going to, though she might not have me now.' That was the next obstacle, but even if she said no, he trusted them to be able to stay professional and get the job done – as they always had.

'Well, I think it's quite ridiculous. I don't know how you can't see what she's doing. It's been obvious from the start this has been her goal.'

'You know what. You're wrong. That was never her goal. Neither of us set out to fall in love but that's what happened. Now, I'm sorry, Mum, but you either accept my choice or I walk away.'

'Walk away? You'd walk away from your family?'

'It's not something I'd do lightly. I love you, both of you, but I'm not your puppet or someone who has to share every misplaced belief you have. And I certainly don't want the love of my life entering into a relationship with me when there's a chance that my own family will abuse her and bring her down.'

Dad downed his tea. 'Come on, Dorothy. Felicity is a charming young woman. She doesn't deserve this from you.'

'You've always had a thing about her, haven't you?'

'Me?' Frank said.

'Don't deny it. Why else did you have her promoted?'

'Because she believed in the company.'

'And she still does,' Gavin said. 'She cared for the future of the business more than I did. She helped me see what was important.' He took a deep breath. 'I'm going to go now. And, Mum, I really hope you decide to change your tune because I'm not going to change my mind.'

She stared as he got to his feet and Frank frowned but there was sadness in his eyes. It was too much to hope that Dorothy would have a sudden epiphany or fall on her knees begging forgiveness. And that wasn't really what Gavin wanted. He just wanted her to give Felicity the respect she deserved. He'd made up his mind. A steely sense of determination surged through him like he was debugging a tricky program. He wouldn't give up until the code was running flawlessly. His relationship with Felicity was going to work, no matter what. He had to make it happen... If that meant cutting off his mother, he would do it. But the biggest barrier might be Felicity herself. Could he blame her if she'd decided against him? He'd been the one to walk away after all and maybe she was quite happy in her new career without him. There was only one way to find out. He was going back to Glenbriar.

CHAPTER TWENTY-NINE

'You've got a keeper there.' Felicity threw her arm around Briony's shoulder. The two of them laughed, watching Zach, as he slowly paced up and down the loch side with a tiny bundle on his shoulder. Indistinct chatter from guests tucking into their breakfast and clinking cutlery filled the sunlit room.

Briony wiped a tear from under her eye.

'Are you ok?' Felicity said. 'I didn't mean to be horrible. I'm serious.'

'It's happy tears. I'm just so emotional these days.'

'Hardly surprising.' Felicity hugged her tighter. Little Leia's earlier than expected arrival had been quite a whirlwind. So much for first labours being long and drawn out, Briony had gone into labour at six in the morning and Leia was in her arms by lunchtime. A week later, and they were all settling into a new routine. Felicity hadn't been over-thrilled at the prospect of living in the attic room at the hotel until she found proper lodgings. But now she was thrilled she could be here to support her friend in these early days. 'His top is just so him.'

The black fitted t-shirt bore the legend, The Dadalorian, and Leia had on a little green baby Yoda hat.

'Isn't it just?' Briony grinned. 'He's already checked the age certificate on all the films and worked out when she can watch them all.'

Felicity beamed. 'I think he's great and I'm so glad you got together, especially after I almost ruined it for you.'

'No, you didn't. You were just looking out for me.' Briony checked around the busy dining room. 'Speaking of which, tell me what's up.'

'What do you mean?' Felicity checked her watch. 'I should get to work.'

'Not yet.' Briony faced her. 'Things have been a bit of a blur the last couple of months. The chronic pelvic pain was so bad I wasn't really thinking straight.'

'I know, that was horrible. But it's all gone now, hasn't it?'

'Yes. Completely. The midwife kept telling me the only cure was having the baby and she was right. I feel so much better. But I also feel well enough to see what I didn't see before.'

'Which is?'

'There's something not right. I know you enjoy this new job but you're not yourself. Is it your granny? Or your dad? What's up? You can tell me anything. I'm just sorry I haven't been as present as I should have been.'

Felicity could easily say she was worried about her family and be done with. But her feelings for Gavin were still sitting there like a vast pile of files and folders to sort through. She didn't know where to start, what to do with them, or why she was still holding on to them. Briony had been her best friend almost since the day they met. She'd helped her through lockdowns and uncertain times. Felicity trusted her but it was so hard to find the words to sum up everything going on in her heart and her head.

'I guess I'm not as happy as I thought I would be. I mean, I love my job. It's everything I ever wanted.' She sighed.

Briony gazed at her with wide eyes. 'But?'

'I miss Gavin.'

'The boss?'

'He was a lot more than that.'

'I kind of guessed that, but I thought you decided it was just a fling.'

'We did… Well, we agreed it would be, then it got bigger really fast. I guess I got carried away thinking somehow we could make it work. We both did. But he… Well, he really wanted me to go for this job, so he left.'

'At least he supported your career.'

'He kept away from everything to do with the job, so I could apply for it and not have people accusing me of sleeping my way to the top. But it doesn't stop me missing him like hell and thinking about what-might-have-beens.'

'Hmm. And are you sure he's not just a commitment-phobe? I mean, he's reached thirty-six and he's not settled.'

'I think it's because of his mum.'

'What?'

'He probably wouldn't agree with me, but I don't think he dares cross her. She doesn't like me. She didn't like the ex he broke up with before and she's always trying to set him up with the "right" people.'

'Look. If he really loved you, he wouldn't let her get in the way.'

Felicity rubbed her forehead. 'I want to believe that and he said he did.'

'Did he?'

'Yes. And I really believed him and I loved him too... Oh god. Am I being an idiot and hanging onto a thread that isn't really there?' Was this her bringing her 'unnecessary drama' to the situation? Her ex had accused her of that and sometimes she couldn't shake the thought he was right. 'I wish I could just forget about Gavin Sinclair, only that's impossible too because he's still my boss.'

'At least you don't have to see him every day.'

'But there's so much that I need to talk to him about and run past him. I end up on calls with him all the time. It's always so awkward and we can't speak freely. I try to email him as much as possible but he calls me instead of replying.'

'Sounds like he still carries a candle for you.' Briony leaned in and hugged her.

'I don't know. He's always so polite. I don't dare mention anything. I'm scared people will find out what happened when we were here and I'll get sacked.'

'Gavin sounds honourable enough to make sure that won't happen.'

'God, I hope so.' She checked the time. 'I really have to go and you should rest before Leia needs her next feed.'

After moaning about Gavin's constant calling, today was the day he didn't. She read a long email from him covering his thoughts on the latest architect's mock-up of the proposed café at Inverbuie, then spent time collating his ideas with hers. After that, she had an in-depth discussion with Alistair Turner to finalise the changes and amendments. If Gavin had his office here, it would be so much easier, but she was glad he didn't. If it was awkward on the phone, how difficult would it be to have to interact personally with him? Always though, that happy feeling like a warm energy rose in her at the thought of him being close by. Awkward or not, his presence was like safety and security.

Before she shut down her computer at the end of the day, she spotted an email marked *urgent* from Gavin Sinclair. She clicked it.

To: felicityswan@Sinclairbros.com; alistairturner@Sinclairbros.com; AGibson@Sinclairbros.com; jerryfaulkner@Sinclairbros.com

From: GWSinclair@Sinclairbros.com

Subject: meeting tomorrow morning

Good afternoon, all.

I'd like to convene a meeting tomorrow at nine thirty. Would be great if I could see you all together. Could you all be at Glenbriar for then? Hope that's convenient. Nothing to worry about but I have a few restructuring issues I'd like to address. Will only take about an hour to run through.

Let me know ASAP if this time doesn't suit.

Thanks

Gavin

Felicity opened her online calendar and put it in. When he said he wanted to see them all together, did that mean he was coming here? Or just wanted them all in the same place, which made no sense. And how could she not worry about restructuring? Had Julian been muttering in his ear and made him change his mind about the upgrades? Dorothy Sinclair had told Felicity Gavin was terrible at making decisions and relied on her to do it for him. Maybe it was the same at work. How ironic that the only decision he'd made himself was to walk away from her.

'Ugh.' She threw her head back and stared at the ceiling. A knock on the door made her jump. Victoria poked her head around.

'This was delivered for you.' Victoria placed a small box, wrapped in pretty, recycled paper with pink flowers on it, on Felicity's desk.

'Who delivered it?' She picked it up and turned it over. All it said on a brown paper gift tag was *Felicity*.

'A woman just came up to the desk and asked if I could give it to Felicity Swan.'

'How mysterious.'

'Open it and see if there's a card or something inside.'

Felicity peeled off the paper and opened the cardboard box inside. She pulled out a delicately wrought tealight holder in the shape of two swans, their necks forming a heart shape. 'I've seen this before...' In the window of Wood 'n' Chic, when she'd walked through town with Gavin. But that didn't explain why it was here. Even if he'd bought it, why had he sent it to her now? Who had delivered it?

'Doesn't it say who sent it?' Victoria asked.

Felicity shook her head.

'A regular little mystery. Looks like you have a secret admirer.' She giggled and let herself out.

As soon as she shut the door, Felicity pulled out a folded bit of paper she'd spotted. She hadn't wanted to open it in front of Victoria. Her feelings were so all over the place, she didn't trust herself not to be crazy or cry or whatever. Her fingers were so shaky, she could hardly open the note. Eventually, she laid it flat and read the typed words.

To Felicity. From someone who:

1. Likes carrot juice

2. Enjoys wild swimming

3. Once walked away from the love of his life for what he thought was her own good and has regretted it ever since.

If you want to see me again, meet me at the wobbly bridge between five and six. No work chat, but I do have some important things to say. x

Felicity checked her watch. It was almost five now. She wasn't going to throw away this chance or give up finding out what he had to say. The lid of her laptop clicked shut and she bundled it into her bag. A few seconds later, she waved goodbye to a somewhat shocked looking Victoria and left the building.

She parked in the centre of Glenbriar and made her way hastily down the path. As soon as the wobbly bridge came in sight, she saw a lone figure in the middle, leaning his forearms on the railing and staring out over the River Briar. She sped up. The bridge wobbled as she moved further along and Gavin was alerted to her presence; he turned to look at her, and a weak smile grew on his handsome face. His white shirt sat slightly open and for a second

Felicity focused on the wedge of skin left bare before shifting her gaze to his eyes.

'Hey, you came,' his voice caught slightly. 'And so soon. I thought I might be in for a long wait.'

'I wanted to see you. I liked the gift. Thank you. You always know what to get me.'

They stood for a moment, simply taking each other in.

'I'm glad you got it. I had to trust a stranger to take it in.' He sighed. 'I might know what to get you but I don't always know what's right for myself or others.'

'How do you mean?' She swallowed, standing close but not so close she could touch him or get full exposure to his scent.

'Ever since I walked away, I've regretted it. The situation and the reasons haven't changed, but I have. Call me unprofessional or whatever, but I'm here to throw myself at your feet and beg for forgiveness.'

Her heart skipped a beat. 'I know why you did it and it meant I could get this job without a shadow of suspicion but if nothing's changed, what can we do?'

'Because I realise now it was a mistake letting you go. That decision shouldn't have been mine alone. I should have asked you what you wanted rather than just assuming.'

'I'm glad you didn't. Because I would have picked you and lost out on the job of a lifetime.' She sucked her lip.

'No. If you'd picked me, I wouldn't have let you lose the job.'

She smiled. 'I think that's kind of what happened anyway, because I would pick you every time.'

'And I choose you, Felicity.'

'But you can't leave either. No way.'

'I would if I had to. You're more important but I think I've finally come up with a better solution. Assuming, well, if you…' He looked away like he was barely holding back a dam of emotions. 'If you still want me.'

'I told you; I'd always choose you. But how can it work? You're in Edinburgh and I don't want to go back there.'

He moved closer, taking hold of her upper arms. 'I should never have lost sight of what was important. I'm moving up here.'

'What?'

'You heard me. Glenbriar and the rural distilleries are the heart of this business. And wherever you are is where my heart is.'

Her eyes filled with tears and she blinked them back, trying to maintain eye contact. When he wrapped her into a warm hug, his arms wholly surrounded her and the tears overflowed, but she smiled through them. 'It's what I want but I still don't see how it'll work. What about everyone else? Your parents? Julian? The managers?'

'My parents already know, so does Julian. Tomorrow, I'm going to tell the managers.'

'About you moving to Glenbriar?'

'Yes, about that.' He pulled back and swept a stray lock of her hair from her tear-stained cheek and pushed it behind her ear. 'And about us.'

'What will you tell them?'

'That I love you.' He dipped in and kissed the corner of her eye, where tears still threatened. 'Because I do love you. I love you more than anyone I've ever loved. It burns so strong in me that I can't bear how pathetic my life is without you. You're my everything and I want to be with you every day of my life.'

'Oh god, Gavin. I love you too.' Her voice trembled. 'But how will that change things? Won't people still say we planned this all from the start?'

'Some people might. But I had nothing to do with you getting this job and Julian will back me up on that.'

'What about your parents?'

'My father doesn't object and my mother… Well, I've stopped seeing her.'

'What? But Gavin.'

'I hope it's not forever. God knows I don't want to break up my family, but I've told her I can't keep seeing her until she respects both you and my decision.'

'I don't want to be the reason your family breaks up.'

'You're not. My mother is the reason and she has the power to fix it.'

'I can hardly believe it. Can we really do this?'

'We can. Look at my parents. They made it work for years. My mum didn't officially work for the company but she attended almost every meeting and made sure her voice was heard. You believe in the company as much as, if not more than, her, and I want you by my side on this journey, but not as someone supporting me from the wings. I want you up here with me, as an equal.'

She leaned her forehead on his shoulder, half laughing, half crying and wholly disbelieving this was real. Gavin held her tightly, his fragrance filling her, calming her and letting her know everything was going to be fine.

He gazed into her eyes, then dipped down and sealed his lips with hers. The intensity took her breath away and she lost herself in the heat of the moment, each tender second pulling them closer.

He drew back first. 'There's something else though.'

'What?' She blinked. What now? Nothing could spoil this moment, could it?

'You might not like this idea and if you don't, you can shove me off this bridge.'

She grinned in spite of herself. 'Just spit it out. What the hell is it?'

'I told you before I was here to throw myself at your feet and...' He took a deep breath '... I would quite literally like to fall on my knees before you.'

Her hand flew to her mouth as he dropped to one knee.

'I know it might seem too soon, too forward, too—'

'Perfect?' She smiled.

'Then let it be perfect. Will you, Felicity Swan, the most amazing woman in the world, marry me, Gavin Sinclair? Just a single man who likes carrot juice, wild swimming, and who doesn't want to throw away a chance at happiness with the woman he adores more than life itself.'

She bent over, laughing through a fresh wave of tears. 'Yes, yes, I will.'

Smiling, he got to his feet and took her face in his hands. 'I love you and I can't wait to move up here and start afresh together.'

'Me neither.' She closed her eyes and smiled. The bridge wobbled slightly, cradling them as they held hands. Life didn't get
much better than this.

Chapter Thirty

Gavin

Gavin took his seat at the head of the conference table and Felicity sat next to him. He smiled at her. This was where he wanted her, always at his side. Even if that was a physical impossibility, just knowing he could go back to her every day and every night was enough. He looked around the room at the managers assembled before him and took a deep breath.

'Thank you all for coming at such short notice today. I could have done this over video link but I think under the circumstances, I'd rather do it in person.'

'That doesn't fill me with confidence,' Angus said. 'Am I getting laid off by any chance?'

'Definitely not,' Felicity said. 'You're the lynchpin at Torrindhu. Without you, the whole place will crumble.'

'Good to know,' he muttered.

'No one's getting laid off,' Gavin continued. 'But there is some important restructuring going on that I want to keep you up to speed with. Julian Morrison, who is currently in charge of the Edinburgh office, is moving into a slightly different role. It won't change much but he'll now be the person at the top in that office.'

'Are you leaving?' Jerry frowned at Gavin.

'No, my role will continue. But instead of being based in Edinburgh, and after much consideration, I've decided to relocate to Glenbriar and carry out my management duties from here.'

There were a few murmurs and raised eyebrows around the table. 'It makes sense from where I'm sitting,' Alistair said. 'Especially with all the work going on at Inverbuie.'

'Exactly. It'll bring me closer to the heart of our operations and allow me to be more hands-on with the day-to-day running of the distilleries.'

'I couldn't agree more,' Jerry said. 'It's a smart move. We've felt a bit isolated in the rural distilleries since your father left and with the business climate changing so much at the moment, having you on site will make all the difference.'

'Sounds sensible,' Alistair agreed.

'Aye, I can't deny it'll be a boost for morale too. Who doesn't like a bit more attention and support?' Angus added.

'Fantastic.' Gavin smiled. 'It's a relief to hear you're all on board. I was worried you might think I was coming up to breathe down your necks and put you under heavy scrutiny but I'm glad you see it in the spirit in which it's intended. I want to be as supportive as possible, especially when so many changes are being implemented.'

'Great,' Jerry said, looking at his colleagues.

'Right.' Gavin took another deep breath. That was the easy bit. Having said that, after telling Julian about his relationship with Felicity, this couldn't be any worse, could it? Thankfully, promotion softened Julian enough and Gavin made a lucky escape, all things considered. He cleared his throat. 'So, there's just one more thing I'd like to tell you.' He glanced at Felicity and she blinked, her cheeks very rosy. 'It's about Felicity.'

Jerry frowned at her and his eyes filled with concern.

'Felicity is... Well, Felicity and I are engaged.'

Three sets of stunned eyes met Gavin's gaze.

'Wow.' Jerry burst out laughing. 'I didn't see that coming.'

'Oh, I don't know.' Angus gave them a cheeky smirk. 'I always saw a twinkle in his eye when he looked at her.'

'Congratulations,' Alistair said.

'Definitely,' Jerry agreed. 'I can't think of a better match, except maybe your parents.'

Felicity beamed at them all. 'Thanks everyone. We appreciate how kind you're all being. I know how it might have been construed.'

'We've both been very aware that you might have concerns about how a personal relationship might impact business, but I want to assure you Felicity won this job on merit. I had nothing to do with her selection for the role and our being engaged won't affect the running of the company. In fact, we believe it'll strengthen it. Just like my parents' relationship did in the past. We're committed to making this work.'

He smiled at Felicity and she beamed back. Under the table, she moved her hand across and squeezed his knee.

August

Gavin and Felicity pulled up in front of his parents' house. 'Back to the scene of the crime,' he said with a wink.

'Oh, don't.' Felicity hid her face. 'Please tell me they don't know what we were doing there.'

He gave a half laugh. 'You can bet your bottom dollar my mum suspected right from the start. She saw the danger long before I did.'

'What danger?'

'The danger that you'd steal my heart.'

She patted his thigh and he gave her hand a gentle squeeze. 'You had mine for a long time. I just didn't want to admit it because the implications were so big.'

'I think we're doing ok.'

'So far, so good.'

His dad was waiting at the door, his arms wide open in welcome. Living here maybe wasn't the best solution long term but in the interim it would work. And as the offer had come from Dorothy, they'd agreed to take it as an olive branch edging in their direction.

'Gavin, Felicity! It's so good to see you both.' His dad embraced them one by one as they approached the door. 'Come in, come in. June has it all looking marvellous.'

Gavin took Felicity's hand and followed his father inside.

'You've been here before, of course.' Dad smiled at Felicity and her cheeks reddened.

Gavin increased the pressure on her hand. 'We were busy, so Felicity didn't get a proper chance to admire the views.'

'Ah yes. And now we know what you were up to.'

Gavin raised an eyebrow and shared a sideways glance with Felicity.

'You were working on the action plan for the upgrades.' Dad grinned as though his meaning had been obvious.

'Yes, exactly.' There had certainly been plenty of action.

'Just take a look at this.' Dad led them into the glass-walled, conservatory-like terrace between the main house and the pool. 'We've had the pool filled, so you can enjoy swimming with a view.'

'It really is stunning,' Gavin said, surveying the stunning green vista of rolling hills, woodland and Loch Briar gleaming in the distance, but tension squeezed his chest. Where was his mum? Was she in hiding? What was he really hoping for?

'You can open the pool house doors and enjoy the outdoors on a day like this.' Dad pointed across the shimmering blue pool. 'And then pull them shut if it starts to rain.'

'Thank you. It's wonderful,' Felicity said. 'And very generous.'

'Not at all.' He waved his hand. 'We hardly use the place these days. It's good to see it being used as a home. I dreamed of moving up here when the kids were young and letting them have this as their backyard.' He gestured at the scenery. 'But it wasn't to be. If you get some use out of it now, I'm more than happy.'

'Thanks, Dad. I think I appreciate it more now than I would have back then.'

A slight cough from behind made them all turn around. Gavin's jaw ached as he ground his teeth together. His mum stood in the doorway, red-faced and flustered.

'Hello, Gavin.' She blinked, then looked at Felicity. 'And Felicity.'

'Hi.' Felicity blinked and rubbed at the base of her neck. Gavin threw his mum a pleading look, begging her to be nice. Felicity was the love of his life and his future lay with her. He didn't want to walk away from his family forever but if he had to, he would. He would take her and walk out of the door that very second.

'I'm sorry, Felicity,' Dorothy said.

'Oh?'

'Yes. I said many things about you that I regret and that weren't worthy of me.'

'I can't deny I always found you intimidating and it was hard not to take it personally.'

'And for that, I'm deeply sorry.'

'Mum, I appreciate you saying that, and as I've said before, I have no desire to break up our family. But I want you to understand that I've chosen Felicity to be my partner for life. My future wife. We're going to be together for a long time. We want to have children and grow old together. If Felicity accepts your apology, I'm happy to accept it too but I'll only accept it for as long as I see it in action.' He put his arm around Felicity's shoulder. 'I'll always stand with Felicity. Always.'

'And I'm not going anywhere without you.' Felicity smiled at him. 'But I would prefer it if we could all be happy, and that includes you, Dorothy.'

'Yes. Yes, of course. That's what I want,' Dorothy said. 'Family has always been the most important thing for me.' She took another deep breath and smiled at Felicity. 'It was my mistake that I believed you were chasing Gavin for the wrong reasons. I didn't fully appreciate how much you cared for him and valued the business. And my loss too. I feel like I've missed out on the opportunity for a good friendship.'

'It doesn't have to be lost, Mum. Like I said, we're going to be together for a very long time. Felicity isn't going away, so if you want me, you've also got her.'

'I understand. I just didn't think... Well, I'm not sure, Felicity, that you'd want that.'

Felicity looked back at his mum. 'I always have room for more friends.'

Dorothy smoothed down the front of her skirt. 'Really? Well, thank you. And Gavin, I think you made the best choice of partner. You're well suited and perfectly matched.' She smiled and her eyes were watery as she turned her gaze to Felicity. 'All I want is for you both to be happy and I hope I can be part of your future.'

Dad clapped his hands.

'Are you ok with that?' Gavin whispered in Felicity's ear.

She nodded. 'Are you?'

'If you're happy, I'm happy,' he said

'I always thought you'd be good for Gavin,' Frank said. 'That's why I wanted you in the job in the first place.'

'Who'd have thought Dad was a closet matchmaker?'

'Oh no,' he said. 'I wouldn't have thought that far. I meant on a purely business level. But sometimes the heart has other ideas. Now, would anyone like a game of golf? We have a mini pitch and putt out front. It's great fun.'

'Why not?' Felicity beamed, and Gavin laughed.

'Pitch and putt it is then. Coming, Mum?'

Dorothy blinked at him, then glanced at Felicity.

'I can't promise to let you win,' Felicity said. 'Sorry if that's a problem.'

'Hmm,' Dorothy said. 'I better accept the challenge then.'

A weight lifted from Gavin's shoulders as they laughed their way round the pitch and putt, then ate lunch together. It was late afternoon before his parents packed up their car, ready to head home.

'And, Mum, just to say, you don't need to send June around every few minutes to check I'm behaving myself.' Because he most certainly wouldn't be. Felicity nudged him.

'All right. I won't.' Mum handed over her keys. 'There you go. Now I can't come in without an invitation.'

'Thanks, Mum.' He hugged her goodbye, then his dad, and watched with a smile as they both hugged Felicity.

'Well, that went better than expected.' Felicity waved them off as the car rolled down the driveway.

'It did. But I'm quite serious. If Mum ever says anything you're unhappy with or makes you feel edgy, tell me. I will not have it.'

'Ok.' She hugged him and he stroked her hair. 'But I sensed she was really trying. It's never easy admitting you were in the wrong. And have you seen how she's stocked the fridge? I know it's a small thing in the grander scheme but she's put a lot of thought into it.'

'Yeah, she's good at stuff like that. And I hope this is just the start. Next up, it'll be my turn meeting your family.'

'They're a bunch of pushovers next to your mum.'

'Really? From what I understand, your father thinks all Scottish men are barbaric peasants who paint their faces blue and charge about the hillside in various states of undress.'

'Well, that's the image he always fed me. Why do you think I was so keen to leave home and come up here?' She assumed an expression of perfect innocence.

Gavin swept the feet from under her and scooped her into his arms. She squealed and grabbed hold of him. 'Maybe I should show you just how rough and ready this Scotsman is.'

'Please be gentle with this poor English lady. She has no experience with these rugged men of the north.'

He chuckled. 'Time we fixed that then. Now, let me carry you across the threshold.' He stepped inside and kicked the door shut behind him. 'I fancy a dip in the pool. How about you?'

'Sounds nice, but maybe we should get undressed first.'

'Even better.' He carried her to one of the lounging chairs in the conservatory and lay her down, then sat at her side, looking into her eyes. 'It's just you and me now.' He tucked a wayward strand of her hair behind her ear and kissed from her cheek, down her neck and along her shoulder, pushing off the strap of her dress with the tip of his nose.

'Yes, Gavin.' She let out a sigh and threaded her fingers into his hair. 'Just you and me. You and me, and the rest of our lives.'

'Let's make those days perfect.' He dipped in and kissed her.

Everything was wonderful.

'Now, I'm just a man who drinks carrot juice with you at breakfast, wild swims with you at weekends and has finally caught the love of my life and will never walk away – ever.'

The End

More Books by Margaret Amatt

Scottish Island Escapes

The Glenbriar Series

1. Stolen Kisses at the Loch View Hotel

2. Just Friends at Thistle Lodge

3. Pitching up at Heather Glen

4. Two's Company at the Forest Light Show

5. Highland Fling on the Whisky Trail

6. Snowdown at the Old Schoolhouse

7. Starting Over at the Crafty Bee Barn

8. A Surprise Proposal in the Rose Garden

9. Cutting it Neat for the Wedding

10. A Classy Affair in the Country

11. Mix Up under the Mistletoe

12. A Fresh Start on the Bridle Path

13. Last First Kiss at the Village Church

14. Fight or Flirt on the Scenic Route

15. Love Match on the Road Home

16. Christmas Wishes at the Station Bookshop

17. Faking the Grade at Glenbriar High

18. Summer Nights at Hillview Farm

19. Love Song at the Music Festival

20. Holly Dates at the Christmas Cottage

Love on the Edge – Barra Series

1. The Castle in the Bay

2. The Lighthouse by the Sea

3. The Gateway on the Sands

ACKNOWLEDGMENTS

Thanks goes to my adorable husband for supporting my dreams and putting up with my writing talk 24/7. Also to my son, whose interest in my writing always makes me smile. It's precious to know I've passed the bug to him – he's currently writing his own fantasy novel and instruction books on how to build Lego!

Throughout the writing process, I have gleaned help from many sources and met some fabulous people. I'd like to give a special mention to Stéphanie Ronckier, my beta reader extraordinaire. Stéphanie's continued support with my writing is invaluable and I love the fact that I need someone French to correct my grammar! Stéphanie, you rock. To my lovely friend, Lyn Williamson, thank you for your continued support and encouragement with all my projects. And to my fellow authors, Evie Alexander and Lyndsey Gallagher – you girls are the best! I love it that you always have my back and are there to help when I need you.

Also, a thanks to the editors at Leannan Press for their work on this novel.

Of course a huge thank you goes to the readers who continue to support me in so many ways. I appreciate each and every one of you and hope that I can keep bringing you more books to enjoy! Big love.

Margaret XX

ABOUT THE AUTHOR
Margaret Amatt

Margaret has told and written stories for as long as she can remember. During her formative years, she spent time on long walks inventing characters and stories to pass the time.

Writing books is Margaret's passion and when she's not doing that, she's often found eating chocolate, walking and taking photographs in the hills around Highland Perthshire. Those long walks still frequently bring inspiration!

It's Margaret's pleasure to bring you the **Scottish Island Escapes** series, **The Glenbriar Series** and the **Love on the Edge — Barra** series. Each series features interconnected stories for those who enjoy inhabiting Margaret's world but each and every book can be read as a standalone if you'd rather dip in and out.

You can find more information about Margaret on her website or by signing up for her newsletter

www.margaretamatt.com